George Ade

# SHORT STORY CLASSICS

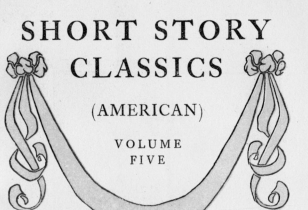

## CLASSICS

(AMERICAN)

VOLUME
FIVE

EDITED BY
William Patten

WITH
AN INTRODUCTION
AND NOTES

P. F. COLLIER & SON
NEW YORK

# CONTENTS—VOLUME V

# "TO MAKE A HOOSIER HOLIDAY"

## BY GEORGE ADE

*The writings of George Ade (born at Kent-
land, Ind., February 9, 1866) have gone far
to justify the claim that America has not only
a literature but a language of its own,
clearly distinct from its English correspond-
ent. Anglo-Saxon nature in this country has
become more effervescent, and its expression
therefore more iridescent. Slang that is the
dull dregs of English wit is the snapping
froth of American humor. And of all our
dispensers of humor George Ade knows best
how to put the sparkling bead of slang on a
draught of good home-brewed philosophy.
While Mr. Ade's fables are all embryo
stories, he has developed few of his conceits
into short stories proper, saving them, it
would seem, for his plays. The present selection is an exceptional "situation" that he has
not yet pressed into dramatic service, letting
it roam temporarily in story guise. It was
published in COLLIER'S WEEKLY.*

# "TO MAKE A HOOSIER HOLIDAY"

## BY GEORGE ADE

I F you will take a map of the State of Indiana and follow with your pencil one of the many railway lines radiating from Indianapolis, you will find, if you are extremely diligent in your search, a black speck marked "Musselwhite." It is not an asterisk, meaning a county seat—simply a speck on the enameled surface. Furthermore, it is one of many specks. A map which shows all of the towns of the Musselwhite kind looks like a platter of caviare—a mere scramble of dark globules, each the same as the others.

As a matter of fact, Musselwhite seemed one of a thousand to the sleepy travelers in the parlor cars. Lying back on their upholstered griddles, slowly baking to a crisp, they would be aroused by a succession of jolts and grinds and would look out with torpid interest at a brindle-colored "depot," a few brick stores ornately faced with cornices of galvanized iron, a straggling row of frame houses prigged out with scallops and protuberant bay windows, a few alert horses at the hitch-rack and a few somnolent Americans punctuated along the platform. Then the train would laboriously push this panorama into the background and whisk away into the cornfields, and the travelers would never again think of Musselwhite. Certainly they would

Reprinted, by permission of the author, from Collier's Weekly for December 17, 1904. Copyright, 1904, by P. F. Collier & Son.

never think of it as a hotbed of politics, an arena of social strivings, a Mecca for the remote farmhand and a headquarters for religious effort. Yet Musselwhite was all of these—and more.

The town had two wings of the Protestant faith, but they did not always flap in unison. They were united in the single belief that the Catholic congregation at the other end of town was intent on some dark plan to capture the government and blow up the public school system.

The Zion Methodist Church stood across the street from the Campbellite structure. Each had a high wooden steeple and a clangorous bell. Zion Church had an undersized pipe-organ which had to be pumped from behind. The Campbellites had merely an overgrown cottage organ, but they put in a cornet to help out—this in the face of a protest from the conservative element that true religion did not harmonize with any "brass-band trimmings."

In the Campbellite Church the rostrum was movable, and underneath was a baptismal pool wherein the newly converted were publicly immersed. Whenever there was to be a Sunday night "baptizing" at the Campbellite Church, the attendance was overflowing. The Methodists could offer no ceremony to compare with that of a bold descent into the cold plunge, but every winter they had a "protracted meeting" which kept the church lighted and warmed for seven nights in the week. During this "revival" period the Campbellites were in partial eclipse.

It must not be assumed that there was any petty

rivalry between the two flocks. It was the strong
and healthy competition between two laborers in the
vineyard, each striving to pick the larger bunch of
grapes. If the Zion Church gave a mush-and-milk
sociable, it was only natural that the Campbellites, in
their endeavor to retain a hold on the friendly sympa-
thies of Musselwhite, should almost immediately make
announcement of a rummage party or an old people's
concert. The Campbellites had their Sunday-school
in the morning, preceding the regular service, and the
Methodists had theirs in the afternoon. The attendance records and missionary collections were zealously
compared. Unusual inducements were offered to the
growing youth of Musselwhite to memorize the golden
text and fight manfully for the large blue card which
was the reward for unbroken attendance. In Musselwhite, as in many other communities, there were parents who believed in permitting the children to attend
two religious services every Sunday, thereby estab-
lishing a good general average for the family, even if
the parents remained at home to read the Sunday
papers. The children found no fault with this arrangement. The morning Sunday-school was a sort
of full-dress rehearsal for the afternoon service, to
which the children flocked in confident possession of
those hidden meanings of the Scripture which can
always be elucidated by a hardware merchant who
wears dark clothes once a week.

At Christmas time the "scholars" found themselves
in a quandary. Each church had exercises Christmas
Eve. A child can not be in two places at the same

time, no matter how busy his effort or how earnest his intention. And so it came about that the congregation offering the more spectacular entertainment and the larger portion of mixed candy drew the majority of the lambkins. The rivalry between the Methodists and the Campbellites touched perihelion on Christmas Eve. An ordinary Christmas tree studded with tapers, festooned with popcorn, and heavy with presents no longer satisfied the junior population, for it had been pampered and fed upon novelty. The children demanded a low-comedy Santa Claus in a fur coat. They had to be given star parts in cantatas, or else be permitted to speak "pieces" in costume. One year the Campbellites varied the programme by having a scenic chimney-corner erected back of the pulpit. There was an open fireplace glowing with imitation coals. In front of the fireplace was a row of stockings, some of which were of most mirth-provoking length and capacity, for the sense of humor was rampant in Musselwhite. A murmur of impatient and restless curiosity rather interfered with the recitations and responsive readings which opened the programme. It rose to a tiptoe of eager anticipation when Mr. Eugene Robinson, the Superintendent of the Sunday-school, arose and, after a few felicitous remarks, which called forth hysterical laughter, read a telegram from Kriss Kringle saying that he would arrive in Musselwhite at 8:30 sharp. Almost immediately there was heard the jingle of sleighbells. The older and more sophisticated boys identified the tone as coming from a strand of bells owned by Henry Boardman, who kept the

livery barn, but the minds of the younger brood were
singularly free from all doubt and questioning. A
distinct "Whoa!" was heard, and then the Saint, swad-
dled in furs and with a most prodigious growth of
cotton whiskers, came right out through the fireplace
with his pack on his back and asked in a loud voice,
"Is this the town of Musselwhite?" His shaggy coat
was sifted with snow, in spite of the fact that the
night was rather warm and muggy, and his whole appearance tallied so accurately with the pictures in the
books that the illusion was most convincing until
"Tad" Saulsbury, aged twelve, piped in a loud voice:
"I know who it is. It's Jake Francis."

His mother moved swiftly down the aisle and
"churned" him into silence, after which the distribu-
tion of presents proceeded with triumphant hilarity.

It was generally conceded that the Campbellite
chimney-corner entertainment rather laid over and
topped and threw into the shade any other Christmas
doings that had been witnessed in Musselwhite. That
is why the Methodists were spurred to unusual effort
one year later, and that is why "Doc" Silverton, Sam
Woodson, and Orville Hufty, as a special committee
on arrangements, met in the doctor's office one evening
in November to devise ways and means.

"They're goin' to give another chimney-corner
show," said "Doc" Silverton. "We've got to do something to offset it. I claim that the Christmas tree is
played out. Since they've started shippin' in these
evergreen trees from Chicago, a good many people
have their own trees right at home. We can't very

well take up the chimney-corner idee. It's too much like trailin' along behind the Campbellites and takin' their dust."

"We've got to give 'em something new and different," said Orville Hufty. "I sent and got a book that's supposed to tell how to get up shows for Christmas, but it's all about singin' songs and speakin' pieces, and we know by experience that such things don't ketch the crowd here in Musselwhite."

"I've been thinkin'," said Sam Woodson, very slowly, "that we might do this: Go to the Campbellites and segest that we take turn about in givin' exhibitions. That is, if they hold off this year, we'll give them a clear field next year."

"Not much!" exclaimed "Doc" Silverton, with great decision. "That'd look like a clean backdown. Don't give 'em anything to crow about. Let's beat 'em at their own game. We can do it if you'll help me on a little scheme that I've been layin' awake nights and thinkin' about. Don't laugh when I tell you what it is. It's nothin' more or less than a weddin'."

"You mean to have somebody get married on Christmas Eve?" asked Mr. Hufty, looking at him coldly.

"That's it exactly," replied "Doc" with a grin of enthusiasm.

"What's gettin' married got to do with Christmas?" asked Sam Woodson.

"People get married every day," added Mr. Hufty.

"Not the people that I'm thinkin' about," said "Doc," leaning back and looking at them serenely. "Can you imagine what kind of a crowd we'll have in that church if we advertise that old 'Baz' Leonard is goin' to get married to Miss Wheatley?"

The other two committeemen gazed at "Doc" in sheer amazement, stunned by the audacity of his suggestion. "Baz" Leonard and Miss Wheatley! It took several moments for them to grasp the Napoleonic immensity of the proposition.

"Well, I'll be jiggered!" said Mr. Hufty. "How did you come to think of anything like that?"

"Is 'Baz' goin' to marry her?" asked Sam Woodson.

"He is," replied "Doc," "but he don't know it—yet. I'm bankin' on the fact that he won't overlook a chance to show off in public, and that Miss Wheatley is about due to get married to some one."

"I think you'd be doin' her a favor if you picked out somebody besides 'Baz,'" suggested the cold and unresponsive Woodson.

"'Baz' is the man," said "Doc" firmly. "If we've got a public character in this town it's 'Baz' Leonard. If there's a woman in town that's supposed to be out of the marryin' class, it's Miss Wheatley. Her gettin' married to any one would be about the biggest piece of news you could spring on Musselwhite. But gettin' married to 'Baz' Leonard! Say! They won't have a handful of peopl at their chimney-corner show. And you can bet they'll never keep Jake Francis over there to play Santa Claus. Any time that old 'Baz' gets married again, Jake'll want to be there to see it."

"I don't see how you're goin' to work it in on a Christmas Eve exhibition," said Woodson, but even as he spoke he chuckled reflectively, and it was evi-

dent that the beautiful possibilities of the plan were
beginning to ramify his understanding.

"Simplest thing in the world," said "Doc." "We
announce that we're goin' to give Miss Wheatley a
Christmas present."

"You'd better postpone the show till April 1," suggested Mr. Hufty, and then all three committeemen
leaned back in their chairs, exchanged glances, and
roared with laughter. It was evident that no vote
would be necessary.

"I've thought it all out," continued "Doc." "We
can have the regular entertainment, then the distribu-
tion of presents. We'll have Santy Claus bring in the
marriage license and present it to 'Baz.' Then we'll
lead the happy couple to the altar, and after Brother
King has done a scientific job of splicin', we'll give
them their combination Christmas and weddin' presents. The different Sunday-school classes can chip in
and buy presents for them. They'll be glad to do it."

"It sounds all right, but can we talk 'em into it?"
asked Mr. Hufty. " 'Baz' has fooled around her a little, but I never thought he wanted to marry her."

"I'll guarantee to have him on hand when the time
comes," said "Doc" confidently. "I want you two fellows to have the women go after Miss Wheatley. We
must take it for granted that they're already engaged.
Have the women go over and congratulate her, and
then convince her that if she has a church weddin'
she'll get a raft of presents. It's the third and last call
with her, and I don't think we'll have to use blinkers
or a curb bit."

And so, next day, there began the strangest campaign that ever Cupid waged by proxy. Rumor—strong, persistent, undeniable—had it that "Baz" Leonard and Miss Beulah Wheatley were to become as one, indivisible. "United in the holy bonds of wedlock" is the way it was put by the editor of the "Courier."

Unless you, indulgent reader, have lived in a Musselwhite, you can not fully comprehend how convulsing was the excitement that laid hold upon the whole township when the story went jumping from house to house, across farm lots, over ditches, through the deep woods, until it was gleefully discussed around the lamplight as far away as Antioch and Burdett's Grove. For "Baz" Leonard was a man who had posed in the fierce light of publicity for many years. In Rome he would have been a senator. In Musselwhite he was a constable. As a war veteran, as a member of the Volunteer Fire Department, as a confirmed juror, as custodian of a bass drum, as judge of elections, as something-or-other, he contrived to be where the common run of mortals had to look at him and rather admire his self-possession and dignified bearing. To be in the foreground of activities, to be in some way connected with every event which partook of the ceremonial, this was the one gnawing ambition of Ballantyne Leonard. His front name, by some system of abbreviation known only to small towns, had been condensed to "Baz." His wife had died soon after the war. He lived in a small frame house, more thoroughly covered by mortgage than by paint. A pension and the occasional fee coming to a constable provided him with the essentials of life—tobacco and one or two other items less important. As a factor in the business life of Musselwhite he was a comparative cipher, but at public functions he shone. Take it on the Fourth of July. On a borrowed horse, with a tri-colored sash once around his waist and once over the shoulder, he led the parade. On election nights he read the returns. The job of pumping the organ in the Zion Church he refused because he could not perform his duties in view of the congregation. Every winter, when the Methodist revival had stirred the town to a high-strung fervor, he walked up the main aisle and joined the church, becoming for a few nights the nucleus of a shouting jubilation. Every summer he attended a soldiers' reunion, drank to the memory of blood-stained battlefields, and was let out of the church as a backslider. If a traveling magician or hypnotist requested "some one from the audience to kindly step upon the stage," "Baz" was always the first to respond. The happiness of his life came from now and then being on a pedestal. "Doc" Silverton knew what he was talking about when he said that on Christmas Eve he would have his man on hand, ready to be married.

As for Miss Beulah Wheatley, she was a small, prim, and exceedingly antique maiden lady who looked out at the world through a pair of bull's-eye spectacles. Those whose memories extended back far enough testified that, as a girl, she had been "not bad lookin'," and they could account for her having been marooned all these years only on the cruel theory that some marry and some don't. Miss Wheatley was a pocket edition of Joan of Arc when it came to church activities, her efforts being concentrated on foreign missionary work. She was a landmark of Zion. "Doc" Silverton once calculated that she had embroidered twenty-seven pairs of slippers for the coming and going preachers. It was known that she owned the house in which she lived, and it was vaguely rumored that she had money invested. In Musselwhite, flitting about like a lonesome and unmated bird among the satisfied and well-fed domestic pigeons, she was a pathetic joke. People respected her because she was pious and a good housekeeper, but likewise they poked fun at her, for the "old maid" is always a fair target.

No two people in Musselwhite were more surprised by the announced engagement than Mr. "Baz" Leonard and Miss Beulah Wheatley. "Baz" met the first congratulations with good nature, his only sensation being one of gratification that the public should be interested in his private affairs. Later on, when his denials were pooh-poohed into silence, and he was given positive proof that Miss Wheatley had been up to Babcock's store, picking out dress goods, he became alarmed. Even this alarm was tempered by the joy of being the most-talked-about man in Musselwhite, and "Doc" Silverton never lost faith. At the first opportunity he called "Baz" into the office and gave him a long and violent handshaking. "It's somethin' you ought to have done years ago, 'Baz,'" he said, leading his visitor over to an operating chair. "She's a fine woman, and she's got a little property, and I don't see that you could do better."

"I'd like to know how them reports got started," said "Baz." "I ain't seen Miss Wheatley for goin' on six weeks, and when I did see her we didn't talk about nothin' except them Plymouth Rock chickens she bought from—"

"That's all right, 'Baz,'" said "Doc," patting him on the shoulder. "You kept it quiet as long as you could, but Miss Wheatley's a woman, you know, and she was so proud of gettin' you away from all these widows around town, you can't blame her for braggin' a little. Now that it's all settled, we're going to give you the biggest weddin' that was ever seen in this neck of the woods."

Thereupon he outlined the plans for Christmas Eve, minimizing the fact that Miss Wheatley would be a party to the exercises, and enlarging upon the glory that would come to the groom. He told how the organ would thunder, how the church would be jammed, how the infant class would strew flowers in the pathway of the hero, and "Baz," listening, was lost.

In the meantime Mrs. Woodson and Mrs. Hufty had been working on Miss Wheatley. They did not falsify to her, but they led her to believe that Mr. Leonard had said many things that were really said by "Doc" Silverton, and they did it in such a way that the feminine conscience did not suffer a single pang Miss Wheatley gathered, from the nature of their conversation, that they were the emissaries of the would-be groom. Certainly their assurances were emphatic, and she, as if in a dream, permitted herself to be measured for a wedding gown.

And so Miss Wheatley and "Baz" Leonard were engaged, and neither had spoken to the other a word that was even remotely suggestive of matrimony. "Doc" Silverton, past-master at politics and all manner of deep scheming, "clinched" the matter by giving a supper at the Commercial Hotel. "Baz" was present and Miss Wheatley was present and many witnesses were present. When the pie had been served, "Doc" arose and made a speech of congratulation to the couple. He referred to the undying splendor of Mr. Leonard's war record, his long and honorable career as a public servant, and the high esteem in which he was held by the beautiful little city of Musselwhite. It was meet and proper, said "Doc," that such a man should choose for his companion and helpmate an estimable lady whose light had never been hidden under a bushel, etc.

"Baz" and Miss Wheatley looked at each other across the celery tops, bewildered, but lacking the moral courage to arise and protest. They were being carried along on a wave of popular enthusiasm. It seemed exhilarating to Miss Wheatley. "Baz" wore an air of melancholy doubt, especially after the supper at the Commercial Hotel, when he had been given the privilege of taking a long, hard, and critical look at Miss Wheatley in her best clothes.

Word came to the committee that the groom was weakening. "Baz" had been meditating and gazing upon two pictures. One was pleasant—he at the church with a yellow rose in his coat and hundreds of people looking at him. The other was a long-drawn vista of straight and narrow matrimony under the supervision of a small but determined woman.

"I guess we'll have to call it off," he said, as he met "Doc" Silverton in front of the post-office, and he looked across the street in a guilty and shamefaced manner.

"You can't call it off," said "Doc." "You've announced your engagement in the presence of witnesses and we've fixed up the whole programme."

"I didn't announce it—you did."

"Well, you were present, and silence gives consent. If you try to back out now she can sue you for breach of promise."

"What'll she git?"

"I'm surprised at you, 'Baz'—after all that your friends have done for you in this thing."

"Baz" studied a display of Christmas goods in a window and rubbed his chin reflectively. Finally he said, "I ain't got any clothes that's fit to wear."

"Doc" hesitated. The committee had not undertaken to outfit the bridegroom. But he knew that the failure of his pet enterprise would fill the town with Campbellite hilarity, so he said, "We'll see that you get a new suit."

Christmas Eve came. It found Musselwhite keyed up to the highest pitch of glad expectation. Every aspiring comic in the town had exhausted his stock of inventive humor in thinking up presents to give to

"Baz" and Miss Wheatley. From cardboard mottoes of satirical character to a nickel-plated kitchen stove, the gifts, large and small, were waiting behind the pulpit of the Zion Church. As many people as could elbow their way into the seats and aisles and corners of the church were waiting. Miss Wheatley, all in white, with smelling salts, also six married women to give her courage, waited in the pastor's study. And down the street, in a small frame house, a grizzled veteran, who had faced death on many fields of carnage, lay back on his bed and told a despairing committee that he was ill, even to the point of death, and that there could be no wedding. He had put on the new black suit. The black bow tie had been carefully balanced by Sam Woodson. "Baz," with the dull horror of impending calamity numbing his resolution, had even combed his hair, and then, when Mr. Hufty looked at his watch and said, "It's about time to start," ."Baz" had been stricken.

"Where does it seem to hurt you?" asked Sam Woodson.

"All over," said "Baz," looking steadfastly at the ceiling. "I'm as weak as a kitten."

"Your pulse is all right," said "Doc" Silverton," "and you've got a good color. Was Freeman Wheatley over to see you to-day?"

"Baz" rolled over and looked at the wall, and then answered hesitatingly, "Yes, I seen him for a little while."

"What did he say to you?"

"He said she didn't have as much property as most

people think, and that no livin' man could get along with her."

"I thought you was slick enough to see through Freeman Wheatley" said Mr. Hufty. "He wants to sidetrack this thing so he'll come into her property."

"This is no time for foolin'," said "Doc" Silverton, arising and rolling up his sleeves. "There's nothin' the matter with 'Baz' except he's a little overheated by the pleasure of this gladsome occasion. I'll bleed him and cool him off a little and he'll be all O. K."

Saying which he produced a pocket surgical case and took out a long, glittering knife.

"Don't you go to cuttin' into me," said "Baz," sitting up in the bed.

"Then you quit this tomfoolin' and come along with us," said "Doc" sternly. "We ain't got a minute to spare."

"Baz" thereupon showed immediate improvement. With a deep sigh he stood up and they bundled him into his overcoat.

The moonlit street was quite deserted. It seemed that every one in town was waiting at the church. "Doc" Silverton walked ahead with the silent victim. Behind, Mr. Hufty and Sam Woodson executed quiet dance steps in the snow, indicative of their joy.

In front of the Gridley house "Baz" stopped. "I need a drink of water," he said. "I think it'd brace me up."

"You can get one at the church," said "Doc."

"I'd rather step in to the Gridley well here. It's the best water in town."

The committee waited at the front gate. "Baz" disappeared around the corner of the house and they heard the dry clanking of the iron pump and the splatter of water, and then there was silence and a pause, but no "Baz" appeared.

"Mebbe he's slipped out the back way," suggested Mr. Hufty in a frightened whisper, and the committee ran for the pump. The Gridley back yard lay quiet in the moonlight and there was neither sound nor sight of bridegroom.

"He couldn't get away so soon," said "Doc." "I don't see any tracks in the snow."

"D'you s'pose—" began Sam Woodson, looking upward, and then he pointed to where Mr. "Baz" Leonard sat in the high crotch of a cherry tree.

"This is a put-up job," said Mr. Leonard. "I'm just gettin' on to it."

" 'Baz,' you're actin' like a child," began Mr. Hufty. "Come on, now; they're waitin' for you."

"Let him stay up there and freeze," said "Doc." "I'm done with him. I didn't think an old soldier would be afraid to face a crowd of people."

"I ain't afraid," said "Baz," shifting his position. "I've had the cards stacked on me, that's all."

"Go over to the church, Sam," said "Doc" Silverton, after an awkward pause. "Tell the whole crowd to come over here and take a look at the bridegroom that's gone to roost like a chicken." Sam started.

"Don't you bring no crowd here," shouted "Baz" as he began to descend. "This is the lowest trick that was ever put up on a human bein'."

Thus ended his resistance. They led him like a lamb to the slaughter.

People in Musselwhite said it was the making of "Baz" Leonard. For years after that he walked a chalk mark and his habits seemed to improve, for he was afraid to attend a soldiers' reunion. He should have been happy, for he lived in a cottage that was spick and span, and had a capable woman to tell him what to do at every turn. And yet there were times when, at Sunday morning services, he would look across at "Doc" Silverton with a reproachful light in his eyes, as if to say, "You did this to me."

# MR. DOOLEY ON THE PURSUIT
## OF RICHES

### BY F. P. DUNNE

*Finley Peter Dunne (born in Chicago, July 10, 1867) is known to all the English-speaking world as the creator of "Mr. Dooley," the Irish philosopher who from his barroom chair delivers* ex cathedrâ *judgments on the actions of humanity moving before him in the panorama of the morning "pa-apers." While the strict canons of literary form must class the creation with the philosophers (Mr. Dooley belongs to the "laughing" school of Democritus), they can not exclude the creator from the ranks of the poets—the "makers" in the realm of literature who in this age are chiefly represented by the story writers. The personality of Mr. Dooley is perhaps as well indicated in his talk, "On the Pursuit of Riches," as in any other selection.*

# MR. DOOLEY ON THE PURSUIT OF RICHES

## RICHES

BY F. P. DUNNE

D EAR me, I wisht I had money," said Mr. Hennessy.

"So do I," said Mr. Dooley. "I need it."

"Ye wudden't get it fr'm me," said Mr. Hennessy.

"If I didn't," said Mr. Dooley, " 'twud be because I was poor or tired. But what d'ye want money f'r? Supposin' I lost me head an' handed over all me accumylated wealth? What wud ye do with that gr-reat fortune? Befure ye had spint half iv it, ye'd be so sick ye'd come to me an' hand me back th' remainin' eighteen dollars.

"A man has more fun wishin' f'r th' things he hasn't got thin injyin' th' things he has got. Life, Hinnissy, is like a Pullman dinin' car: a fine bill iv fare, but nawthin' to eat. Ye go in fresh an' hungry, tuck ye'er napkin in ye'er collar, an' square away at th' list iv groceries that th' black man hands ye. What'll ye have first? Ye think ye'd like to be famous an' ye ordher a dish iv fame an' bid th' waither make it good an' hot. He's gone an age, an' whin he comes back ye'er appytite is departed. Ye taste th' ordher an' says ye: 'Why, it's cold an' full iv broken glass.' 'That's th' way we always sarve Fame on this car,'

(1423)

says th' coon. 'Don't ye think ye'd like money f'r th' sicond coorse? Misther Rockyfellar over there has had forty-two helpin's,' says he. 'It don't seem to agree with him,' says ye, 'but ye may bring me some,' ye say. Away he goes an' stays till ye're bald an' ye'er teeth fall out, an' ye set dhrummin' on th' table an' lookin' out at th' scenery. By an' by he comes back with ye'er ordher, but jus' as he's goin' to hand it to ye, Rockyfellar grabs th' plate. 'What kind iv a car is this?' says ye. 'Don't I get annything to eat? Can't ye give me a little happiness?' 'I wudden't ricommend th' happiness,' says th' waither. 'It's canned an' it kilt th' las' man that thried it.' 'Well, gracious,' says ye, 'I've got to have something. Give me a little good health an' I'll thry to make a meal out iv that.' 'Sorry, sir,' says th' black man, 'but we're all out iv good health. Besides,' he says, takin' ye gintly by th' ar-rm, 'we're goin' into th' deepo an' ye'll have to get out,' he says.

"An' there ye ar-re. Ye'll niver get money onless ye fix th' waither an' grab th' dishes away fr'm th' other passengers. An' ye won't do that. So ye'll niver be rich. No poor man iver will be. Wan iv th' sthrangest things about life is that th' poor who need th' money th' most ar-re th' very wans that niver have it. A poor man is a poor man an' a rich man is a rich man. Ye're ayether born poor or rich. It don't make anny diff'rence whether or not ye have money to begin with. If ye're born to be rich, ye'll be rich, an' if ye're born to be poor, ye'll be poor. Th' buttons on ye'er vest tell th' story. Rich man, poor man, beggar man, rich man,

F. P. Dunne.

or wurruds to that effect. I always find that I have
ayether two buttons or six.

"A poor man is a man that rayfuses to cash in. Ye
don't get annything f'r nawthin', an' to gather in a
millyon iv thim beautiful lithographs iv Salmon P.
Chase, ye have to go down ivry day with something
undher ye'er ar-rm to th' great pawnshop. Whin
Hogan wants four dollars, he takes th' clock down to
Moses. Whin Rockyfellar wants tin millyon, he puts
up his peace iv mind or his health or something akelly
valyable. If Hogan wud hock his priceless habit iv
sleepin' late in th' mornin', he wud be able to tell th'
time iv day whin he got up without goin' to th' corner
dhrug store.

"Look at McMullin. He's rowlin' in it. It bulges
his pocket an' inflates his convarsation. Whin he looks
at me, I always feel that he's wondhrin' how much I'd
bring at a forced sale. Well, McMullin an' I had th'
same start, about forty yards behind scratch an' Vanderbilt to beat. They always put th' best man in anny
race behind th' line. Befure McMullin gets through
he'll pass Vanderbilt, carry away th' tape on his shoul-
dhers, an' run two or three times around th' thrack.
But me an' him started th' same way. Th' on'y diff'-
rence was that he wud cash in an' I wudden't. Th'
on'y thing I iver ixpicted to get money on was me
dhream iv avarice. I always had that. I cud dhream
iv money as hard as anny man ye iver see an' can still.
But I niver thought iv wurrukin' f'r it. I've always
looked on it as dishon'rable to wurruk f'r money. I
wurruk f'r exercise an' I get what th' lawyers call an

honoraryium be dilutin' th' spirits. Th' on'y way I iver expict to make a cint is to have it left to me be a rich relation, an' I'm th' pluthycrat iv me fam'ly, or to stub me toe on a gambler's roll or stop a runaway horse f'r Pierpont Morgan. An' th' horse mustn't be runnin' too fast. He must be jus' goin' to stop, on'y Morgan don't know it, havin' fainted. Whin he comes to, he finds me at th' bridle, modestly waitin' f'r him to weep on me bosom. But as f'r scramblin' down town arly in th' mornin' an' buyin' chattel morgedges, I niver thought iv it. I get up at siven o'clock. I wudden't get up at a quarther to siven f'r all th' money I dhream about. I have a lot iv things ar-round here I cud cash in if I cared f'r money. I have th' priceless gift iv laziness. It's made me what I am, an' that's th' very first thing ivry rich man cashes in. Th' millyonaires ye r-read about thryin' to give th' rest iv th' wurruld a good time be runnin' over thim in autymobills all started with a large stock iv indolence which they cashed in. Now, whin they cud enjoy it, they can't buy it back. Thin I have me good health. Ye can always get money on that. An' I have me frinds; I rayfuse to cash thim in. I don't know that I cud get much on thim, but if I wanted to be a millyonaire, I'd tuck you an' Hogan an' Donahue undher me ar-rm an' carry ye down to Mose.

"McMullin did cash. He had no more laziness thin me, but he cashed it in befure he was twinty-wan. He cashed in his good health, a large stock iv fam'ly ties, th' affiction if his wife, th' comforts iv home, an' wan frind afther another. Wanst in a while, late in life, he'd thry to redeem a pledge, but he niver cud. They wasn't annything in th' wurruld that McMullin wudden't change f'r th' roly-boly. He cashed in his vote, his pathreetism, his rellijon, his rilitives, an' fin'lly his hair. Ye heerd about him, didn't ye? He's lost ivry hair on his head. They ain't a spear iv vigitation left on him. He's as arid as th' desert iv Sahara. His head looks like an iceberg in th' moonlight. He was in here th' other day, bewailin' his fate. 'It's a gr-reat misfortune,' says he. 'What did ye get f'r it?' says I. 'That's th' throuble,' says he. 'Well, don't complain,' says I. 'Think what ye save in barber's bills,' I says, an' he wint away lookin' much cheered up.

"No, Hinnissy, you an' I, me frind, was not cut out be Provydence to be millyionaires. If ye had nawthin' but money, ye'd have nawthin' but money. Ye can't ate it, sleep it, dhrink it, or carry it away with ye. Ye've got a lot iv things that McMullin hasn't got. Annybody that goes down to Mose's won't see ye'er peace iv mind hangin' in th' window as an unredeemed pledge. An' annyhow, if ye're really in search iv a fortune, perhaps I cud help ye. Wud a dollar an' a half be anny use to ye?"

"Life is full iv disappointments," said Mr. Hennessy.

"It is," said Mr. Dooley, "if ye feel that way. It's thrue that a good many have thried it an' none have come back f'r a post-gradjate coorse. But still it ain't so bad as a career f'r a young man. Ye niver get what ye ordher, but it's pretty good if ye'er appytite ain't keen an' ye care f'r th' scenery."

# A CHRISTMAS PRESENT FOR A LADY

## BY MYRA KELLY

*Myra Kelly (born in Dublin, Ireland, about 1880) spent two years as a public school teacher in the East Side of New York—a region inhabited chiefly by Russian Jews. The stories she brought home of her experiences with the children and their parents were so full of humor and character that certain of her friends persuaded her to write one down and send it to some periodical. "McClure's" was the fortunate magazine to secure this contribution, which proved to be the first of a series of stories that, though varying in style from the purely humorous to the romantic and pathetic, possess the common flavor of the author's individuality. The present selection ripples down the limited gamut of the emotions of the poor, from the high notes of sheer joy to tones of love made tender by pathetic penury. Miss Kelly was married during the present year (1905) to Allan Macnaughton.*

# A CHRISTMAS PRESENT FOR A LADY

## BY MYRA KELLY

IT was the week before Christmas, and the First
Reader Class, in a lower East Side school, had,
almost to a man, decided on the gifts to be lav-
ished on "Teacher." She was quite unprepared for
any such observance on the part of her small adhe-
rents, for her first study of the roll book had shown
her that its numerous Jacobs, Isidores, and Rachels
belonged to a class to which Christmas Day was much
as other days. And so she went serenely on her way,
all unconscious of the swift and strict relation between her manner and her chances. She was, for instance, the only person in the room who did not know
that her criticism of Isidore Belchatosky's hands and
face cost her a tall "three for ten cents" candlestick
and a plump box of candy.

But Morris Mogilewsky, whose love for Teacher
was far greater than the combined loves of all the
other children, had as yet no present to bestow. That
his "kind feeling" should be without proof when the
lesser loves of Isidore Wishnewsky, Sadie Gonorowsky, and Bertha Binderwitz were taking the tan-
gible but surprising forms which were daily exhibited
to his confidential gaze was more than he could bear.

The knowledge saddened all his hours, and was the more maddening because it could in no wise be shared by Teacher, who noticed his altered bearing and tried with all sorts of artful beguilements to make him happy and at ease. But her efforts served only to increase his unhappiness and his love. And he loved her! Oh, how he loved her! Since first his dreading eyes had clung for a breath's space to her "like man's shoes" and had then crept timidly upward past a black skirt, a "from silk" apron, a red "jumper," and "from gold" chain to her "light face," she had been mistress of his heart of hearts. That was more than three months ago. How well he remembered the day!

His mother had washed him horribly, and had taken him into the big red schoolhouse, so familiar from the outside, but so full of unknown terrors within. After his dusty little shoes had stumbled over the threshold he had passed from ordeal to ordeal until, at last, he was torn in mute and white-faced despair from his mother's skirts.

He was then dragged through long halls and up tall stairs by a large boy, who spoke to him disdainfully as "greenie," and cautioned him as to the laying down softly and taking up gently of those poor, dusty shoes, so that his spirit was quite broken and his nerves were all unstrung when he was pushed into a room full of bright sunshine and of children who laughed at his frightened little face. The sunshine smote his timid eyes, the laughter smote his timid heart, and he turned to flee. But the door was shut, the large boy gone, and despair took him for its own.

Down upon the floor he dropped, and wailed, and wept, and kicked. It was then that he heard, for the first time, the voice which now he loved. A hand was forced between his aching body and the floor, and the voice said:

"Why, my dear little chap, you mustn't cry like that. What's the matter?"

The hand was gentle and the question kind, and these, combined with a faint perfume suggestive of drug stores and barber shops—but nicer than either—made him uncover his hot little face. Kneeling beside him was a lady, and he forced his eyes to that perilous ascent; from shoes to skirt, from skirt to jumper, from jumper to face, they trailed in dread uncertainty, but at the face they stopped—they had found rest.

Morris allowed himself to be gathered into the lady's arms and held upon her knee, and when his sobs no longer rent the very foundations of his pink and wide-spread tie, he answered her question in a voice as soft as his eyes, and as gently sad.

"I ain't so big, and I don't know where is my mama."

So, having cast his troubles on the shoulders of the lady, he had added his throbbing head to the burden, and from that safe retreat had enjoyed his first day at school immensely.

Thereafter he had been the first to arrive every morning, and the last to leave every afternoon; and under the care of Teacher, his liege lady, he had grown in wisdom and love and happiness, but the greatest of these was love. And now, when the other boys and girls were planning surprises and gifts of price for Teacher, his hands were as empty as his heart was full. Appeal to his mother met with denial prompt and energetic.

"For what you go and make, over Christmas, presents? You ain't no Krisht; you should better have no kind feelings over Krishts, neither; your papa could to have a mad."

"Teacher ain't no Krisht," said Morris stoutly; "all the other fellows buys her presents, und I'm loving mit her; it's polite I gives her presents the while I'm got such a kind feeling over her."

"Well, we ain't got no money for buy nothing," said Mrs. Mogilewsky sadly. "No money, und your papa, he has all times a scare he shouldn't to get no more, the while the boss"—and here followed incomprehensible, but depressing, financial details, until the end of the interview found Morris and his mother sobbing and rocking in one another's arms. So Morris was helpless, his mother poor, and Teacher all unknowing.

. . . . . . . .

And now the great day, the Friday before Christmas, has come, and the school is, for the first half hour, quite mad. Doors open suddenly and softly to admit small persons, clad in wondrous ways and bearing wondrous parcels. Room 18, generally so placid and so peaceful, is a howling wilderness full of brightly colored, quickly changing groups of children, all whispering, all gurgling, and all hiding queer bun-

dles.  A new-comer invariably causes a diversion; the
assembled multitude, athirst for novelty, falls upon
him and clamors for a glimpse of his bundle and a
statement of its price.

Teacher watches in dumb amaze.  What can be the
matter with the children?  They can't have guessed
that the shrouded something in the corner is a Christmas tree?  What makes them behave so queerly, and
why do they look so strange?  They seem to have
grown stout in a single night, and Teacher, as she
notes this, marvels greatly.  The explanation is
simple, though it comes in alarming form.  The
sounds of revelry are pierced by a long, shrill yell, and
a pair of agitated legs spring suddenly into view between two desks.  Teacher, rushing to the rescue,
notes that the legs form the unsteady stem of an up-
turned mushroom of brown flannel and green braid,
which she recognizes as the outward seeming of her
cherished Bertha Binderwitz; and yet, when the desks
are forced to disgorge their prey, the legs restored to
their normal position are found to support a fat child
—and Bertha was best described as "skinny"—in a
dress of the Stuart tartan tastefully trimmed with purple.  Investigation proves that Bertha's accumulative
taste in dress is an established custom.  In nearly all
cases the glory of holiday attire is hung upon the solid
foundation of every-day clothes as bunting is hung
upon a building.  The habit is economical of time,
and produces a charming embonpoint.

Teacher, too, is more beautiful than ever.  Her
dress is blue, and "very long down, like a lady," with

bands of silk and scraps of lace distributed with the eye of art. In her hair she wears a bow of what Sadie Gonorowsky, whose father "works by fancy goods," describes as "black from plush ribbon—costs ten cents."

Isidore Belchatosky, relenting, is the first to lay tribute before Teacher. He comes forward with a sweet smile and a tall candlestick—the candy has gone to its long home—and Teacher for a moment can not be made to understand that all that length of bluish-white china is really hers "for keeps."

"It's to-morrow holiday," Isidore assures her; "and we gives you presents, the while we have a kind feeling. Candlesticks could to cost twenty-five cents."

"It's a lie. Three for ten," says a voice in the background, but Teacher hastens to respond to Isidore's test of her credulity:

"Indeed, they could. This candlestick could have cost fifty cents, and it's just what I want. It is very good of you to bring me a present."

"You're welcome," says Isidore, retiring; and then, the ice being broken, the First Reader Class in a body rises to cast its gifts on Teacher's desk, and its arms round Teacher's neck.

Nathan Horowitz presents a small cup and saucer; Isidore Applebaum bestows a large calendar for the year before last; Sadie Gonorowsky brings a basket containing a bottle of perfume, a thimble, and a bright silk handkerchief; Sarah Schodsky offers a penwiper and a yellow celluloid collar-button, and Eva Kidansky gives an elaborate nasal douche, under the pleasing delusion that it is an atomizer.

Once more sounds of grief reach Teacher's ears. Rushing again to the rescue, she throws open the door and comes upon woe personified. Eva Gonorowsky, her hair in wildest disarray, her stocking fouled, ungartered, and down-gyved to her ankle, appears before her teacher. She bears all the marks of Hamlet's excitement, and many more, including a tear-stained little face and a gilt saucer clasped to a panting breast.

"Eva, my dearest Eva, what's happened to you *now?*" asks Teacher, for the list of ill chances which have befallen this one of her charges is very long. And Eva wails forth that a boy, a very big boy, had stolen her golden cup "what I had for you by present," and has left her only the saucer and her undying love to bestow.

Before Eva's sobs have quite yielded to Teacher's arts, Jacob Spitsky presses forward with a tortoise-shell comb of terrifying aspect and hungry teeth, and an air showing forth a determination to adjust it in its destined place. Teacher meekly bows her head; Jacob forces his offering into her long-suffering hair, and then retires with the information, "Costs fifteen cents, Teacher," and the courteous phrase—by etiquette prescribed—"Wish you health to wear it." He is plainly a hero, and is heard remarking to less favored admirers that "Teacher's hair is awful softy, and smells off of perfumery."

Here a big boy, a very big boy, enters hastily. He does not belong to Room 18, but he has long known Teacher. He has brought her a present; he wishes her a merry Christmas. The present, when produced, proves to be a pretty gold cup, and Eva Gonorowsky, with renewed emotion, recognizes the boy as her assailant and the cup as her property. Teacher is dreadfully embarrassed; the boy not at all so. His policy is simple and entire denial, and in this he perseveres, even after Eva's saucer has unmistakably proclaimed its relationship to the cup.

Meanwhile the rush of presentation goes steadily on. Other cups and saucers come in wild profusion. The desk is covered with them, and their wrappings of purple tissue paper require a monitor's whole attention. The soap, too, becomes urgently perceptible. It is of all sizes, shapes, and colors, but of uniform and dreadful power of perfume. Teacher's eyes fill with tears of gratitude as each new piece, or box, is pressed against her nose, and Teacher's mind is full of wonder as to what she can ever do with all of it. Bottles of perfume vie with one another and with the all-pervading soap until the air is heavy and breathing grows laborious, while pride swells the hearts of the assembled multitude. No other teacher has so many helps to the toilet. None other is so beloved.

Teacher's aspect is quite changed, and the "blue long down like a lady dress" is almost hidden by the offerings she has received. Jacob's comb has two massive and bejeweled rivals in the "softy hair." The front of the dress, where aching or despondent heads are wont to rest, is glittering with campaign buttons of American celebrities, beginning with James G. Blaine and extending into modern history as far as

Patrick Divver, Admiral Dewey, and Captain Drey-
fus. Outside the blue belt is a white one, nearly clean,
and bearing in "sure 'nough golden words" the curt,
but stirring, invitation, "Remember the Maine."
Around the neck are three chaplets of beads, wrought
by chubby fingers and embodying much love, while
the waist-line is further adorned by tiny and berib-
boned aprons. Truly, it is a day of triumph.

When the waste-paper basket has been twice filled
with wrappings and twice emptied; when order is
emerging out of chaos; when the Christmas tree has
been disclosed and its treasures distributed, a timid
hand is laid on Teacher's knee and a plaintive voice
whispers, "Say, Teacher, I got something for you";
and Teacher turns quickly to see Morris, her dearest
boy charge, with his poor little body showing quite
plainly between his shirtwaist buttons and through
the gashes he calls pockets. This is his ordinary costume, and the funds of the house of Mogilewsky are
evidently unequal to an outer layer of finery.

"Now, Morris, dear," says Teacher, "you shouldn't
have troubled to get me a present; you know you and
I are such good friends that —"

"Teacher, yis, ma'am," Morris interrupts, in a bewitching rising inflection of his soft and plaintive
voice; "I know you got a kind feeling by me, and I
couldn't to tell even how I'm got a kind feeling by
you. Only it's about that kind feeling I should give
you a present. I didn't"—with a glance at the
crowded desk—"I didn't to have no soap nor no perfumery, and my mama, she couldn't to buy none by

the store; but, Teacher, I'm got something awful nice
for you by present."

"And what is it, deary?" asks the already rich and
gifted young person. "What is my new present?"

"Teacher, it's like this: I don't know; I ain't so big
like I could to know"—and, truly, God pity him! he is
passing small—"It ain't for boys—it's for ladies.
Over yesterday on the night comes my papa on my
house, and he gives my mama the present. Sooner
she looks on it, sooner she has a awful glad; in her
eye stands tears, und she says, like that—out of Jewish—'Thanks,' un' she kisses my papa a kiss. Und
my papa, *how* he is polite! he says—out of Jewish,
too—'You're welcome, all right,' un' he kisses my
mama a kiss. So my mama, she sets and looks on
the present, und all the time she looks she has a glad
over it. Und I didn't to have no soap, so you could to
have the present."

"But did your mother say I might?"

"Teacher, no ma'am; she didn't say like that un'
she didn't to say *not* like that. She didn't to know.
But it's for ladies, un' I didn't to have no soap. You
could to look on it. It ain't for boys."

And here Morris opens a hot little hand and dis-
closes a tightly-folded pinkish paper. As Teacher
reads it he watches her with eager, furtive eyes, dry
and bright, until hers grow suddenly moist, when his
promptly follow suit. As she looks down at him, he
makes his moan once more:

"It's for ladies, und I didn't to have no soap."

"But, Morris, dear," cries Teacher unsteadily,

laughing a little, and yet not far from tears, "this is ever so much nicer than soap—a thousand times better than perfume; and you're quite right, it is for ladies, and I never had one in all my life before. I am so very thankful."

"You're welcome, all right. That's how my papa says; it's polite," says Morris proudly. And proudly he takes his place among the very little boys, and loudly he joins in the ensuing song. For the rest of that exciting day he is a shining point of virtue in a slightly confused class. And at three o'clock he is at Teacher's desk again, carrying on the conversation as if there had been no interruption.

"Und my mama," he says insinuatingly—"she kisses my papa a kiss."

"Well?" says Teacher.

"Well," says Morris, "you ain't never kissed me a kiss, und I seen how you kissed Eva Gonorowsky. I'm loving mit you too. Why don't you never kiss me a kiss?"

"Perhaps," suggests Teacher mischievously, "perhaps it ain't for boys."

But a glance at her "light face," with its crown of surprising combs, reassures him.

"Teacher, yis, ma'am; it's for boys," he cries as he feels her arms about him, and sees that in her eyes, too, "stands tears."

"It's polite you kisses me a kiss over that for ladies' present."

Late that night Teacher sat in her pretty room— for she was, unofficially, a great pampered young person—and reviewed her treasures. She saw that they were very numerous, very touching, very whimsical, and very precious. But above all the rest she cherished a frayed pinkish paper, rather crumpled and a little soiled. For it held the love of a man and woman and a little child, and the magic of a home, for Morris Mogilewsky's Christmas present for ladies was the receipt for a month's rent for a room on the top floor of a Monroe Street tenement.

# THE SPIRAL STONE

## BY ARTHUR COLTON

*Arthur Willis Colton (born at Washing-ton, Ct., May 22, 1868) was for several years after his graduation from Yale an instructor in English literature at that institution. For the last ten years he has devoted himself to authorship, contributing to the leading magazines stories and what might be called studies in story style, which, later, he has gathered into books. The present selection is a short one—a bat's flight, as it were, in the dusk of the graveyard. Yet longer attempts of the same order invariably end in Icarian failure. The wings of imagination must be a natural growth to bear one safely into the realm of the unknown.*

# THE SPIRAL STONE

## BY ARTHUR COLTON

THE graveyard on the brow of the hill was white with snow. The marbles were white, the evergreens black. One tall spiral stone stood painfully near the centre. The little brown church outside the gates turned its face in the more comfortable direction of the village.

Only three were out among the graves: "Ambrose Chillingworth, ætat 30, 1675"; "Margaret Vane, ætat 19, 1839"; and "Thy Little One, O God, ætat 2," from the Mercer Lot. It is called the "Mercer Lot," but the Mercers are all dead or gone from the village.

The Little One trotted around busily, putting his tiny finger in the lettering and patting the faces of the cherubs. The other two sat on the base of the spiral, which twisted in the moonlight over them.

"I wonder why it is?" Margaret said. "Most of them never come out at all. We and the Little One come out so often. You were wise and learned. I knew so little. Will you tell me?"

"Learning is not wisdom," Ambrose answered. "But of this matter it was said that our containment in the grave depended on the spirit in which we departed. I made certain researches. It appeared

From "Tioba and Other Tales," copyright, 1903, by Henry Holt & Co. This story originally appeared in 1901, in the "Atlantic Monthly," and was copyrighted that year by Messrs. Houghton, Mifflin & Co.

by common report that only those came out whom
desperate sin tormented, or labors incomplete and
great desire at the point of death made restless. I
had doubts the matter were more subtle, the reasons
of it reaching out distantly." He sighed faintly, following with his eyes, tomb by tomb, the broad white
path that dropped down the hillside to the church.
"I desired greatly to live."

"I too. Is it because we desired it so much, then?
But the Little One—"

"I do not know," he said.

The Little One trottted gravely here and there,
seeming to know very well what he was about, and
presently came to the spiral stone. The lettering on
it was new, and there was no cherub. He dropped
down suddenly on the snow with a faint whimper.
His small feet came out from under his gown, as
he sat upright gazing at the letters with round,
troubled eyes, and up to the top of the monument,
for the solution of some unstated problem.

"The stone is but newly placed," said Ambrose,
"and the new-comer would seem to be of those who
rest in peace."

They went and sat down on either side of him, on
the snow. The peculiar cutting of the stone, with
spirally ascending lines, together with the moon's
illusion, gave it a semblance of motion. Something
twisted and climbed continually, and vanished continually from the point. But the base was broad,
square, and heavily lettered: "John Mareschelli
Vane."

"Vane? That was thy name," said Ambrose.

1890.   ÆTAT 72.

AN EMINENT CITIZEN, A PUBLIC BENEFAC-
TOR AND WIDELY ESTEEMED.

FOR THE LOVE OF HIS NATIVE PLACE RE-
TURNED TO LAY HIS DUST THEREIN.

THE JUST MADE PERFECT.

"It would seem he did well and rounded his labors
to a goodly end, lying down among his kindred as a
sheaf that is garnered in the autumn.  He was fortunate."

And Margaret spoke, in the thin, emotionless voice
which those who are long in the graveyard use: "He
was my brother."

"Thy brother?" said Ambrose.

The Little One looked up and down the spiral with
wide eyes.  The other two looked past it into the
deep white valley, where the river, covered with ice
and snow, was marked only by the lines of skeleton
willows and poplars.  A night wind, listless but con-
tinual, stirred the evergreens.  The moon swung low
over the opposite hills, and for a moment slipped behind a cloud.

"Says it is not so, 'For the Love of his Native
Place'?" murmured Ambrose.

And as the moon came out, there leaned against
the pedestal, pointing with a finger at the epitaph,
one that seemed an old man, with bowed shoulders
and keen, restless face, but in his manner cowed and
weary.

"It is a lie," he said slowly. "I hated it, Margaret. I came because Ellen Mercer called me."

"Ellen isn't buried here."

"Not here?"

"Not here."

"Was it you, then, Margaret? Why?"

"I didn't call you."

"Who then?" he shrieked. "Who called me?"

The night wind moved on monotonously, and the moonlight was undisturbed, like glassy water.

"When I came away," she said, "I thought you would marry her. You didn't, then? But why should she call you?"

"I left the village suddenly!" he cried. "I grew to dread and then to hate it. I buried myself from the knowledge of it, and the memory of it was my enemy. I wished for a distant death, and these fifty years have heard the summons to come and lay my bones in this graveyard. I thought it was Ellen. You, sir, wear an antique dress; you have been long in this strange existence. Can you tell who called me? If not Ellen, where is Ellen?" He wrung his hands, and rocked to and fro.

"The mystery is with the dead as with the living," said Ambrose. "The shadows of the future and the past come among us. We look in their eyes, and understand them not. Now and again there is a call even here, and the grave is henceforth untenanted of its spirit. Here, too, we know a necessity which binds us, which speaks not with audible voice and will not be questioned."

"But tell me," moaned the other, "does the weight of sin depend upon its consequences? Then what weight do I bear? I do not know whether it was ruin or death, or a thing gone by and forgotten. Is there no answer here to this?"

"Death is but a step in the process of life," answered Ambrose. "I know not if any are ruined or anything forgotten. Look up, to the order of the stars, and handwriting on the wall of the firmament. But who hath read it? Mark this night wind, a still small voice. But what speaketh it? The earth is clothed in white garments as a bride. What mean the ceremonials of the seasons? The will from without is only known as it is manifested. Nor does it manifest where the consequences of the deed end or its causes began. Have they any end or a beginning? I can not answer you."

"Who called me, Margaret?"

And she said again monotonously:

"I didn't call you."

The Little One sat between Ambrose and Margaret, chuckling to himself and gazing up at the newcomer, who suddenly bent forward and looked into his eyes, with a gasp.

"What is this?" he whispered.

" 'Thy Little One, O God, ætat 2,' from the Mercer Lot," returned Ambrose gently.

"He is very quiet. Art not neglecting thy business, Little One? The lower walks are unvisited to-night."

"They are Ellen's eyes!" cried the other, moaning and rocking. "Did you call me? Were you mine?"

"It is written, 'Thy Little One, O God,'" murmured Ambrose.

But the Little One only curled his feet up under his gown, and now chuckled contentedly.

# JEAN MICHAUD'S LITTLE SHIP

## BY CHARLES G. D. ROBERTS

*Charles George Douglas Roberts (born at Douglas, New Brunswick, Canada, January 10, 1860) is an American author in the continental rather than national sense of that term. By birth a Canadian, his work in history and historical fiction has naturally been concerned with British America; but his purely imaginative writings, his prose idyls, and his animal stories, no less than his verse, deal with forests and streams whose position on either side of a political boundary is indifferent, and the allegiance of whose denizens, men or beasts, is to nature alone. Of fiction in the latter vein only an entire book of Mr. Roberts's, such as his "Red Fox," would be adequately representative. Accordingly the present selection has been made from his romantic stories which have a connection with Canadian history.*

# JEAN MICHAUD'S LITTLE SHIP

## BY CHARLES G. D. ROBERTS

PATIENTLY, doggedly, yet with the light in his eyes that belongs to the enthusiast and the dreamer, young Jean Michaud had worked at it. Throughout the winter he had hewed the seasoned timbers and the diminutive hackmatack "knees" from the swamp far back in the Equille Valley; and whenever the sledding was good with his yoke of black oxen he had hauled his materials to the secret place of his shipbuilding by the winding shore of a deep tidal tributary of the Port Royal. In the spring he had laid the keel and riveted securely to it the squared hackmatack knees. It was unusual to use such sturdy and unmanageable timbers as these hackmatack knees for a craft so small as this which the young Acadian was building; but Jean Michaud's thoughts were long thoughts and went far ahead. He was putting all his hopes as well as all his scant patrimony into this little ship; and he was resolved that it should be strong to carry his fortunes.

Through all the green and blue and golden Acadian summer he had toiled joyously at bending the thin planks and riveting them soundly to the ribs, the stem and the sternpost. It was hot work, but white and savory, the clean spruce planks that he wrought

with breathing sweet scents to his lungs as adze and
chisel and saw set free the tonic spirit of their fibres.
His chips soon spread a yellow carpet over the mossy
sward and the tree-roots.    The yellow sides of his
graceful craft presently arose high among the green
kissing branches of the water-ash and Indian pear.
The tawny golden shimmering current of the creek
lipped up at high tide close under the stern of the
little ship and set afloat the lowest layers of the chips;
while at ebb a gleaming abyss of red mud with walls
sloping sharply to a mere rivulet at their foot seemed
to tempt the structure to a premature launching and
a wild swooping rush to oozy doom.    Very secluded,
far apart from beaten highway or forest byway, and
quite aside from all the river traffic, was the place of
Jean Michaud's shipbuilding.    And so it came about
that the clear ringing blows of his adze, the sharp
staccato of his diligent hammer and the strident cry-
ing of his saw brought no answer but the chatter of
the striped chipmunks among the near tree-roots, or
the scolding of the garrulous and inquisitive red squirrels from the branches overhead.    At the quiet of the
noon hour, while Jean lay in the shade contemplating
his handiwork, and weaving his many-colored dreams,
and munching his brown-bread cakes and pale cheese,
the clucking partridge hen would lead her brood out
to investigate the edges of the chip-strewn open,
where insects gathered in the heat.    And afterward,
when once more Jean's hammering set up its brisk
and cheerful echoes, the big golden-wing wood-
peckers would promptly accept the sound as a

challenge, and begin an emolous rat-tat-tat-tat-ing
on the resonant sound-board of a dead beech not
far off.

By the time the partridge brood had taken to whir-
ring up into the maple branches when alarmed, instead of scurrying to cover in the underbrush, the
hull was completed; and a smell of smoking pitch
drowned the woodsy odors as Jean calked the seams.
Then the pale yellow of the timbers no more shone
through the reddening leafage, but a sombre black
bulk loomed impressively above the chips, daunting
the squirrels for a few days with its strange shadow.
By the time of the moose-calling, when the rowan-
berries hung in great scarlet bunches and half the
red leafage was turning brown, and the pale gold
birch leaves fell in fluttering showers at every gust,
two slim masts had raised their tops above the trees,
and a white bowsprit was thrusting its nose into the
branches of the nearest red maple. Under the bowsprit glittered a carved and gilded Madonna, the most
auspicious figurehead to which, in Jean's eyes, he
could intrust the fortunes of his handiwork. A few
days more and the ship was done—so nearly complete
that three or four hours of work would make her
ready for sea. Being so small, it was feasible to
launch her in this advanced state of equipment; and
the conditions under which she had been built made it
necessary that she should be prepared to hurry
straight from the greased ways of the launching to
the security of the open sea. The tidal creek in which
she would first take water could give her no

safe harborage; and once out of the creek she would have to make all speed, under cover of night, till Port Royal River and the sodded ramparts of Annapolis town should be left many miles astern.

Having made his preparations and gathered his materials far ahead, and devised his precautions with subtlety, and accustomed his neighbors to the idea that he was an erratic youth, given to long absences and futile schemes, not worth gossip, Jean had succeeded in keeping his enterprise a secret from all but two persons. These two, deep in his counsels from the first, were Barbe Dieudonné, his sweetheart, and Mich' Masson, his friend and ally.

Mich' Masson—whose home, which served him best as a place to stay away from, was in the village of Grand Pré, far up on the Basin of Minas—had been Jean's close friend since early boyhood, in the days before Port Royal town had been captured by the English and found its name changed to Annapolis. He was a daring adventurer, hunter, woods-ranger, an implacable partisan of the French cause, and just now deeply interested in the traffic between Acadie and the new French fortress city of Louisburg—a traffic which the English Governor was angrily determined to break up. Mich' Masson could sail a ship as well as set a dead-fall or lay an ambush. He had kept bright in Jean's heart the flame of hatred against the English conquerors of Acadie. It was he who had come to the aid of Jean's shipbuilding from time to time, when timbers had to be put in place which

were too heavy for one pair of hands to work with.
It was, indeed, at his suggestion that Jean had finally
decided to sell his cottage on the outskirts of
Annapolis town, his scrap of upland with its apple
trees in full bearing, his strip of rich dikeland by the
riverside—secretly to build his little ship for the forbidden traffic—and to settle under the walls of Louisburg, where the flag he loved should always wave
over his roof-tree. It was Mich' Masson who had
shown Jean how by this course he could quickly
grow rich, and make a home for Barbe which that
somewhat disconcerting and incomprehensible maiden
would not scorn to accept. Mich' Masson loved his
own honor. He loved Jean. He hated the English.
Jean's secret was safe with him.

Mademoiselle Barbe, under a disguise of indifference which sometimes reduced Jean to the not un-
profitable condition wherein hard work is the sole refuge from despair, hid a passionate interest in her
lover's undertaking. She, too, hated the new domina-
tion. She, too, chafed to escape from Annapolis and
take up life anew under her old Flag of the Fleur-de-
lis. Moreover, her restless and fiery spirit could accept
no contented tiller of green Acadian acres for a mate;
and she was resolved that Jean's courageous heart and
stirring dreams should translate themselves into action.
She would have him not only the daring dreamer but
the daring doer—the successful smuggler, the shrewd
foiler of the English watch-dogs, the admired and con-
sulted partisan leader. That he had it in him to be all
these things she felt utterly convinced; but she pro-

posed that the debilitating effects of too much happiness should have no chance of postponing his success. Her keen watchfulness detected every weak spot in Jean's enterprise, every unguarded point in his secret; and her two-edged mockery, which seemed as careless and inconsequent as the wind, at once accomplished the effects she had in view. Her fickleness of mood, her bewildering caprice, were the iridescent foam-bubbles veiling a deep and steady current. She knew that she loved Jean's love for her, of which she felt as certain as dawn does of the sunrise. She had a suspicion in the deep of her heart that she might be in love with Jean himself; but of this she was in no haste to be assured. She was loyal in every fibre. And Jean's secret was safe with her.

Thus the wonder came to pass that Jean's secret, though known to three people, yet remained so long a secret. Had the English Governor, behind his sodded ramparts overlooking the tide, got wind of it, never would Jean Michaud's little ship have sailed the open, save with an English captain and an English crew. It would have been confiscated, on the not unreasonable presumption that it was intended for the forbidden trade.

Early in the afternoon, on a day of mid-October, Jean stepped down the ladder which leaned against the starboard bow of his ship, and contemplated with satisfaction the name, "Mon Rêve," which he had just painted in strong, gold lettering. The exultation in his eyes became a passion of love and worship, as he turned to the slim girl who lay curled up luxuriously on a sweet-smelling pile of dried ferns and marsh-grass, watching him.

"Since you won't let me name her directly after you, that is the nearest I can come to it, Barbe," he said. "You can't find fault with that. You are my dream—and all else besides."

For a moment she watched him in silence. Her figure was of a childish slenderness, and there was a childish abandon in her attitude. The small hands crossed idly in her lap were very dark and thin and long-fingered, with rosy nails. She was dressed in skirt and bodice of the creamy Acadian homespun linen, the skirt reaching not quite to her slim ankles. Her mouth was full and red, half sorrowful, half mocking. Her face, small and rather thin, was tanned to a clear, dark brown, and of a type that suggested a strain of the ancient blood of the Basques. The thick black masses of her hair, with a rebel wave in them, and here and there a glint of flame, half covered her little ears and were gathered into a knot at the back of her neck. The brim of her low-crowned hat of quilted linen was tilted far down to shade her face; and her eyes, very green and clear and large, made a bewildering brilliance in the shadow.

The light in her eyes softened presently, and she said in a low voice:

"Poor boy, a very sharp reality you find me most of the time, I'm afraid."

For this unexpected utterance Jean had no words of answer ready, but his look was a sufficiently eloquent refutation. He took a few eager steps toward her;

then, reading inhibition in the sudden gravity of her mouth, he checked himself.

"Day after to-morrow, about sundown," said he, "our Lady and St. Joseph permitting, we will get her launched. The tide will be full then, and we will run down with it, and pass the fort before moonrise. If the wind's fair we will get out of the Basin and off to sea that same night; but if it fails us there'll be tide enough to get us round the Island and into a hidden anchorage in Hibert River. Then—a cargo of Acadian beef and barley for Louisburg! And then— money! And then—and then—you!"

He looked at her with pleading and longing in his eyes, but with a doggedness about his mouth which told of much pain endured and a determination which might bide its time, indeed, but would not be balked. The look of the mouth she was conscious of, deep down in her heart, and she in reality rested upon it; but it was the look in his eyes which she answered. She answered it lightly. A mocking smile played about the corners of her lips and her eyes sparkled upon him whimsically. The look both repulsed and invited him; and he hung for some moments, as it were, trembling midway between the promise and the denial.

"Don't be too sure of—me!" she said at last. And his face fell—not so much at the words themselves as at their discouraging accent.

"But," he protested, "it is all planned, all done, just for you, Barbe. There is nothing in it at all, except you. It is all you. That is understood between us from the first, and all the time."

Still her mouth mocked him; and still her eyes gleamed upon him with their enigmatic light.

"You will have your beautiful little ship," she said slowly. "You will have wonderful adventures—and little time to think of me at all. You will make a wonderful deal of money. You will make your name famous and hated among these English. I am expecting you to do great things. But as for me—I am not won yet, Jean."

His eyes glowed upon her, and the lines of his face set themselves with a sudden masterfulness. He gave a little, soft laugh.

"You are mine! You will be my wife before I make my second voyage."

"If you believe that, you ought to be a very happy man," she retorted, and her smile softened almost imperceptibly as she said it. "You don't look quite as happy as you ought to, Jean!"

"*Don't* make me wait for my second voyage! Let me take you away from this unhappy country. Come with me—come with me now!"

He spoke swiftly, his voice thick with the sudden outburst of passion long held in check; and he strode forward to catch her in his arms.

Instantaneous as a darting bird, or a flash of light on a wave, she was up from her resting-place and away behind the pile of grass and ferns.

"Stay there!" she commanded, "or I'll go home at once!" And Jean stayed.

She laughed at him gayly, mercilessly.

"Would you have me take you on trust, Jean?" she

questioned, with her head on one side. "How do I know that you are going to be brave enough to fight the English, or clever enough to outwit them? How do I know you will really do the great things I'm expecting of you? I know your dreams are fine, Boy; but you must show me deeds."

"I will," he answered quietly. "Come here, Sweet, just for one minute!"

"No," she said with a very positive shake of her small head. "You must go on with your work. You have more to do yet than you realize. And *I've* something to do, too. I must go home at once."

"That's not fair, Barbe!" he pleaded.

"I don't care! It is good for you. No, don't come one step with me. Not one step. Go on with your work. I'm going to fly."

She ran lightly across the chips, at a safe distance from Jean's outstretched arms, and turned into the trail among the maples. There she paused, gave her lover one melting, caressing, but still half-mocking glance, and cried to him:

"I am making a flag for 'Mon Rêve,' and it's not *nearly* done yet, Jean."

Then she disappeared among the bright branches. With a tumult in his heart Jean turned back to his ladder and paint-pot. Little twinges of angry disappointment ran along his nerves, only to be smothered straightway in a flood of passionate tenderness.

"Next voyage, anyway!" he muttered to himself as he worked feverishly. "I couldn't *live* longer than that without her!" And he went over and over in his imagination every detail of the girl's appearance, the changing moods of her radiant dark face, her hair, her hands, the tones of her voice.

Along the trail through the autumn maples, meanwhile Mademoiselle Barbe was speeding on light feet. The little smile was gone from the corners of her mouth, and into her eyes, now that Jean could no longer see them, was come a great gentleness. Her mockery, her impatience, her picturesque asperity were a kind of game which she played with herself, to disguise, sometimes even from herself, the greatness and the oversensitiveness of her heart. At this moment she was feeling sore at the nearness of Jean's departure, and was conscious of the pressure of his will urging her to go with him. This she was resolved she would not do; but she was equally resolved that her flag should be ready and go in her place. As for the next voyage—well, she thought to herself that Jean might persuade her by that time, if he tried hard. As to his success she had not really a grain of doubt. She knew well enough the quality of his fibre. Her light feet, as she hurried, made hardly a sound upon the soft mould of the trail, which was half-hidden by the bright autumn carpeting of the leaves. But presently she heard the noise of heavier footfalls approaching. Just ahead of her the trail turned sharply. Peering through the tangle of branches and thinned leafage, she caught glimpses of something that caused her face to grow pale, her heart to throb up into her throat; and she stepped behind the thick shelter of a fir bush to consider what was to be done.

The sight that so disturbed her was in itself no terrible one. A tall, ruddy-faced, keen-eyed man, carelessly dressed, but of erect, military bearing, came striding up the trail, a gun over his arm, a brown dog at his heels. Barbe recognized him at once—the English officer in command of the fort at Annapolis. She saw that he was out for partridges —but she saw, also, that he was walking at a pace that would speedily devour the scant two miles that divided him from the shipyard of "Mon Rêve." It was evident that he had forgotten his shooting in his interest in this unknown trail upon which he had stumbled. If he went on the game was up for Jean's little ship!

She resolved that he should not go on. It took her just five seconds to decide the whole question. There was a large fallen tree close beside the trail, two or three paces from where she hid. Over this she threw herself discreetly, with a little choking scream, and lay moaning among the leaves beside it.

The Englishman darted forward and was at her side in a moment, bending over her with a mingling of alarm and admiration in his gray eyes.

"Mademoiselle," he cried, "what has happened? Are you much hurt?"

Receiving no answer, but more faint moans, he lifted her gently and stood her on her feet; but the instant he released her she collapsed upon the leaves, an appealing but intoxicating confusion of skirts, and slim brown hands, and crinkly dark hair, and the corner of a red mouth, and the glimpse of an ankle.

"Mademoiselle! Tell me what is the matter. Tell me what can I do. Let me do something, I beg of you!" Lifting her again, he seated her beside him on the fallen tree; and this time he did not at once release her. At first, her eyes closed and her face a little drawn as with pain, she clung instinctively to his arm, with hands that seemed to him the most maddening that he had ever seen. Then, after several minutes which were very agreeable to him in spite of his anxiety, she appeared to pull herself together with a mighty effort. She moved away from his clasp, sat up straight, and opened upon him great eyes of pain and gratitude.

"Oh, thank you, Monsieur!" she said simply. "I'm afraid I have been very troublesome. But, indeed, I thought I was going to die."

"But what is the matter, Mademoiselle? Tell me, and let me help you."

She sat cringing and setting her teeth hard. He noticed how white were the teeth, how scarlet the full lips.

"It is just my heart," she said. "I was looking through the bushes to see who was coming. Something startled me, I think; and the pain clutched at my heart so I could not breathe, and I fell off."

She paused, to moan a little softly and catch her breath. Before he could say anything she went on:

"It's better now, but it hurts horribly."

"Let me support you, Mademoiselle," he urged with eager courtesy.

But she shrank away from the approaching ministration.

"No, Monsieur, I am better, really. But I must get home as quick as I can." She arose unsteadily.

The Englishman arose at the same time. The next moment Barbe sank back again, biting her lips to keep back a cry.

"Oh," she gasped, "I *can't* stand it! How can I get home?"

"You must let me see you home, Mademoiselle," said the officer, authority blending with palpable enthusiasm in his tones.

"You are so good, Monsieur," she murmured gratefully. "But I could not think of taking you away back so far, almost to the village. It will spoil your afternoon's sport."

The sympathy of the Englishman's face gave way to amusement, and he hastened to assure her of her mistake.

"Not at all, indeed, Mademoiselle. It will be quite as much my pleasure as my duty to see you safely home. Your misfortune—if not too serious— is my great good fortune!"

Thanking him with a look, Barbe arose weakly and took the proffered arm. At first the homeward journey was very slow; but as the afternoon deepened, and the miles gathered between the English commandant and Jean's little ship, the girl began to let herself recover. By this time she felt that there was

no danger of her escort leaving her one minute before
he was obliged to; and she knew that now, for this
night, the ship was safe.  At last, as they emerged
from the woods into a high pasture-ground, behind
the cottage where Barbe lived with her aunt and
uncle, the Englishman threw off the gallant for a
moment and became the wide-awake officer.  He
paused, took his bearings carefully, and scrutinized
the trail behind him with searching eyes.

"I have not seen this road before, Mademoiselle,"
he remarked, "and it interests me.  It is not down on
our map of the Annapolis district.  Whither does it
lead, may I ask?"

Barbe's heart grew faint within her; but she answered lightly, with a look that somehow conveyed to
him the impression that he should not be interested
in roads when she was by.

"They haul wood over it, my uncle and his neighbors, in the winter," she answered, "and black mud
in summer from the swamp back there."

The Englishman appeared satisfied; but she felt
that his curiosity was aroused, and with all her arts
she strove to divert his thoughts exclusively to herself.  She succeeded in this to a degree that presently
began to stir her apprehensiveness, and at her doorway she made her grateful farewells a trifle hurried.
But the Englishman would listen to nothing more
discouraging than *au revoir*.  At last he said:

"I shall be shooting over these woods again to-
morrow"—Barbe clutched hard upon the latch and
held her breath—"and shall give myself the pleasure

of calling to ask after—but no!" he corrected himself.
"You are making me forget, Mademoiselle. I have a
council-meeting to fill my day with drudgery to-
morrow." (Barbe breathed again at this respite.) "I
must deny myself till the day after. I may call then,
may I not?"

There was a moment's pause, and in that moment
the girl's swift brain made its decision.

"Certainly, Monsieur le Commandant," she said,
sweeping his face with a brilliant glance that made
his nerves tingle sweetly; "I shall be much honored.
My aunt and I will be much honored!" And with
a curtsy half mocking, half formal, and a disastrous
curving of her scarlet lips, she slipped into the house.

"By—Jove!" muttered the Englishman, as he
strode away in a daze.

From the window, behind the bean vines, Barbe
watched him go. The instant he was out of sight
she darted from the door, sped swiftly over the rough
pasture-lot, and disappeared among the twilights of
the trail, where the afternoon shadows were already
darkening to purple. She ran with the endurance of
health and practice and a clean-breathing outdoor
life; but presently her breath began to fail, her heart
to thump madly against her slim sides. Then—
around a bend of the trail came Jean, returning earlier than his wont. With an exclamation of glad
surprise he sprang forward to meet her. Still more
was his surprise when she caught him by the shoulders with both hands and leaned, gasping and sobbing, against his breast.

After one fierce clasp he held her lightly and tenderly like a child, and anxiously scanned her face.

"What is it, Barbe, beloved?  What is the matter?" he questioned eagerly.

"The ship," she panted, "must go!  You must go —*to-morrow* night!"

"Why?  But it is impossible!" he protested, bewildered.  "Mich' won't be here till the day after—and one man can't launch her, and can't sail her all by himself."

"I tell you, it must be done," she cried imperiously. "You must, you must!"  And then, in a few edged words, she explained the situation.  "If you can't, all is lost," she concluded, "for they will discover you, and seize the ship, the day after to-morrow.  Jean, I would never believe that you had any such word as 'can't.' "

By this time Jean's face was white and his jaw was set.

"Of course," he said quietly, "it will be done somehow.  I'm not beaten till I'm dead.  But the chances are, Sweet, that after I get the little ship launched I'll run her aground somewhere down the river, and be caught next day like a rat in a barrel.  It's ticklish navigating at best, down the river, and one man can't rightly manage even the foresail alone, and steer, in those eddies and twists in the channel.  But—"

"But, Jean—" she interrupted, and then paused, leaning close against him, and looking up at him with eyes that seemed to him to make a brightness in the dark.

"But what, beautiful one?" he questioned, leaning his face over her, and growing suddenly tremulous with a vague, wonderful expectancy.

"*I* can help! Take me!" And she hid her eyes against his rough shirt-sleeve.

For one moment Jean stood tense, moveless, unable to apprehend this sudden realization of his dreams. Then he swung her light figure up into his arms, and covered her face and hair with kisses. With a little smile of content upon her lips she suffered his madness for a while. Then she made him put her down.

"There is no time now to make love to me," she said. "We've so much to do and plan. You've never run away with a ship and a girl before, Jean, and we must make sure you know just how to go about it."

That night Barbe snatched a few hours of sleep, being mindful of the witchery of her eyes. But Jean toiled all night long, driving his yoke of oxen to and fro between his cabin and his shipyard in the forest. And he was not weary. His heart was light as air and sang with every pulse. His strength and his star—he felt them equal to any crisis.

On the following afternoon, when it wanted yet an hour of high tide, and the shadows of the maples were beginning to creep over the yellow chips, all was ready. Full of a wild gayety, and untiring as a boy, Barbe had worked all day, getting the sails bent, the stores on board, the last of block and tackle into place. Suddenly, from a post of vantage in the high-pointing bowsprit, she looked down the trail and clapped her brown hands with a shout of delight.

"Mich' has come!" she cried. And Mich' Masson, striding into the open, threw down a big red bundle on the chips.

"Pretty nigh ready?" he inquired. "Why, what is the matter, *mon gar'?*"

Jean's face had fallen like his heart. There was no longer any necessity of Barbe's sharing his adventure. But he hurried forward and clasped his friend's hand.

"We've got to get away to-night," he stammered, struggling bravely to make his voice sound cheerful. "The English are coming over here to-morrow to find out what's going on—so it's time for us to be going off! Barbe was to help me through with it."

Mich' held to Jean's hand, and glanced questioningly from his troubled face to the girl's teasing one. But Barbe had burned her bridges and saw no reason to be unmerciful.

"I suppose I'll have to be just crew and cabin-boy now, Mich'," she pouted. "Jean was going to let me be first mate, and there wasn't to be any crew."

A great joy broke over Jean's face, and Mich' removed his gray woolen cap with a sweeping bow. But before either could reply there came from a little way up the trail the excited yapping as of a dog that has treed a partridge. The three looked at each other, their eyes wide with apprehension. Then the report of a gun.

"The Englishman!" gasped Barbe. "He has not waited. Quick, hide, one each side of the trail, and take him prisoner. Don't shoot him. He was kind to me."

Jean snatched up his musket and the two men darted into the bush. By a rope from the bulwarks Barbe swung herself lightly to the ground. In haste she crossed the chip-strewn open, and then, carelessly swinging her hat in her hand, and singing a fitful snatch of song, she sauntered up the trail to meet the intruder.

The trail wound rapidly, so that before she had gone twoscore paces the ship was hid from her view. A few steps more and the Englishman came in sight, swinging forward alertly, a fluff of brown feathers dangling from his right hand. He was face to face with Barbe; and the delighted astonishment that came into his eyes was dashed with a faint chill of suspicion.

"How fate favors me, Mademoiselle!" he exclaimed, doffing his cap. "Gad, you are a brave girl to wander so far into the woods alone!"

"No, Monsieur, fate does not favor you," retorted Barbe with a sort of intimate petulance, holding out her brown fingers. "You had no business coming to-day when you said you were not coming till to-morrow. Now, you are going to find out a secret of mine which I didn't want any one to find out."

"But you are not angry at seeing me," he protested.

"N-n-o-o!" she answered, her head upon one side in doubt, while she bewildered him with her eyes. "But I'm sorry in a way! Well, come and I'll show you. Forgive me for lying to you yesterday about this road!"

And she turned to accompany him, walking very close to his side, so that her slim shoulder touched his arm and blurred his sagacity.

The next instant came the sharp order: "Halt! Don't stir, or you're dead!"

The Englishman found himself facing two leveled muskets. At the same moment his own weapon went flying into the underbrush, twitched from his hold by a dexterous catch of Barbe's fingers.

He stood still and very straight, his arms at his sides, eying his assailants steadily. His first impulse was to dart upon them with his naked hands; but he saw the well-knit form of Jean, almost his own height, the lean, set face, a certain exultation in the eyes which he read aright; and he saw the shrewd, dark, confident look of Mich', the experienced master of situations. The red mounted slowly to his face, and he turned upon Barbe a look wherein reproach at once gave way to scorn and a kind of shame.

Barbe herself flushed under that look.

"You wrong me, Monsieur!" she cried impetuously. "I did it to save you. You are a brave man, and would have tried to fight, and they would have killed you!"

He bowed stiffly and turned to the men.

"What do you want of me?"

"Your parole!" said Jean. "Give us your word

that you will come with us quietly, making no resistance and no effort to escape."

The Englishman shut his lips doggedly.

"Then you must be bound," said Mich' with curt decision. "We've no time to waste."

"Let *me* bind you, Monsieur," said Barbe, taking his wrists gently and putting them behind his back. "It is no dishonor to be captive to a woman."

With a silk scarf from her waist, and a feminine cunning in knots, she quickly tied his hands together so that he felt himself quite hopeless of escape. Then, in a cold wrath, he was led forward, with no constraint but Barbe's touch upon his arm. The ship, high on her stocks, came into view. And he understood.

Seating him upon a log, with his back against a tree, Mich' passed a rope about his waist and made him fast to the trunk. There he sat and chewed his indignation, while his captors went in haste about their work. But presently he grew interested. He saw the blocks knocked out from under the little ship's sides, so that she came down upon the greased ways and slid smoothly into the flood. He saw her checked gradually by a rope turned once around a tree trunk, so that she was kept from running aground on the opposite side of the Basin. He saw a small boat dragged down from the bushes to the edge of the tide, and oars put into it. By this time he had revolved many aspects of the case in his mind. Then came to him Barbe and Jean.

"Monsieur," said Jean, "I regret to have incon-

venienced you in this way. But you would without
mercy have wrecked all my hopes. I have put all my
means into this little ship, built with my own hands.
My heart is set on removing from the land of Acadie,
to live once more under my own flag of France. But
I do not wish to take you a prisoner to Louisburg, or
to put you to any further annoyance. To Mademoiselle Dieudonné you showed yourself yesterday a
most kind and courteous gentleman. All Acadie
knows you are brave. Give me your word that you
will in no way seek to stop or hinder our departure,
and let me set you free!"

"Give your parole, Monsieur!" begged Barbe, "or
you will have to devote yourself to entertaining me
all the way to Louisburg."

The Englishman's face brightened.

"Almost you make me wish to go to Louisburg,
Mademoiselle. With the duty you apportion me I
should be much happier, I assure you, than here in
Annapolis trying to govern your good fellow-coun-
trymen. But I will give my parole. I promise you,
sir," and he turned his face to Jean, "that I will not
in any way interfere with the departure of you and
your ship from Acadie."

"Thank you," said Jean, and he undid the rope and
the scarf.

The Englishman arose, walked down to the wa-
terside with Barbe, and with elaborate courtesy
helped her into the boat. He bent his lips over her
hand as he said good-by, and stood bareheaded as
women spectators.

Turning upon him then a laughing face of farewell, Barbe cried:

"Never, never will I pardon you, Monsieur, for consenting to give your parole!"

"Mademoiselle," he answered, "I am your prisoner still, and always."

# MRS. PROTHEROE

## BY BOOTH TARKINGTON

*Newton Booth Tarkington (born in Indiana, July 29, 1869) was not able to resist the desire, which soon or late attacks all Hoosiers, to "dabble in politics," and recently accepted a nomination for State Legislator. However, being by nature a virtuoso in dabbling, he emerged from the contest not only victor, but with no more soot and soil than, transferred by his artist finger tips from the political to the literary canvas, sufficed to give delicate shading to the strong crayon strokes of certain fictitious sketches suggested by his experience. These political pastels appear in a volume entitled "In the Arena." Of them the author has designated "Mrs. Protheroe" as most suitable for inclusion in the present series.*

# MRS. PROTHEROE

## BY BOOTH TARKINGTON

WHEN Alonzo Rawson took his seat as the Senator from Stackpole in the upper branch of the General Assembly of the State, an expression of pleasure and of greatness appeared to be permanently imprinted upon his countenance. He felt that if he had not quite arrived at all which he meant to make his own, at least he had emerged upon the arena where he was to win it, and he looked about him for a few other strong spirits with whom to construct a focus of power which should control the Senate. The young man had not long to look, for within a week after the beginning of the session these others showed themselves to his view, rising above the general level of mediocrity and timidity, party leaders and chiefs of factions, men who were on their feet continually, speaking half a dozen times a day, freely and loudly. To these, and that house at large, he felt it necessary to introduce himself by a speech which must prove him one of the elect, and he awaited impatiently an opening.

Alonzo had no timidity himself. He was not one of those who first try their voices on motions to adjourn, written in form and handed out to novices by presiding officers and leaders. He was too con-

From "In the Arena." Copyright, 1905, by McClure, Phillips & Co.

scious of his own gifts, and he had been "accustomed
to speaking" ever since his days in the Stackpole
City Seminary. He was under the impression, also,
that his appearance alone would command attention
from his colleagues and the gallery. He was tall; his
hair was long, with a rich waviness, rippling over
both brow and collar, and he had, by years of endeavor, succeeded in molding his features to present
an aspect of stern and thoughtful majesty whenever
he "spoke."

The opportunity to show his fellows that new greatness was among them was delayed not over-long, and
Senator Rawson arose, long and bony in his best
clothes, to address the Senate with a huge voice in denunciation of the "Sunday Baseball Bill," then upon
second reading. The classical references, which, as
a born orator, he felt it necessary to introduce, were
received with acclamations which the gavel of the
Lieutenant-Governor had no power to still.

"What led to the De-cline and Fall of the Roman
Empire?" he exclaimed. "I await an answer from
the advocates of this *de*-generate measure! I *de-
mand* an answer from them! Let me hear from
them on *that* subject! Why don't they speak up?
They can't give one. Not because they ain't familiar
with history—no, sir! That's not the reason! It's
because they *daren't,* because their answer would have
to go on record *against* 'em! Don't any of you try
to raise it against me that I ain't speaking to the
point, for I tell you that when you encourage Sunday
Baseball, or any kind of Sabbath-breakin' on Sunday

you're tryin' to start the State on the downward path
that beset Rome! *I'll* tell you what ruined it. The
Roman Empire started out to be the greatest nation on
earth, and they had a good start, too, just like the
United States has got to-day. Then what happened
to 'em? Why, them old ancient fellers got more interested in athletic games and gladiatorial combats and
racing and all kinds of outdoor sports, and bettin'
on 'em, than they were in oratory, or literature, or
charitable institutions and good works of all kinds.
At first they were moderate and the country was prosperous. But six days in the week wouldn't content
'em, and they went at it all the time, so that at last
they gave up the seventh day to their sports, the
way this bill wants *us* to do, and from that time on
the result was *de*-generacy and *de*-gradation! You
better remember *that* lesson, my friends, and don't
try to sink this State to the level of Rome!"

When Alonzo Rawson wiped his dampened brow,
and dropped into his chair, he was satisfied to the
core of his heart with the effect of his maiden effort.
There was not one eye in the place that was not
fixed upon him and shining with surprise and delight, while the kindly Lieutenant-Governor, his face
very red, rapped for order. The young Senator
across the aisle leaned over and shook Alonzo's hand
excitedly.

"That was beautiful, Senator Rawson!" he whispered. "I'm *for* the bill, but I can respect a masterly
opponent."

"I thank you, Senator Truslow," Alonzo returned

graciously. "I am glad to have your good opinion, Senator."

"You have it, Senator," said Truslow enthusiastically. "I hope you intend to speak often."

"I do, Senator. I intend to make myself heard," the other answered gravely, "upon all questions of moment."

"You will fill a great place among us, Senator!"

Then Alonzo Rawson wondered if he had not underestimated his neighbor across the aisle; he had formed an opinion of Truslow as one of small account and no power, for he had observed that, although this was Truslow's second term, he had not once demanded recognition nor attempted to take part in a debate. Instead, he seemed to spend most of his time frittering over some desk work, though now and then he walked up and down the aisles talking in a low voice to various Senators. How such a man could have been elected at all, Alonzo failed to understand. Also, Truslow was physically inconsequent, in his colleague's estimation—"a little, insignificant, dudish kind of a man," he had thought; one whom he would have darkly suspected of cigarettes had he not been dumfounded to behold Truslow smoking an old black pipe in the lobby. The Senator from Stackpole had looked over the other's clothes with a disapproval that amounted to bitterness. Truslow's attire reminded him of pictures in New York magazines, or the dress of boys newly home from college, he didn't know which, but he did know that it was contemptible. Consequently, after receiving the young man's congratulations, Alonzo was conscious of the keenest surprise at his own feeling that there might be something in him after all.

He decided to look him over again, more carefully to take the measure of one who had shown himself so frankly an admirer. Waiting, therefore, a few moments until he felt sure that Truslow's gaze had ceased to rest upon himself, he turned to bend a surreptitious but piercing scrutiny upon his neighbor. His glance, however, sweeping across Truslow's shoulder toward the face, suddenly encountered another pair of eyes beyond, so intently fixed upon himself that he started. The clash was like two searchlights meeting—and the glorious brown eyes that shot into Alonzo's were not the eyes of Truslow.

Truslow's desk was upon the outer aisle, and along the wall were placed comfortable leather chairs and settees, originally intended for the use of members of the upper house, but nearly always occupied by their wives and daughters, or "lady-lobbyists," or other women spectators.

Leaning back with extraordinary grace, in the chair nearest Truslow, sat the handsomest woman Alonzo had ever seen in his life. Her long coat of soft gray fur was unrecognizable to him in connection with any familiar breed of squirrel; her broad flat hat of the same fur was wound with a gray veil, underneath which her heavy brown hair seemed to exhale a mysterious glow, and never, not even in a lithograph, had he seen features so regular or a skin so clear! And to look into her eyes seemed to

Alonzo like diving deep into clear water and turning
to stare up at the light.

His own eyes fell first.   In the breathless awkward-
ness that beset him they seemed to stumble shamefully down to his desk, like a country boy getting back
to his seat after a thrashing on the teacher's platform.
For the lady's gaze, profoundly liquid as it was, had
not been friendly.

Alonzo Rawson had neither the habit of petty anal-
ysis, nor the inclination toward it; yet there arose
within him a wonder at his own emotion, at its strangeness and the violent reaction of it.   A moment ago
his soul had been steeped in satisfaction over the figure
he had cut with his speech and the extreme enthusiasm which had been accorded it—an extraordinarily
pleasant feeling: suddenly this was gone, and in its
place he found himself almost choking with a dazed
sense of having been scathed, and at the same time
understood in a way in which he did not understand
himself.   And yet—he and this most unusual lady had
been so mutually conscious of each other in their
mysterious interchange that he felt almost acquainted
with her.   Why, then, should his head be hot with
resentment?   Nobody had *said* anything to him!

He seized upon the fattest of the expensive books
supplied to him by the State, opened it with emphasis
and began not to read it, with abysmal abstraction,
tinglingly alert to the circumstance that Truslow was
holding a low-toned but lively conversation with the
unknown.   Her laugh came to him, at once musical,
quiet, and of a quality which irritated him into say-

ing bitterly to himself that he guessed there was just
as much refinement in Stackpole as there was in the
Capital City, and just as many old families! The
clerk calling his vote upon the "Baseball Bill" at that
moment, he roared "No!" in a tone which was pro-
fane. It seemed to him that he was avenging himself
upon somebody for something and it gave him a great
deal of satisfaction.

He returned immediately to his imitation of Archi-
medes, only relaxing the intensity of his attention to
the text (which blurred into jargon before his fixed
gaze) when he heard that light laugh again. He
pursed his lips, looked up at the ceiling as if slightly
puzzled by some profound question beyond the reach
of womankind; solved it almost immediately, and, setting his hand to pen and paper, wrote the capital letter
"O" several hundred times on note paper furnished
by the State. So oblivious was he, apparently, to
everything but the question of statecraft which occupied him that he did not even look up when the morning's session was adjourned and the law-makers began to pass noisily out, until Truslow stretched an arm
across the aisle and touched him upon the shoulder.

"In a moment, Senator!" answered Alonzo in his
deepest chest tones. He made it a very short moment, in deed, for he had a wild, breath-taking suspicion of what was coming.

"I want you to meet Mrs. Protheroe, Senator,"
said Truslow, rising, as Rawson, after folding his
writings with infinite care, placed them in his breast
pocket.

"I am pleased to make your acquaintance, ma'am," Alonzo said in a loud, firm voice, as he got to his feet, though the place grew vague about him when the lady stretched a charming, slender, gloved hand to him across Truslow's desk. He gave it several solemn shakes.

"We shouldn't have disturbed you, perhaps?" she asked, smiling radiantly upon him. "You were at some important work, I'm afraid."

He met her eyes again, and their beauty and the thoughtful kindliness of them fairly took his breath. "I am the chairman, ma'am," he replied, swallowing, "of the committee on drains and dikes."

"I knew it was something of great moment," she said gravely, "but I was anxious to tell you that I was interested in your speech."

A few minutes later, without knowing how he had got his hat and coat from the cloak-room, Alonzo Rawson found himself walking slowly through the marble vistas of the State-house to the great outer doors with the lady and Truslow. They were talking inconsequently of the weather, and of various legislators, but Alonzo did not know it. He vaguely formed replies to her questions, and he hardly realized what the questions were; he was too stirringly conscious of the rich quiet of her voice and of the caress of the gray fur of her cloak when the back of his hand touched it—rather accidentally—now and then, as they moved on together.

It was a cold, quick air to which they emerged, and Alonzo, daring to look at her, found that she had pulled the veil down over her face, the color of which, in the keen wind, was like that of June roses seen through morning mists. At the curb a long, low, rakish black automobile was in waiting, the driver a mere indistinguishable cylinder of fur.

Truslow, opening the little door of the tonneau, offered his hand to the lady. "Come over to the club, Senator, and lunch with me," he said. "Mrs. Protheroe won't mind dropping us there on her way."

That was an eerie ride for Alonzo, whose feet were falling upon strange places. His pulses jumped and his eyes swam with the tears of unlawful speed, but his big ungloved hand tingled not with the cold so much as with the touch of that divine gray fur upon his little finger.

"You intend to make many speeches, Mr. Truslow tells me," he heard the rich voice saying.

"Yes ma'am," he summoned himself to answer. "I expect I will. Yes, ma'am." He paused, and then repeated, "Yes, ma'am."

She looked at him for a moment. "But you will do some work, too, won't you?" she asked slowly.

Her intention in this passed by Alonzo at the time. "Yes, ma'am," he answered. "The committee work interests me greatly, especially drains and dikes."

"I have heard," she said, as if searching his opinion, "that almost as much is accomplished in the committee-rooms as on the floor? There—and in the lobby and in the hotels and clubs?"

"I don't have much to do with that!" he returned

quickly. "I guess none of them lobbyists will get much out of me! I even sent back all their railroad tickets. They needn't come near me!"

After a pause which she may have filled with unexpressed admiration, she ventured, almost timidly: "Do you remember that it was said that Napoleon once attributed the secret of his power over other men to one quality?"

"I am an admirer of Napoleon," returned the Senator from Stackpole. "I admire all great men."

"He said that he held men by his reserve."

"It can be done," observed Alonzo, and stopped, feeling that it was more reserved to add nothing to the sentence.

"But I suppose that such a policy," she smiled upon him inquiringly, "wouldn't have helped him much with women?"

"No," he agreed immediately. "My opinion is that a man ought to tell a *good* woman everything. What is more sacred than—"

The car, turning a corner much too quickly, performed a gymnastic squirm about an unexpected street-car and the speech ended in a gasp, as Alonzo, not of his own volition, half rose and pressed his cheek closely against hers. Instantaneous as it was, his heart leaped violently, but not with fear. Could all the things of his life that had seemed beautiful have been compressed into one instant it would not have brought him even the suggestion of the wild shock of joy of that one, wherein he knew the glamourous perfume of Mrs. Protheroe's brown hair and felt her

cold cheek firm against his, with only the gray
veil between.

"I'm afraid this driver of mine will kill me
some day," she said, laughing and composedly
straightening her hat.  "Do you care for big
machines?"

"Yes, ma'am," he answered huskily.  "I haven't
been in many."

"Then I'll take you again," said Mrs. Protheroe.
"If you like I'll come down to the State-house and
take you out for a run in the country."

"When?" said the lost young man, staring at her
with his mouth open.  "When?"

"Saturday afternoon if you like.  I'll be there at
two."

They were in front of the club and Truslow had
already jumped out.  Mrs. Protheroe gave him her
hand and they exchanged a glance significant of something more than a friendly good-by.  Indeed, one
might have hazarded that there was something almost
businesslike about it.  The confused Senator from
Stackpole, climbing out reluctantly, observed it not,
nor could he have understood, even if he had seen,
that delicate signal which passed between his two com-
panions.

When he was upon the ground, Mrs. Protheroe
extended her hand without speaking, but her lips
formed the word "Saturday."  Then she was carried
away quickly, while Alonzo, his heart hammering,
stood looking after her, born into a strange world, the
touch of the gray fur upon his little finger, the odor

of her hair faintly about him, one side of his face red, the other pale.

"To-day is Wednesday," he said, half aloud.

"Come on, Senator." Truslow took his arm and turned him toward the club doors.

The other looked upon his new friend vaguely. "Why, I forgot to thank her for the ride," he said.

"You'll have other chances, Senator," Truslow assured him. Mrs. Protheroe has a hobby for studying politics and she expects to come down often. She has plenty of time—she's a widow, you know."

"I hope you didn't think," exclaimed Alonzo indignantly, "that I thought she was a married woman!"

After lunch they walked back to the State-house together, Truslow regarding his thoughtful companion with sidelong whimsicalness. Mrs. Protheroe's question, suggestive of a difference between work and speechmaking, had recurred to Alonzo, and he had determined to make himself felt, off the floor as well as upon it. He set to this with a fine energy that afternoon in his committee-room, and the Senator from Stackpole knew his subject. On drains and dikes he had no equal. He spoke convincingly to his colleagues of the committee upon every bill that was before them, and he compelled their humblest respect. He went earnestly at it, indeed, and sat very late that night in his room at a nearby boarding-house, studying bills, trying to keep his mind upon them and not to think of his strange morning and of Saturday. Finally his neighbor in the next room, Senator Ezra Trumbull, long abed, was awakened by his praying and groaned

slightly.    Trumbull meant to speak to Rawson about
his prayers, for Trumbull was an early one to bed and
they woke him every night.    The partition was flimsy
and Alonzo addressed his Maker in the loud voice of
those accustomed to talking across wide out-of-door
spaces.    Trumbull considered it especially unnecessary
in the city; though, as a citizen of a county which
loved but little his neighbor's district, he felt that in
Stackpole there was good reason for a person to shout
his prayers at the top of his voice and even then have
small chance to carry through the distance.    Still, it
was a delicate matter to mention, and he put it off
from day to day.

Thursday passed slowly for Alonzo Rawson, nor
was his voice lifted in debate.    There was little but
routine; and the main interest of the chamber was in
the lobbying that was being done upon the "Sunday
Baseball Bill," which had passed to its third reading
and would come up for final disposition within a fort-
night.    This was the measure which Alonzo had set
his heart upon defeating.    It was a simple enough bill:
it provided, in substance, that baseball might be played
on Sunday by professionals in the State capital, which
was proud of its league team.    Naturally, it was denounced by clergymen, and deputations of ministers
and committees from women's religious societies were
constantly arriving at the State-house to protest against
its passage.    The Senator from Stackpole reassured
all of these with whom he talked, and was one of
their staunchest allies and supporters.    He was active
in leading the wavering among his colleagues, or even

the inimical, out to meet and face the deputations.  It
was in this occupation that he was engaged, on Friday
afternoon, when he received a shock.

A committee of women from a church society was
waiting in the corridor, and he had rounded up a reluctant half-dozen senators and led them forth to be
interrogated as to their intentions regarding the bill.
The committee and the lawmakers soon distributed
themselves into little argumentative clumps, and Alonzo
found himself in the centre of these, with one of
the ladies who had unfortunately—but, in her enthusiasm, without misgivings—begun a reproachful
appeal to an advocate of the bill whose name was
Goldstein.

"Senator Goldstein," she exclaimed, "I could not
believe it when I heard that you were in favor of this
measure!   I have heard my husband speak in the
highest terms of your old father.   May I ask you what
*he* thinks of it?   If you voted for the desecration of
Sunday by a low baseball game, could you dare go
home and face that good old man?"

"Yes, madam," said Goldstein mildly; "we are *both*
Jews."

A low laugh rippled out from near-by, and Alonzo,
turning almost violently, beheld his lady of the furs.
She was leaning back against a broad pilaster, her
hands sweeping the same big coat behind her, her
face turned toward him, but her eyes, sparklingly delighted, resting upon Goldstein.   Under the broad fur
hat she made a picture as engaging, to Alonzo Rawson,
as is was bewitching.   She appeared not to see him, to

be quite unconscious of him—and he believed it. Truslow and five or six members of both houses were about her, and they all seemed to be bending eagerly toward her. Alonzo was furious with her.

Her laugh lingered upon the air for a moment, then her glance swept round the other way, omitting the Senator from Stackpole, who, immediately putting into practice a reserve which would have astonished Napoleon, swung about and quitted the deputation without a word of farewell or explanation. He turned into the cloak-room and paced the floor for three minutes with a malevolence which awed the colored attendants into not brushing his coat; but, when he returned to the corridor, cautious inquiries addressed to the tobacconist elicited the information that the handsome lady with Senator Truslow had departed.

Truslow himself had not gone. He was lounging in his seat when Alonzo returned and was genially talkative. The latter refrained from replying in kind, not altogether out of reserve, but more because of a dim suspicion (which rose within him the third time Truslow called him "Senator" in one sentence) that his first opinion of the young man as a light-minded person might have been correct.

There was no session the following afternoon, but Alonzo watched the street from the windows of his committee-room, which overlooked the splendid breadth of stone steps leading down from the great doors to the pavement. There were some big bookcases in the room, whose glass doors served as mirrors in which he more and more sternly regarded the soft image of an entirely new gray satin tie, while the conviction grew within him that (arguing from her behavior of the previous day) she would not come, and that the Stackpole girls were nobler by far at heart than many who might wear a king's-ransom's-worth of jewels round their throats at the opera-house in a large city. This sentiment was heartily confirmed by the clock when it marked half-past two. He faced the bookcase doors and struck his breast, his open hand falling across the gray tie with tragic violence; after which, turning for the last time to the windows, he uttered a loud exclamation and, laying hands upon an ulster and a gray felt hat, each as new as the satin tie, ran hurriedly from the room. The black automobile was awaiting.

"I thought it possible you might see me from a window," said Mrs. Protheroe as he opened the little door.

"I was just coming out," he returned, gasping for breath. "I thought—from yesterday—you'd probably forgotten."

"Why 'from yesterday'?" she asked.

"I thought—I thought—" He faltered to a stop as the full glorious sense of her presence overcame him. She wore the same veil.

"You thought I did not see you yesterday in the corridor?"

"I thought you might have acted more—more—"

"More cordially?"

"Well, he said, looking down at his hands, "more like you knew we'd been introduced."

At that she sat silent, looking away from him, and he, daring a quick glance at her, found that he might let his eyes remain upon her face. That was a dangerous place for eyes to rest, yet Alonzo Rawson was anxious for the risk. The car flew along the even asphalt on its way to the country like a wild goose on a long slant of wind, and, with his foolish fury melted inexplicably into honey, Alonzo looked at her—and looked at her—till he would have given an arm for another quick corner and a streetcar to send his cheek against that veiled, cold cheek of hers again. It was not until they reached the alternate vacant lots and bleak Queen Anne cottages of the city's ragged edge that she broke the silence.

"You were talking to some one else," she said almost inaudibly.

"Yes, ma'am, Goldstein, but—"

"Oh, no!" She turned toward him, lifting her hand. "You were quite the lion among ladies."

"I don't know what you mean, Mrs. Protheroe," he said, truthfully.

"What were you talking to all those women about?"

"It was about the 'Sunday Baseball Bill.'"

"Ah! The bill you attacked in your speech last Wednesday?"

"Yes, ma'am."

"I hear you haven't made any speeches since then," she said indifferently.

"No, ma'am," he answered gently. "I kind of

got the idea that I'd better lay low for a while, at first, and get in some quiet, hard work."

"I understand. You are a man of intensely reserved nature."

"With men," said Alonzo, "I am. With ladies I am not so much so. I think a good woman ought to be told—"

"But you are interested," she interrupted, "in defeating that bill?"

"Yes, ma'am," he returned. "It is an iniquitous measure."

"Why?"

"Mrs. Protheroe!" he exclaimed, taken aback. "I thought all the ladies were against it. My own mother wrote to me from Stackpole that she'd rather see me in my grave than votin' for such a bill, and I'd rather see myself there!"

"But are you sure that you understand it?"

"I only know it desecrates the Sabbath. That's enough for me!"

She leaned toward him and his breath came quickly.

"No. You're wrong," she said, and rested the tips of her fingers upon his sleeve.

"I don't understand why—why you say that," he faltered. "It sounds kind of—surprising to me—"

"Listen," she said. Perhaps Mr. Truslow told you that I am studying such things. I do not want to be an idle woman; I want to be of use to the world, even if it must be only in small ways."

"I think that is a noble ambition!" he exclaimed. "I think all good women ought—"

"Wait," she interrupted gently. "Now, that bill is a worthy one, though it astonishes you to hear me say so. Perhaps you don't understand the conditions. Sunday is the laboring man's only day of recreation—and what recreation is he offered?"

"He ought to go to church," said Alonzo promptly.

"But the fact is that he doesn't—not often—not at *all* in the afternoon. Wouldn't it be well to give him some wholesome way of employing his Sunday afternoons? This bill provides for just that, and it keeps him away from drinking, too, for it forbids the sale of liquor on the grounds."

"Yes, I know," said Alonzo plaintively. "But it ain't *right!* I was raised to respect the Sabbath and—"

"Ah, that's what you should do! You think *I* could believe in anything that wouldn't make it better and more sacred?"

"Oh, no, ma'am!" he cried reproachfully. "It's only that I don't see—"

"I am telling you." She lifted her veil and let him have the full dazzle of her beauty. "Do you know that many thousands of laboring people spend their Sundays drinking and carousing about the low country road-houses because the game is played at such places on Sunday? They go there because they never get a chance to see it played in the city. And don't you understand that there would be no Sunday liquor trade, no workingmen poisoning themselves every seventh day in the low groggeries, as hundreds of them do now, if they had something to see that would interest them?—something as wholesome and fine as this sport would be, under the conditions of this bill; something to keep them in the open air, something to bring a little gayety into their dull lives!" Her voice had grown louder and it shook a little, with a rising emotion, though its sweetness was only the more poignant. "Oh, my dear Senator, she cried, "don't you *see* how wrong you are? Don't you want to *help* these poor people?"

Her fingers, which had tightened upon his sleeve, relaxed and she leaned back, pulling the veil down over her face as if wishing to conceal from him that her lips trembled slightly; then resting her arm upon the leather cushions, she turned her head away from him, staring fixedly into the gaunt beech woods lining the country road along which they were now coursing. For a time she heard nothing from him, and the only sound was the monotonous chug of the machine.

"I suppose you think it rather shocking to hear a woman talking practically of such commonplace things," she said at last, in a cold voice, just loud enough to be heard.

"No, ma'am," he said huskily.

"Then what *do* you think?" she cried, turning toward him again with a quick, imperious gesture.

"I think I'd better go back to Stackpole," he answered very slowly, "and resign my job. I don't see as I've got any business in the Legislature."

"I don't understand you."

He shook his head mournfully. "It's a simple enough matter. I've studied out a good many bills and talked 'em over and I've picked up some influence and—"

"I know you have," she interrupted eagerly. "Mr. Truslow says that the members of your drains-and-dikes committee follow your vote on every bill."

"Yes, ma'am," said Alonzo Rawson meekly, "but I expect they oughtn't to. I've had a lesson this afternoon."

"You mean to say—"

"I mean that I didn't know what I was doing about that baseball bill. I was just pig-headedly goin' ahead against it, not knowing nothing about the conditions, and it took a lady to show me what they were. I would have done a wrong thing if you hadn't stopped me."

"You mean," she cried, her splendid eyes widening with excitement and delight; "you mean that you—that you—"

"I mean that I will vote for the bill!" He struck his clinched fist upon his knee. "I come to the Legislature to do *right!*"

"You will, ah, you *will* do right in this!" Mrs. Protheroe thrust up her veil again and her face was flushed and radiant with triumph. "And you'll work, and you'll make a speech for the bill?"

At this the righteous exaltation began rather abruptly to simmer down in the soul of Alonzo Rawson. He saw the consequences of too violently reversing, and knew how difficult they might be to face.

"Well, not—not exactly," he said weakly. "I expect our best plan would be for me to lay kind of low and not say any more about the bill at all. Of course, I'll quit workin' against it; and on the roll-call I'll edge close up to the clerk and say 'Aye' so that only him'll hear me. That's done every day— and I—well, I don't just exactly like to come out too publicly for it, after my speech and all I've done against it."

She looked at him sharply for a short second, and then offered him her hand and said: "Let's shake hands *now* on the vote. Think what a triumph it is for me to know that I helped to show you the right."

"Yes, ma'am," he answered confusedly, too much occupied with shaking her hand to know what he said. She spoke one word in an undertone to the driver and the machine took the very shortest way back to the city.

After this excursion several days passed before Mrs. Protheroe came to the State-house again. Rawson was bending over the desk of Senator Josephus Battle, the white-bearded leader of the opposition to the "Sunday Baseball Bill," and was explaining to him the intricacies of a certain drainage measure, when Battle, whose attention had wandered, plucked his sleeve and whispered:

"If you want to see a mighty pretty woman that's doin' no good here, look behind you, over there in the chair by the big fireplace at the back of the room."

Alonzo looked.

It was she whose counterpart had been in his dream's eye every moment of the dragging days which had been vacant of her living presence. A number of his colleagues were hanging over her almost idiotically; her face was gay and her voice came to his ears, as he turned, with the accent of her cadenced laughter running through her talk like a chime of tiny bells flitting through a strain of music.

"This is the third time she's been here," said Battle, rubbing his beard the wrong way. "She's lobbyin' for that infernal Sabbath-Desecration bill, but we'll beat her, my son."

"Have you made her acquaintance, Senator?" asked Alonzo stiffly.

"No, sir, and I don't want to. But I knew her father—the slickest old beat and the smoothest talker that ever waltzed up the pike. She married rich; her husband left her a lot of real estate around here, but she spends most of her time away. Whatever struck her to come down and lobby for that bill I don't know —yet—but I will! Truslow's helping her to help himself; he's got stock in the company that runs the baseball team, but what she's up to—well, I'll bet there's a nigger in the woodpile *some*where!"

"I expect there's a lot of talk like that!" said Alonzo, red with anger, and taking up his papers abruptly.

"Yes, *sir!*" said Battle emphatically, utterly misunderstanding the other's tone and manner. "Don't you worry, my son. We'll kill that venomous bill right here in this chamber! We'll kill it so dead that it won't make one flop after the axe hits it. You and me and some others'll tend to *that!* Let her work that pretty face and those eyes of hers all she wants to! I'm keepin' a little lookout, too—and I'll—"

He broke off, for the angry and perturbed Alonzo had left him and gone to his own desk. Battle, slightly surprised, rubbed his beard the wrong way and sauntered out to the lobby to muse over a cigar. Alonzo, loathing Battle with a great loathing, formed bitter phrases concerning that vicious-minded old gentleman, while for a moment he affected to be setting his desk in order. Then he walked slowly up the aisle, conscious of a roaring in his ears (though not aware how red they were) as he approached the semicircle about her.

He paused within three feet of her in a sudden panic of timidity, and then, to his consternation, she looked him squarely in the face, over the shoulders of two of the group, and the only sign of recognition that she exhibited was a slight frown of unmistakable repulsion, which appeared between her handsome eyebrows.

It was very swift; only Alonzo saw it; the others had no eyes for anything but her, and were not aware of his presence behind them, for she did not even pause in what she was saying.

Alonzo walked slowly away with the wormwood in his heart. He had not grown up among the young people of Stackpole without similar experiences, but it had been his youthful boast that no girl had ever "stopped speaking" to him without reason, or "cut a dance" with him and afterward found opportunity to repeat the indignity.

"What have I *done* to *her?*" was perhaps the hottest cry of his bruised soul, for the mystery was as great as the sting of it.

It was no balm upon that sting to see her pass him at the top of the outer steps, half an hour later, on the arm of that one of his colleagues who had been called the "best-dressed man in the Legislature." She swept by him without a sign, laughing that same laugh at some sally of her escort, and they got into the black automobile together and were whirled away and out of sight by the impassive bundle of furs who manipulated the wheel.

For the rest of that afternoon and the whole of that night no man, woman, or child heard the voice of 'Alonzo Rawson, for he spoke to none. He came not to the evening meal, nor was he seen by any who had his acquaintance. He entered his room at about midnight, and Trumbull was awakened by his neighbor's overturning a chair. No match was struck, however, and Trumbull was relieved to think that the Senator from Stackpole intended going directly to bed without troubling to light the gas, and that his prayers would soon be over. Such was not the case, for no other sound came from the room, nor were Alonzo's prayers uttered that night, though the unhappy statesman in the next apartment could not get to sleep for several hours on account of his nervous expectancy, of them.

After this, as the day approached upon which hung the fate of the bill which Mr. Josephus Battle was fighting, Mrs. Protheroe came to the Senate Chamber nearly every morning and afternoon. Not once did she appear to be conscious of Alonzo Rawson's presence, nor once did he allow his eyes to delay upon her, though it can not be truthfully said that he did not always know when she came, when she left, and with whom she stood or sat or talked. He evaded all mention or discussion of the bill or of Mrs. Protheroe; avoided Truslow (who, strangely enough, was avoiding *him*) and, spending upon drains and dikes all the energy that he could manage to concentrate, burned the midnight oil and rubbed salt into his wounds to such marked effect that by the evening of the Governor's Reception—upon the morning following which the mooted bill was to come up—he offered an impression so haggard and worn that an actor might have studied him for a make-up as a young statesman going into a decline.

Nevertheless he dressed with great care and bitterness, and placed the fragrant blossom of a geranium— taken from a plant belonging to his landlady—in the lapel of his long coat before he set out.

And yet, when he came down the Governor's broad stairs, and wandered through the big rooms, with the glare of lights above him and the shouting of the guests ringing in his ears, a sense of emptiness beset him; the crowded place seemed vacant and without meaning. Even the noise sounded hollow and remote —and why had he bothered about the geranium? He hated her and would never look at her again—but why was she not there?

By and by, he found himself standing against a wall, where he had been pushed by the press of people. He was wondering drearily what he was to do with a clean plate and a napkin which a courteous negro had handed him, half an hour earlier, when he felt a quick jerk at his sleeve. It was Truslow, who had worked his way along the wall, and who now, standing on tiptoe, spoke rapidly but cautiously, close to his ear.

"Senator, be quick," he said sharply, at the same time alert to see that they were unobserved. "Mrs. Protheroe wants to speak to you at once. You'll find her near the big palms under the stairway in the hall."

He was gone—he had wormed his way half across the room—before the other, in his simple amazement, could answer. When Alonzo at last found a word, it was only a monosyllable, which, with his accompanying action, left a matron of years, who was at that moment being pressed fondly to his side, in a state of mind almost as dumfounded as his own. *"Here!"* was all he said as he pressed the plate and napkin into her hand and departed forcibly for the hall, leaving a spectacular wreckage of trains behind him.

The upward flight of the stairway left a space underneath, upon which, as it was screened (save for a narrow entrance) by a thicket of palms, the crowd had not encroached. Here were placed a divan and a couple of chairs; there was shade from the glare of gas, and the light was dim and cool. Mrs. Protheroe had risen from the divan when Alonzo entered this grotto, and stood waiting for him.

He stopped in the green entrance-way with a quick exclamation.

She did not seem the same woman who had put such slights upon him, this tall, white vision of silk, with the summery scarf falling from her shoulders. His great wrath melted at the sight of her; the pain of his racked pride, which had been so hot in his breast, gave way to a species of fear. She seemed not a human being, but a white spirit of beauty and goodness who stood before him, extending two fine arms to him in long, white gloves.

She left him to his trance for a moment, then seized both his hands in hers and cried to him in her rapturous, low voice: "Ah, Senator, you have come! I *knew* you understood!"

"Yes ma'am," he whispered chokily.

She drew him to one of the chairs and sank gracefully down upon the divan near him.

"Mr. Truslow was so afraid you wouldn't," she went on rapidly, "but I was sure. You see I didn't want anybody to suspect that I had any influence with you. I didn't want them to know, even, that I'd talked to you. It all came to me after the first day that we met. You see I've believed in you, in your power and in your reserve, from the first. I want all that you do to seem to come from yourself and not from me or any one else. Oh, I *believe* in great, strong men who stand upon their own feet and conquer the world for themselves! That's *your* way, Senator Rawson. So, you see, as they think I'm lobbying for the bill, I wanted them to believe that your speech for it to-morrow comes from your own great, strong mind and heart and your sense of right, and not from any suggestion of mine."

"My speech!" he stammered.

"Oh, I know," she cried; "I know you think I don't believe much in speeches, and I don't ordinarily, but a few simple, straightforward and vigorous words from you, to-morrow, may carry the bill through. You've made such *progress,* you've been so *reserved,* that you'll carry great weight—and there are three votes of the drains-and-dikes that are against us now, but will follow yours absolutely. Do you think I would have 'cut' *you* if it hadn't been *best?*"

"But I—"

"Oh, I know you didn't actually promise me to speak, that day. But I knew you would when the time came! I knew that a man of power goes over *all* obstacles, once his sense of *right* is aroused! I *knew*—I never doubted it, that once *you* felt a thing to be right you would strike for it, with all your great strength—at all costs—at all—"

"I can't—I—I—can't!" he whispered nervously. "Don't you see—don't you see—I—"

She leaned toward him, lifting her face close to his. She was so near him that the faint odor of her hair came to him again, and once more the unfortunate Senator from Stackpole risked a meeting of his eyes with hers, and saw the light shining far down in their depths.

At this moment the shadow of a portly man who was stroking his beard the wrong way projected itself upon them from the narrow, green entrance to the grotto. Neither of them perceived it.

Senator Josephus Battle passed on, but when Alonzo Rawson emerged, a few moments later, he was pledged to utter a few simple, straightforward, and vigorous words in favor of the bill. And—let the shame fall upon the head of the scribe who tells it— he had kissed Mrs. Protheroe!

The fight upon the "Sunday Baseball Bill" the next morning was the warmest of that part of the session, though for a while the reporters were disappointed. They were waiting for Senator Battle, who was famous among them for the vituperative vigor of his attacks and for the kind of personalities which made valuable copy. And yet, until the debate was almost over, he contented himself with going quietly up and down the aisles, whispering to the occupants of the desks, and writing and sending a multitude of notes to his colleagues. Meanwhile, the orators upon both sides harangued their fellows, the lobby, the unpolitical audience, and the patient presiding officer to no effect, so far as votes went. The general impression was that it would be close.

Alonzo Rawson sat bent over his desk, his eyes fixed with gentle steadiness upon Mrs. Protheroe, who occupied the chair wherein he had first seen her. A senator of the opposition was finishing his denunciation, when she turned and nodded almost imperceptibly to the young man.

He gave her one last look of pathetic tenderness and rose.

"The Senator from Stackpole!"

"I want," Alonzo began, in his big voice—"I want to say a few simple, straightforward but vigorous words about this bill. You may remember I spoke against it on its second reading—"

"You did *that!*" shouted Senator Battle suddenly.

"I want to say now," the Senator from Stackpole continued, "that at that time I hadn't studied the subject sufficiently. I didn't know the conditions of the case, nor the facts, but since then a great light has broke in upon me—"

"I should say it had! I saw it break!" was Senator Battle's second violent interruption.

When order was restored, Alonzo, who had become very pale, summoned his voice again. "I think we'd ought to take into consideration that Sunday is the working-man's only day of recreation and not drive him into low groggeries, but give him a chance in the open air to indulge his love of wholesome sport—"

"Such as the ancient Romans enjoyed!" interposed Battle vindictively.

"No, sir!" Alonzo wheeled upon him, stung to the quick. "Such a sport as free-born Americans and *only* free-born Americans can play in this wide world

—the American game of baseball, in which no other nation of the *Earth* is our equal!"

This was a point scored and the cheering lasted two minutes. Then the orator resumed:

"I say: 'Give the working-man a chance!' Is his life a happy one? You know it ain't! Give him his one day. *Don't* spoil it for him with your laws —he's only got one! I'm not goin' to take up any more of your time, but if there's anybody here who thinks my well-considered opinion worth following I say: *'Vote for this bill.'* It is right and virtuous and ennobling, and it ought to be passed! I say: *'Vote for it.'"*

The reporters decided that the Senator from Stackpole had "wakened things up." The gavel rapped a long time before the chamber quieted down, and when it did, Josephus Battle was on his feet and had obtained the recognition of the chair.

"I wish to say, right here," he began, with a rasping leisureliness, "that I hope no member of this honored body will take my remarks as personal or unparliamentary—*but"*—he raised a big forefinger and shook it with menace at the presiding officer at the same time suddenly lifting his voice to an unprintable shriek—"I say to *you,* sir, that the song of the siren has been *heard* in the land, and the call of Delilah has been answered! When the Senator from Stackpole rose in his chamber, less than three weeks ago, and denounced this iniquitous measure, I heard him with pleasure—we *all* heard him with pleasure—*and* respect! In spite of his youth and the poor quality of

his expression, *we* listened to him. *We* knew he was
sincere! What has caused the change in him? What
*has*, I ask? I shall not tell you, upon this floor, but
I've taken mighty good care to let most of you know,
during the morning, either by word of mouth or by
*note* of hand! Especially those of you of the drains-
and-dikes and others who might follow this young
Samson, whose locks have been shore! *I've* told
you all about that, and more—*I've* told you the
*inside* history of some *facts* about the bill that I
will not make public, because I am too confident of
our strength to defeat this devilish measure, and prefer to let our vote speak our opinion of it! Let me
not detain you longer. *I* thank you!"

Long before he had finished, the Senator from
Stackpole was being held down in his chair by Truslow and several senators whose seats were adjacent;
and the vote was taken amid an uproar of shouting
and confusion. When the clerk managed to proclaim
the result over all other noises, the bill was shown to
be defeated and "killed," by a majority of five votes.

A few minutes later, Alonzo Rawson, his neck-
wear disordered and his face white with rage, stumbled out of the great doors upon the trail of Battle,
who had quietly hurried away to his hotel for lunch as
soon as he had voted.

The black automobile was vanishing round a corner. Truslow stood upon the edge of the pavement
staring after it ruefully:

"Where is Mrs. Protheroe?" gasped the Senator
from Stackpole.

"She's gone," said the other.

"Gone where?"

"Gone back to Paris. She sails day after to-mor-row. She just had time enough to catch her train for New York after waiting to hear how the vote went. She told me to tell you good-by, and that she was sorry. Don't stare at me, Rawson! I guess we're in the same boat!— Where are you going?" he finished abruptly.

Alonzo swung by him and started across the street. "To find Battle!" the hoarse answer came back.

The conquering Josephus was leaning meditatively upon the counter of the cigar-stand of his hotel when Alonzo found him. He took one look at the latter's face and backed to the wall, tightening his grasp upon the heavy-headed ebony cane it was his habit to carry, a habit upon which he now congratulated himself.

But his precautions were needless. Alonzo stopped out of reaching distance.

"You tell me," he said in a breaking voice; "you tell me what you meant about Delilah and sirens and Samsons and inside facts! You tell me!"

"You wild ass of the prairies," said Battle, "I saw you last night behind them pa'ms! But don't you think I told it—or ever will! I just passed the word around that she'd argued you into her way of thinkin', same as she had a good many others. And as for the rest of it, I found out where the nigger in the woodpile was, and I handed that out, too. Don't you take it hard, my son, but I told you her husband left her a good deal of land around here. She owns the ground that they use for the baseball park, and her lease would be worth considerable more if they could have got the right to play on Sundays!"

Senator Trumbull sat up straight, in bed, that night, and, for the first time during his martyrdom, listened with no impatience to the prayer which fell upon his ears.

"O Lord Almighty," through the flimsy partition came the voice of Alonzo Rawson, quaveringly, but with growing strength: "Aid Thou me to see my way more clear! I find it hard to tell right from wrong, and I find myself beset with tangled wires. O God, I feel that I am ignorant, and fall into many devices. These are strange paths wherein Thou hast set my feet, but I feel that through Thy help, and through great anguish, I am learning!"

# HOW THE RAVEN DIED

## BY ALFRED HENRY LEWIS

*Mr. Lewis is from Missouri, and is con-*
*victed only on demonstration. He has long*
*been a metropolitan journalist, and has no*
*illusions. As a reporter, he wrote up his in-*
*terviews of "distinguished citizens" with a*
*pencil of lunar caustic. As the editor of a*
*satirical paper ("The Verdict") he wetted that*
*pencil's point from a tongue fluent with acer-*
*bity—for Mr. Lewis possesses the most copious*
*vocabulary of all writers of picturesque de-*
*nunciation. Of Mr. Lewis's work in fiction,*
*a cycle of three books is especially notable—*
*"Wolfville," "Wolfville Days," and "Wolf-*
*ville Nights." These are composed of tales*
*of life on the plains. The present selection*
*has admirably caught the spirit of Indian le-*
*gend, and is, therefore, in its way as great*
*a triumph as Lafcadio Hearn's Chinese le-*
*gend, "The Soul of the Great Bell."*

# HOW THE RAVEN DIED

## BY ALFRED HENRY LEWIS

"WHICH if you-all is out to hear of Injuns, son," observed the Old Cattleman, doubtfully, "the best I can do is shet my eyes an' push along regyardless, like a cayouse in a storm of snow. But I don't guarantee no facts; none whatever; I never does bend myse'f to severe study of savages, an' what notions I packs concernin' 'em is the casual frootes of what I accidental hears an' what I sees. It's only now an' then, as I observes former, that Injuns invades Wolfville; an' when they does, we-all scowls 'em outen camp— sort o' makes a sour front, so as to break 'em early of habits of visitin' us. We shore don't hone none to have 'em hankerin' 'round.

"Nacherally, I makes no doubt that if you goes clost to Injuns an' studies their little game you finds some of 'em good an' some bad, some gaudy an' some sedate, some cur'ous an' some indifferent, same as you finds among shore-enough folks. It's so with mules an' broncos; wherefore, then, may not these differences exist among Injuns? Come squar' to the turn, you-all finds white folks separated the same. Some gents follows off one wagon track an' some another; some even makes a new trail.

"Speakin' of what's opposite in folks, I one time an' ag'in sees two white chiefs of scouts who frequent comes pirootin' into Wolfville from the Fort. Each has mebby a score of Injuns at his heels who pertains to him personal. One of these scout chiefs is all buckskins, fringes, beads an' feathers from y'ears to hocks, while t'other goes garbed in a stiff hat with a little jim-crow rim—one of them kind you deenom'nates as a darby—an' a diag'nal overcoat; one chief looks like a dime novel on a spree an' t'other as much like the far East as he saveys how. An' yet, son, this voylent person in buckskins is a Second Lootenant—a mere boy, he is—from West P'int; while that outcast in the reedic'lous hat is foaled on the plains an' never does go that clost to the risin' sun as to glimpse the old Missouri. The last form of maverick bursts frequent into Western bloom; it's their ambition, that a-way, to deloode you into deemin' 'em as fresh from the States as one of them tomatter airtights.

"Thar's old gent Jeffords; he's that sort. Old Jeffords lives for long with the Apaches; he's found among 'em when Gen'ral Crook—the old 'Gray Fox' —an' civilization and Gatlin' guns comes into Arizona arm in arm. I used to note old Jeffords hibernatin' about the Oriental over in Tucson. I shore reckons he's procrastinatin' about thar yet, if the Great Sperit ain't done called him in. As I says, old Jeffords is that long among the Apaches back in Cochise's time that the mem'ry of man don't run none to the contrary. An' yet no gent ever sees old Jeffords wearin' anything more savage than a long-tail black surtoot an' one of them stove-pipe hats. Is Jeffords dangerous? No, you-all couldn't call him a distinct peril; still, folks who goes devotin' themse'fs to stirrin' Jeffords up jest to see if he's alive gets disastrous action. He has long gray ha'r an' a tangled white beard half-way down his front; an' with that old plug hat an' black coat he's a sight to frighten children or sour milk! Still, Jeffords is all right. As long as towerists an' other inquisitive people don't go pesterin' Jeffords, he shore lets 'em alone. Otherwise, you might as well be up the same saplin' with a cinnamon b'ar; which you'd most likely hear something drop a lot!

"For myse'f, I likes old Jeffords, an' considers him a pleasin' conundrum. About tenth drink time he'd take a cha'r an' go camp by himse'f in a far corner, an' thar he'd warble hymns. Many a time as I files away my nosepaint in the Oriental have I been regaled with

> " 'Jesus, Lover of my soul,
>   Let me to Thy bosom fly,
> While the nearer waters roll,
>   While the tempest still is high,'

as emanatin' from Jeffords where he's r'ared back conductin' some personal services. Folks never goes buttin' in interferin' with these concerts; which it's cheaper to let him sing.

"Speakin' of Injuns, as I su'gests, I never does see overmuch of 'em in Wolfville. An' my earlier experiences ain't thronged with 'em neither, though

while I'm workin' cattle along the Red River I
does carom on Injuns more or less. Thar's one
old hostile I recalls speshul; he's a fool Injun
called Black Feather—Choctaw, he is. This Black
Feather's weakness is fire-water; he thinks more of
it than some folks does of children.

"Black Feather used to cross over to where Dick
Stocton maintains a store an' licker house on the
Upper Hawgthief. Of course, no gent sells these
Injuns licker. It's ag'in the law; an' onless you-all
is onusual eager to make a trip to Fort Smith with
a marshal ridin' herd on you doorin' said visit, im-
partin' of nosepaint to aborigines is a good thing
not to do. But Black Feather, he'd come over to
Dick Stocton's an' linger 'round the bar'ls of Valley
Tan, an' take a chance on stealin' a snifter or two
while Stocton's busy.

"At last Stocton gets tired an' allows he'll lay for
Black Feather. This yere Stocton is a mighty reck-
less sport; he ain't carin' much whatever he does do;
he hates Injuns an' shotguns, an' loves licker, seven-
up, an' sin in any form; them's Stocton's prime char-
acteristics. An' he gets mighty weary of the whis-
key-thievin' Black Feather, an' lays for him.

"One evenin' this aggravatin' Black Feather
crosses over an' takes to ha'ntin' about Dick Stocton's licker room, as is his wont. It looks like Black
Feather has already been buyin' whiskey of one of
them boot-laig parties who takes every chance an'
goes among the Injuns an' sells 'em nosepaint on the
sly. 'Fore ever he shows up on the Upper Hawg-

thief that time, this Black Feather gets nosepaint some'ers an' puts a whole quart of it away in the shade; an' he shore exhibits symptoms. Which for one thing he feels about four stories tall!

"Stocton sets a trap for Black Feather. He fills up the tin cup into which he draws that Valley Tan with coal-oil—karoseen you-all calls it—an' leaves it, temptin' like, settin' on top a whiskey bar'l. Shore! it's the first thing Black Feather notes. He sees his chance an' grabs an' downs the karoseen; an' Stocton sort o' startin' for him, this Black Feather gulps her down plump swift. The next second he cuts loose the yell of that year, burns up about ten acres of land, and starts for Red River. No, I don't know whether the karoseen hurts him none or not; but he certainly goes squatterin' across the old Red River like a wounded wild-duck, an' he never does come back no more.

"But, son, as you sees, I don't know nothin' speshul or much touchin' Injuns, an' if I'm to dodge the disgrace of ramblin' along in this desultory way, I might better shift to a tale I hears Sioux Sam relate to Doc Peets one time in the Red Light. This Sam is a Sioux, an' a mighty decent buck, considerin' he's Injun; Sam is servin' the Great Father as a scout with the diag'nal-coat, darby-hat sharp I mentions. Peets gives this saddle-tinted longhorn a four-bit piece, an' he tells this yarn. It sounds plenty-child-ish, but you oughter b'ar in mind that savages' mental ain't no bigger nor older than ten-year-old young ones among the palefaces.

" 'This is the old story my mother tells me,'
says Sioux Sam, 'to show me the evils of curiosity.
"The Great Sperit allows to every one the right to
ask only so many questions," says my mother,
"an' when they ask one more than is their right, they
die."

" 'This is the story of the fate of *Kaw-kaw-chee,*
the Raven, a Sioux chief who died long ago exackly
as my mother told me. The Raven died because he
asked too many questions an' was too cur'ous. It
began when Sublette, who was a trader, came up the
*Mitchi-zoor-rah,* the Big-Muddy, an' was robbed by
the Raven's people. Sublette was mad at this, an'
said next time he would bring the Sioux a present so
they would not rob him. So he brought a little cask
of firewater an' left it on the bank of the Big-Muddy.
Then Sublette went away, an' twenty of the Raven's
young men found the little cask. An' they were
greedy an' did not tell the camp; they drank the firewater where it was found.

" 'The Raven missed his twenty young men an'
when he went to spy for them, behold! they were dead,
with their teeth locked tight an' their faces an' bodies
writhen an' twisted as the whirlwind twists the cot-
tonwoods. Then the Raven thought an' thought; an'
he got very cur'ous to know why his young men died
so writhen an' twisted. The firewater had a whirlwind in it, an' the Raven was eager to hear. So he
sent for Sublette.

" 'Then the Raven an' Sublette had a big talk. They
agreed not to hurt each other; an' Sublette was to

come an' go an' trade with the Sioux; an' they would never rob him.

" 'At this, Sublette gave the Raven some of the whirlwind that so killed an' twisted the twenty young men. It was a powder, white; an' it had no smell. Sublette said its taste was bitter; but the Raven must not taste it or it would lock up his teeth an' twist an' kill him. For to swallow the white powder loosed the whirlwind on the man's heart an' it bent him an' twisted him like the storms among the willows.

" 'But the Raven could give the powder to others. So the Raven gave it in some deer's meat to his two squaws; an' they were twisted till they died; an' when they would speak they couldn't, for their teeth were held tight together an' no words came out of their mouths—only a great foam. Then the Raven gave it to others that he did not love; they were twisted an' died.. At last there was no more of the powder of the whirlwind; the Raven must wait till Sublette came up the Big-Muddy again an' brought him more.

" 'There was a man, the Gray Elk, who was of the Raven's people. The Gray Elk was a *Choo-ayk-eed,* a great prophet. And the Gray Elk had a wife; she was wise an' beautiful, an' her name was Squaw-who-has-dreams. But the Gray Elk called her *Kee-nee-moo-sha,* the Sweetheart.

" 'While the Raven waited for Sublette to bring him more powder of the whirlwind, a star with a long tail came into the sky. This star with the tail made the Raven heap cur'ous. He asked Gray Elk to tell him about it, for he was a prophet. The Raven asked many questions; they fell from him like leaves from a tree in the month of the first ice. So the Gray Elk called *Chee-bee,* the Spirit; an' the Spirit told the Gray Elk. Then the Gray Elk told the Raven.

" 'It was not a tail, it was blood—star blood; an' the star had been bit an' was wounded, but would get well. The Sun was the father of the stars, an' the Moon was their mother. The Sun, *Gheezis,* tried ever to pursue an' capture an' eat his children, the stars. So the stars all ran an' hid when the Sun was about. But the stars loved their mother who was good an' never hurt them; an' when the Sun went to sleep at night an' *Coush-ee-wan,* the Darkness, shut his eyes, the Moon an' her children came together to see each other. But the star that bled had been caught by the Sun; it got out of his mouth, but was wounded. Now it was frightened, so it always kept its face to where the Sun was sleeping over in the west. The bleeding star, *Sch-coo-dah,* would get well an' its wound would heal.

" 'Then the Raven wanted to know how the Gray Elk knew all this. An' the Gray Elk had the Raven into the medicine lodge that night; an' the Raven heard the spirits come about an' heard their voices; but he could not understand. Also, the Raven saw a wolf all fire, with wings like the eagle which flew overhead. Also he heard the Thunder, *Boom-wa-wa,* talking with the Gray Elk; but the Raven couldn't understand. The Gray Elk told the Raven to draw his knife an' stab with it in the air outside the medicine lodge. An' when he did, the Raven's blade an' hand came back covered with blood. Still, the Raven was cur'ous an' kept askin' to be told how the Gray Elk knew these things. An' the Gray Elk at last took the Raven to the Great Bachelor Sycamore that lived alone, an' asked the Raven if the Bachelor Sycamore was growing. An' the Raven said it was. Then Gray Elk asked him how he knew it was growing. An' the Raven said he didn't know. Then Gray Elk said he did not know how he knew about *Sch-coo-dah*, the star that was bit. This made the Raven angry, for he was very cur'ous; an' he thought the Gray Elk had two tongues.

" 'Then it came the month of the first young grass an' Sublette was back for furs. Also he brought many goods; an' he gave to the Raven more of the powder of the whirlwind in a little box. At once the Raven made a feast of ducks for the Gray Elk; an' he gave him of the whirlwind powder; an' at once his teeth came together an' the Gray Elk was twisted till he died.

" 'Now no one knew that the Raven had the powder of the whirlwind, so they could not tell why all these people were twisted and went to the Great Spirit. But the Squaw-who-has-dreams saw that it was the Raven who killed her husband, the Gray Elk, in a vision. Then the Squaw-who-has-dreams went into the mountains four days an' talked with *Moh-kwa*, the Bear who is the wisest of the beasts. The Bear said it was the Raven who killed the Gray Elk an' told the Squaw-who-has-dreams of the powder of the whirlwind.

" 'Then the Bear an' the Squaw-who-has-dreams made a fire an' smoked an' laid a plot. The Bear did not know where to find the powder of the whirlwind which the Raven kept always in a secret place. But the Bear told the Squaw-who-has-dreams that she should marry the Raven an' watch until she found where the powder of the whirlwind was kept in its secret place; an' then she was to give some to the Raven, an' he, too, would be twisted an' die. There was a great danger, though; the Raven would, after the one day when they were wedded, want to kill the Squaw-who-has-dreams. So to protect her, the Bear told her she must begin to tell the Raven the moment she was married to him the Story-that-never-ends. Then, because the Raven was more cur'ous than even he was cruel, he would put off an' put off giving the powder of the whirlwind to the Squaw-who-has-dreams, hoping to hear the end of the Story-that-never-ends. Meanwhile the Squaw-who-has-dreams was to watch the Raven until she found the powder of the whirlwind in its secret place.

" 'Then the wise Bear gave the Squaw-who-has-dreams a bowlful of words as seed, so she might plant them an' raise a crop of talk to tell the Story-that-never-ends. An' the Squaw-who-has-dreams planted the seed-words, an' they grew an' grew, an' she gathered sixteen bundles of talk an' brought them to her wigwam. After that she put beads in her hair, an' dyed her lips red, an' rubbed red on her cheeks, an' put on a new blanket; an' when the Raven saw her, he asked her to marry him. So they were wedded;

an' the Squaw-who-has-dreams went to the teepee of the Raven an' was his wife.

" 'But the Raven was old an' cunning like *Yah-mee-kee*, the Beaver, an' he said, "He is not wise who keeps a squaw too long!" An' with that he thought he would kill the Squaw-who-has-dreams the next day with the powder of the whirlwind. But the Squaw-who-has-dreams first told the Raven that she hated *When-dee-goo,* the Giant; an' that she should not love the Raven until he had killed *When-dee-goo*. She knew the Giant was too big an' strong for the Raven to kill with his lance, an' that he must get his powder of the whirlwind; she would watch him an' learn its secret place. The Raven said he would kill the Giant as the sun went down next day.

" 'Then the Squaw-who-has-dreams told the Raven the first of the Story-that-never-ends an' used up one bundle of talk; an' when the story ended for that night, the Squaw-who-has-dreams was saying: "An' so, out of the lake that was red as the sun came a great fish that was green, with yellow wings, an' it walked also with feet, an' it came up to me an' said:" But then she would tell no more that night; nor could the Raven, who was crazy with cur'osity, prevail on her. "I must now sleep an' dream what the green fish with the yellow wings said," was the reply of the Squaw-who-has-dreams, an' she pretended to slumber. So the Raven, because he was cur'ous, put off her death.

" 'All night she watched, but the Raven did not go to the secret place where he had hidden the powder of the whirlwind. Nor the next day, when the sun went down, did the Raven kill the Giant. But the Squaw-who-has-dreams took up again the Story-that-never-ends an' told what the green fish with the yellow wings said; an' she used up the second bundle of talk. When she ceased for that time, the Squaw-who-has-dreams was saying: "An' as night fell, *Moh-kwa,* the Bear, called to me from his canyon, an' said for me to come an' he would show me where the treasure of fire-water was buried for you who are the Raven. So I went into the canyon, an' *Moh-kwa,* the Bear, took me by the hand an' led me to the treasure of firewater which was greater an' richer than was ever seen by any Sioux."

" 'Then the Squaw-who-has-dreams would tell no more that night, while the Raven eat his fingers with cur'osity. But he made up a new plan not to twist the Squaw-who-has-dreams until she showed him the treasure of firewater an' told him the end of the Story-that-never-ends. On her part, however, the Squaw-who-has-dreams, as she went to sleep, wept an' tore the beads from her hair an' said the Raven did not love her, for he had not killed the Giant, as he promised. She said she would tell no more of the Story-that-never-ends until the Giant was dead; nor would she show to a husband who did not love her the great treasure of firewater which *Moh-kwa,* the Bear, had found. At this, the Raven, who was hot to have the treasure of firewater an' whose ears rang with cur'osity to hear the end of the Story-that-never-ends, saw that he must kill the Giant. Therefore, when the Squaw-who-has-dreams had ceased to sob and re=

vile him, an' was gone as he thought asleep, the Raven
went to his secret place where he kept the powder of
the whirlwind an' took a little and wrapped it in a
leaf an' hid the leaf in the braids of his long hair.
Then the Raven went to sleep.

" 'When the Raven was asleep the Squaw-who-has-
dreams went also herself to the secret place an' got
also a little of the powder of the whirlwind.  An' the
next morning she arose early an' gave the powder of
the whirlwind to the Raven on the roast buffalo, the
*Pez-hee-kee,* which was his food.

" 'When the Raven had eaten, the Squaw-who-has-
dreams went out of the teepee among the people an'
called all the Sioux to come an' see the Raven die.
So the Sioux came gladly, an' the Raven was twisted
an' writhen with the powder of the whirlwind wrench-
ing at his heart; an' his teeth were tight like a trap;
an' no words, but only foam, came from his mouth;
an' at last the Spirit, the *Chee-bee,* was twisted out of
the Raven; an' the Squaw-who-has-dreams was re-
venged for the death of the Gray Elk whom she loved
an' who always called her *Kee nee-moo-sha,* the
Sweetheart, because it made her laugh.

" 'When the Raven was dead, the Squaw-who-has-
dreams went to the secret place an' threw the powder
of the whirlwind into the Big-Muddy; an' after that
she distributed her fourteen bundles of talk that were
left among all the Sioux so that everybody could tell
how glad he felt because the Raven was twisted and
died.  An' for a week there was nothing but happiness an' big talk among the Sioux; an' *Moh-kwa,* the

Bear, came laughing out of his canyon with the wonder of listening to it; while the Squaw-who-has-dreams now, when her revenge was done, went with *When-dee-goo*, the Giant, to his teepee and became his squaw. So now everything was ended save the Story-that-never-ends.'

"When Sioux Sam gets this far," concluded the Old Cattleman, "he says, 'an' my mother's words at the end were: An' boys who ask too many questions will die, as did the Raven whose cur'osity was even greater than his cruelty.'"

# AT THE END OF HIS ROPE

## BY FLORENCE MORSE KINGSLEY

*Florence Morse (born near Medina, Ohio, July 14, 1859; married in 1882 to Charles R. Kingsley) entered into authorship in 1894 with a religious novel entitled "Titus, a Comrade of the Cross," which rivaled "Ben Hur" in popularity. She followed up her success with a number of religious and altruistic novels, all of which were constructed with an ingenuity that is rarely found in this order of fiction. She has written a number of short stories in which her especial gift of clever invention is strikingly displayed. The present selection is an example of the manner in which the hackneyed "vacation love-story" can be freshly treated by the introduction of a new and ingenious situation.*

# AT THE END OF HIS ROPE

BY FLORENCE MORSE KINGSLEY

## I

MR. PERCY ALGERNON SMITH, familiarly known as "Cinnamon" Smith, thrust his hands deeper into his trousers pockets. "I am not going," he remarked with an air of decision.

"Not going!" cried the joint proprietors of Lone Pine Camp in a chorus. "Not going! Why?"

Mr. Smith vouchsafed no immediate reply; he had fixed an experienced eye upon the coffee-pot, which at the moment threatened to inundate the camp-fire with its furious contents. "Here, you, Jake," he said peremptorily; "the coffee's boiling over!"

The campers at Lone Pine were on the point of starting out for an all-day's fishing excursion up Sunday Brook. It may as well be explained right here that the party consisted of four undergraduates of C—— University who were temporarily pursuing their education in the bracing air of the Adirondacks.

That these young gentlemen were thus studiously engaged during that portion of the year commonly exempt from mental pursuits argues nothing. Great minds have ever been remarkable for concentration of purpose; and everybody knows that the late football, rowing, and bicycle seasons were of unusual and engrossing interest. It is to be hoped that a future and more enlightened generation will so arrange the dull and comparatively unimportant scholastic pursuits that they shall not clash with live interests. In a word, to quote from their own forceful if inelegant phraseology—Messrs. "Cinnamon" Smith, "Piggy" Brewster, "Herodotus" Jones, and "Tommy" Pettigrew had been "plucked" in their examinations, and were now "cramming" with more or less enthusiasm and diligence under the able direction of Prof. John Gearing.

Mr. Smith's announcement occasioned considerable badinage of a personal and even damaging nature, all of which was received by that young man with commendable stoicism and equanimity.

"Cin's lazy!" drawled "Piggy" Brewster, as he ensconced himself comfortably in the stern of the boat, armed with the lightest paddle.

"Cinnamon's going to write to his best girl!" shouted Herodotus Jones, shying a mighty quid of spruce-gum at the auburn head of the young gentleman on the shore. "Do it in poetry on birch-bark, old boy! Little wavelets a-kissin' the beach; green leaves all whisperin' of thee; my heart a-tremblin' with rapture at the call of the lone loon across the moonlit waters! Hey, Cin?"

"Aw—get along with you!" growled the recipient of these graceful sallies. "I'm going to bone all day on Greek—that's what I'm going to do."

A burst of derisive laughter greeted this saying. Then the boat shot out into the sparkling waters of

Beaver Lake, and speedily disappeared behind the wooded island.

Left to himself, it appeared that Mr. Smith had not remained behind to indulge in solitary ease, for no sooner did the last echo of oars and voices die away than he fell to work with extraordinary energy and diligence. He swept out the camp—being not over-particular as to corners—gathering in the process a goodly heap of bacon-rinds, egg-shells, torn paper, and tin cans, which he bestowed in the bushes. A motley array of old shoes of various sizes, four and one-half pairs of ragged socks, a nondescript assortment of party-colored garments in various stages of dilapidation were retired, in company with the camp frying-pan, to a dark corner under the bunks, this position being further defended by an artistic arrangement of balsam boughs. As a finishing touch, two pairs of muddy trousers, a half-emptied tin of condensed milk—to the wrath and discomfiture of an industrious swarm of Adirondack flies— and three dog-eared novels followed the bacon-rinds into the comfortable obscurity of the huckleberry bushes.

Mr. Smith paused long enough to wipe his heated brow. "It looks pretty slick," he murmured approvingly. "And now for the grub; girls are always hungry."

A rapid but thoughtful investigation of the camp cupboard ensued, with the following-named results: item—two small and somewhat wizened lemons; item—one damp and dubious paper bag, containing ginger-snaps minus the snap; item—one box of marshmallows.

"The lemonade'll be on the Sunday-school-picnic order," meditated the youth, as he surveyed these tempting articles with a doubtful grimace; "and the less said about the snaps the better; but they'll cotton to the marshmallows all right.—Jerusalem crickets! there they are now, t'other side of the lake, and I haven't even washed my hands!"

Exactly seven minutes later, Mr. Percy Algernon Smith, arrayed in a golf suit of the latest fashionable cut and an immaculate flannel shirt, set off by a necktie of flaming red—which, he flattered himself, subdued the tint of his auburn locks to a positive brown —sauntered jauntily down to the boat-landing.

"How de do, Miss Daisy! (Jove, but she's a stunner, and no mistake!) Glad to see you, Miss Terrill! Won't you come ashore?"

The elder of the two young persons in the boat hesitated; but the one addressed as Miss Daisy was on her feet in a twinkling.

"Just for an instant, Kate!" she said deprecatingly. "What a *sweet* place for a camp—ours isn't nearly so pretty!—Lemonade?" went on this sprightly damsel, fanning her flushed face with a big green fan; "yes, indeed, and it's awfully kind of you to think of it, Mr. Smith! Aren't you thirsty, Kate?"

The person addressed as Kate looked about her tentatively. "It certainly is a very pretty place," she said sedately; "but we ought not to stop, Margaret."

"The fellows are all off on the trail to Sunday

Brook," remarked the astute Mr. Smith, setting out three glasses on the pine board which did duty as a table. "They won't be back before evening. The old man's out bug-hunting."

"Who is the old man?" cried Miss Margaret with and irrelevant gurgle of laughter. "And bug-hunting—ugh! Who ever heard of such a thing!"

"Oh, I mean Gearing! He's bossing the cramming for exams.," replied Mr. Smith with elegant brevity. "Two lumps of sugar, or three, Miss Daisy?"

"Three, please. Is he married?"

"Married! Who—the old man? Ha! ha!—that's a good one! Why, Miss Daisy, Gearing never even looks at anything but books and bugs, and is more afraid of a pretty girl than he'd be of a boa constrictor!"

"The idea! How funny! Kate, do look at that big spool up there on the tree! What is that for, Mr. Smith?"

"That spool? Aw—that's another of Gearing's notions. He likes to get off all by himself after his bugs—don't want even a guide along to bother him. So he ties up one end of a string in camp and unwinds a monstrous spool as he goes along. When he gets through with his investigations he winds up, and the string brings him into camp again as right as a trivet. See?"

"The very idea!"

"Bright man!" chorused the fair voyagers.

"His spools hold a mile of string, and he generally carries his pockets full of 'em," pursued Mr.

Smith, gallantly presenting a toasted marshmallow to
each of his guests. "You can bet the fellows don't
raise many objections to his travels!—I say, Miss
Margaret," he added guilelessly, "don't you want
some pink water-lilies? I know where there's a grist
of 'em—beauties too."

"You go, Margaret," said Miss Terrill indulgently;
"I'll stop here and rest. I'm too deliciously comfortable to move."

And producing a volume from the pocket of her
jacket, the young lady settled back in her luxurious
chair—cunningly fashioned out of a barrel and a
piece of burlap—with the air of an experienced
chaperon.

Before proceeding further with this narrative, it
must be distinctly understood that Miss Katherine
Terrill was a young person in whose veins ran certain saving streams of genuine blue blood. Not only
was she a Colonial dame by virtue of both lines of
descent, but through her maternal grandmother she
was still further linked with greatness in a manner
which defied question.

To quote the often-repeated admonition of Madam
Carter Stockard herself, "You must never forget, my
dear Katherine, what your position as a descendant
of Col. Brayton Carter, of Virginia, implies."

"I should require a memory as long as that of
Methuselah, dear grandmama, if I remembered all
that it implies," was the somewhat flippant answer.

"I am grieved and astonished, my dear Katherine,"
once remarked Miss Penelope Scidmore, principal of

the Scidmore Select School for Young Ladies, "to learn that *you,* a young person of the most admirable birth and breeding, should for one moment have countenanced such a breach of the proprieties!"  Miss Scidmore had made the painful discovery that certain of her "select" young ladies, under the leadership of Miss Terrill, had walked out of the protecting walls of the S. S. S. Y. L. *without a chaperon;* and that, thus alone and unprotected, they had pressed into service a team of horses and an empty hay-wagon which they found on a side street, and had actually taken a ride therein through the principal street of the little town, to the consternation (when he saw them) of the old farmer who owned the wagon, and to the still greater consternation (when she heard of it) of Miss Scidmore.

"*Why,*" continued that lady in impassioned tones, "have you thus forgotten what is due to yourself and your family?"

"I am sure I don't know, Miss Scidmore," Katherine had replied with honest contrition; "I—I just did it!"  By which it will be seen that this young lady of high birth was, on occasion, as much the sport of freakish impulse as Katie O'Flarity, the daughter of the gardener at Brayton manor.  All this by way of explanation—though it is in no sense an excuse—for what is to follow.

The day was warm, as has been intimated, and the claims of "The Scarlet Doom" on the interest of the reader wavered after a little.  Historical novels, dealing with the sanguinary past from a cold-blooded

American standpoint, were decidedly out of place—
thought this sapient young person—amid the fresh,
breezy wilds of the Adirondacks.  She dropped the
book, to fix her undivided attention upon the antics
of a pair of squirrels which were frisking in primal
gladness from bough to bough of the big pine.  Her
eyes followed them with a certain distinct satisfaction in the lawless freedom of these creatures of the
wilderness, whose ancestors cast no chilling shadow
upon the joyous present.

At this point in the course of her aimless medita-
tions her vagrant fancy was again arrested by the big
spool dangling by a scarlet thread from the branch
just above her head.  As she gazed at this simple
object, Miss Terrill completely forgot her position in
society and the august character of her lineage. After
full five minutes of reflection, which—as subsequent
events proved—might have been spent to better advantage, the descendant of the Brayton Carters deliberately stood up on her chair and detached the big
spool from its position.

"This is a cobweb party," she said solemnly; "the
scientific old professor and his box of bugs is the prize."
With that, this "model of all the proprieties" began to
walk away into the woods, winding up the scarlet
cord as she went.

From fragrant, low-dropping balsam to white-limbed
birch; from sunny knoll, crowded with purple-fruited
huckleberries, to solemn stretches of forest, where the
winds loitered in the odorous branches of the pines,
whispering strange, ancient secrets of earth and sky;

through trackless wastes of sweet fern, where the gnats bit fiercely; through dense blackberry thickets, which clutched her savagely in their thorny arms; over fallen logs, half rotted away and carpeted deep with softest emerald mosses; past swampy spots, where the trim boots sank ankle deep in the black mud—deeper and deeper into the pathless wilderness led the slender clew.

"It's simply barrels of fun!" sighed the bold adventurer, lapsing into the camp vernacular, as she sank breathless on to a bank to rest, "but—I believe I'll go back without my prize.   It must be nearly dinner-time."

She reached out after a sprig of wintergreen, where gay scarlet berries glimmered like live coals amid the overarching ferns, her brown cheeks dimpling as she reflected upon the undoubted consternation of the water-lily hunters.   Then she sprang to her feet with an air of decision.   "I must go back at once; we ought not to have stopped at all."

She glanced down at the bulky form of the big brown spool, and the full extent of her folly dawned suddenly upon her.   "How can I go back?   I've *wound up the cord!*"

It was characteristic of this young person that, preliminarily to a careful consideration of the question, she sank down and laughed—till she cried; this to the great astonishment and dismay of divers small woodsfolk, who paused in the business of the hour to observe the new and peculiar animal which produced such strange noises.

"I have come a mile," she reflected, sitting up and wiping her eyes; "for this spool is full, and number two hangs in the bushes yonder."

The idea of surprising an elderly student of science at his labors had been gradually growing less and less attractive; and now after a period of serious reflection it ceased to appear either funny or fascinating in the slightest degree.

"He is undoubtedly a person who would be politely, sarcastically, and crushingly disagreeable because I had ventured to meddle with his absurd spools," decided Miss Terrill soberly. "I am very glad that I stopped in time; I shall have no trouble in reaching the camp from this point. Of course I shall put the spool exactly where I found it."

She rose slowly to her feet and looked meditatively about her. "I came by that big tree; I remember the dead branch hanging down to the ground."

Ah, foolish maid! keener eyes than those pretty brown ones of yours have been deceived by the wonderful likeness of everything to every other thing in the big woods. The tree with the dead branch certainly led to a perfectly familiar-looking bush; and the bush beguiled the weary little feet to an odorous group of balsams, where bright-eyed squirrels chattered angrily at the wearer of the jaunty red tam. And beyond the balsams there was a cup-like hollow where the beautiful deadly "Fly Amanita" thrust its golden globes through the black-leaf mould. Then the brambles clutched at her with their thorny fingers, and the treacherous mud tried to hold her away from the ripe huckleberries.    And all the while the gnats and mosquitoes followed hard after—like the hosts of an avenging fate.

But, yes; it was all perfectly plain and not at all far.    She would soon catch a sparkle of blue water through the trees, and then dinner and a long, delicious rest in the hammock!    The grewsome tales of wayfarers lost and starving in the woods were—she decided—simply figments of weak and elderly imaginations; mere bugaboos to keep small children within bounds.    Any person of sound judgment and educated powers of observation could easily—

"Gracious!"    Miss Terrill rarely made use of such vulgar exclamations, but the exigency of the occasion wrung it from her lips.    The spool was again empty! She looked wildly about her; there was no welcome glimmer of blue water, no pervasive odor of a smoky camp-fire, no dinner, no hammock anywhere in sight.

"Well, there is only one thing to do," decided the girl after a second period of reflection, during which the humorous nature of the adventure did not once recur to her mind.    "I will go back to the second spool once more, and try again.    One can always do what one must do," she added sententiously, and with the air of one who combats an unpleasant suggestion.

Two hours later, as she wearily retraced her steps for the third time to the spot where the second spool hung in the bushes, the situation had resolved itself in her mind (she had been a "special" in mathematics) into the following concise form:

"Let A represent the camp, and B the position of

the second spool, one mile distant from A. How many miles might a person travel in endeavoring to reach A, supposing he started from B in a different direction each time?"

"If the traveler started out from B and traveled in a perfectly straight line each time," she murmured —a diagram of the problem presenting itself with appalling distinctness before her mental vision—"he might easily travel several hundred miles without reaching A. If he traveled in curved lines—as he certainly would—why—"

The undeniable conclusions were too harrowing to contemplate with calmness, therefore Miss Katherine Carter Terrill sat down upon a mossy log and shed tears for full five minutes. She beheld herself, as it were, the wandering radius of an unknown circle, returning innumerable times to point B, and at last lying cold and unconscious on the forest leaves, the fatal spool clutched tight in her stiffened fingers.

"I shall never find it—never!" she wailed, grinding the innocent cause of her misadventure beneath her boot-heels. "But, oh, how can I let that man find me, as he certainly will, if I hold on to this wretched spool! I *can't*, if I have to die of slow starvation—and I am so hungry! But suppose I leave the spool here, the unsuspecting old gentleman will wind up to it, and then he will have nothing to go by—not even point B!"

A vision of her own revered grandparent wandering gaunt and famished through interminable wastes of desolate forest filled her with a lively anguish.

"No, I must not leave him to perish—it would be murder!" she said with a shudder. "I will find him and tell him what I have done."

## II

John Gearing glanced hastily over the closely written pages of his note-book by the waning light, snapped the cover of his tin specimen case with a well-satisfied air, and rose to his feet.

"It must be getting along toward sunset," he reflected, with a cursory glance at his watch. "Capital day's work, though; I shouldn't like to have missed that scarlet-headed arachnid. As for the coleopteron, I doubt if it has been generally recognized as a genuine crotylid—which it unquestionably is."

He paused to drop a full spool into his pocket and disengage an empty one from the limb of a mighty spruce which stood among its fellows weeping odorous tears of purest gum. The bug-hunter eyed it thoughtfully, a cheerful vision of the camp frying-pan, replete with sizzling slices of fragrant bacon, to be succeeded by a long procession of substantial slapjacks, rising alluringly before him.

"Jove!" he muttered, "I forgot to eat my lunch!"

The reflections of the hungry scientist as he strode rapidly onward winding up his second spool were both comfortable and complacent. "A more useful device to save valuable time than this simple system of spools was never devised," he decided. "At this moment I am—approximately—one and one-half miles from supper; with no doubtful trail to follow, no delays to puzzle over direction, no uncertainty whatever as to the exact point at which I shall—" He stopped short; his keen ear had caught the sound of crackling branches.

"A deer!" he muttered; "and coming right this way!"

Arachnida, coleoptera, spools, and even supper were forgotten on the instant; and the bug-hunter, alert and silent, stood grasping his rifle, his eyes fixed on the low-growing tangle of evergreens from which the suspicious sounds had proceeded. A moment later and he was staring with undisguised amazement at the small figure which limped rapidly toward him.

"You are *not* Professor Gearing—I am so glad!" were the astonishing words with which the apparition introduced itself. It pushed back a scarlet tam-o'-shanter from a tangle of brown curls, and continued: "I don't know who you are, but I am Katherine Terrill and I am lost in these dreadful woods. Do take me home!" With that the figure sank back against a tree with a sound suspiciously like a sob.

"I—I do not understand," stammered the astounded bug-hunter lamely. "I can take you home, certainly; but I must acknowledge that I am John Gearing."

The wearer of the scarlet tam started up with a hysterical laugh. "Professor Gearing is an old man!" she cried, "and *you*—you are quite—quite young! I took his spool out of the camp, and I can't find the way back!"

"The spool—eh! You don't mean—"

"Yes, I do. I took it and wound it up to point B —I mean the second spool," faltered the mischief-maker, her cheeks dyed with penitent blushes. "I—I was stopping at the camp, you see, for a few moments with a friend, and I saw the spool. I can't tell you why I did it." This last with a vain clutch after her vanished dignity. "It—it just occurred to me that it might be—"

"I hung that empty spool there merely as a tag at the end of my string," remarked John Gearing meditatively. "I certainly—"

"Say anything you like to me," interrupted Miss Terrill solemnly; "I deserve it. We shall never get home alive—never!"

John Gearing stared at the speaker for a full minute, then he threw back his head and laughed long and loud. "I—I beg your pardon, Miss Terrill," he said at length; "but really—"

"Oh, yes, you may laugh!" said the young lady with an indignant shrug. "I laughed too—at first. But it hasn't seemed a bit funny for at least six hours. I tell you we *can't* get back! We shall starve to death; and it's—it's getting dark!"

The bug-hunter was sobered in an instant by the pitiful quiver in the tired voice.

"You don't mean to say that you have been wandering about since morning with nothing to eat?" he asked anxiously.

"Nothing but huckleberries—and I loathe huckleberries!"

John Gearing hastily swung his pack-basket to the ground. "These sandwiches"—producing a parcel of dubious aspect—"have suffered somewhat, I fear, knocking about all day among my traps; but if you will accept them—"

"They look perfectly delicious!" declared the young lady with unconcealed delight. "But I shall eat only one—it is just possible, you know, that we might—in time—"

"I beg that you will give yourself no further anxiety on that score!" cried John Gearing confidently. "We are only a trifle over a mile from camp; we'll be there inside of an hour."

The girl shook her head mournfully. "That we are so near is just the most dreadful part of it," she said, winking rapidly to keep back two big tears which were trying hard to pass the barrier of her long lashes. "But if you really think you can find the way, do let us start at once. Of course we can reach the second spool," she added. "I—I was frightened when I saw how late it was growing, so I came to meet you. I thought it was my duty to—to tell you—"

John Gearing surveyed the speaker in puzzled silence. "Do you—er—mind telling me," he burst out after a long pause, during which the stealthy twilight made perceptible advances, "what—that is—why you were so sure that I was somebody else—at first, you know?"

"What *must* you think of me!" exclaimed Miss Terrill irrelevantly, stopping short in the midst of a vicious tangle of blackberry bushes for no other purpose, it appeared, than to wring her small hands. "It has all been so dreadful that I haven't realized *that!* You must think me bold and meddlesome and—and generally horrid!"

"I have thought nothing of the kind!" retorted the bug-hunter with unnecessary warmth. "It was all the fault of those infernal spools! I wouldn't mind this" —with a comprehensive wave of the hand which seemed to include all the hostile forces of nature—"if it were not for you. I should get into camp all right, some time; but—"

"You may think so, but you couldn't," said the girl with a pitying glance at the stalwart figure. "It will be all the harder for you to bear; and when I think that I did it—that it is all my fault! But of course I didn't think—I could never have imagined—what a fatal thing I was doing when I touched that spool. No, wait till I have told you all." With that she poured forth the tale of the day's adventures, closing with a statement of the problem which she had spent six unhappy hours in trying to solve.

"Don't you see," she said in a shaking voice, "how utterly improbable it is that we shall *ever* reach point A?"

John Gearing had smiled more than once during this recital; he also frowned as he stared anxiously into the black depths of the forest which shut them in like a wall.

"Miss Terrill," he said gravely, "your conclusions are undeniably logical and unpleasantly correct—from your premises; but luckily there are other factors which you have overlooked, and which must be introduced. One is, that the guides are sure to beat the woods for miles about point A. There is, therefore, not the slightest danger of our becoming either variable or permanent radii of point B. The only question to be considered at present is, shall we make any immediate attempt to solve the problem ourselves? You are already weary, and—"

"You might attach a second spool at point B," interrupted the girl, knitting her pretty brows; "our chances would then be multiplied by two."

"But I object to the preliminary division," said John Gearing decidedly; "it simply isn't to be thought of. The darkness has closed in upon us at an unconscionably early hour," he went on rapidly. "I can not understand it, unless, to add to our perplexity, it is about to—" A drop of water which landed squarely on the tip of his nose explained the phenomenon.

"It is raining," observed Miss Terrill with the calmness of despair. "But of course that was to be expected. We will go on," she added firmly. "No—I am not at all tired, and I am quite accustomed to the woods." This last with a superb gesture of refusal as her victim offered his arm.

Two minutes later her foot slipped on a treacherous log, and with a cry she plunged forward into the darkness.

John Gearing was at her side in an instant. "My poor little girl," he murmured, lifting her with all possible gentleness, "are you much hurt?"

"At all events I have not sprained my ankle," said the girl with a faint laugh. "But I slipped once before to-day, and—"

John Gearing groaned. "I shall never forgive my-self for my outrageous folly!" he declared savagely, and quite involuntarily he tightened the clasp of his strong arms.

Miss Terrill laughed again in spite of herself. "Put me down, please, Mr. Gearing," she said. "If you should change most of the pronouns in your last state-ment to the second person, it would be quite what I deserve. I fear I shall have to stop where I am; but you must go on. Please go at once before it gets any darker."

"And leave you here alone?"

"Yes."

By way of answer, John Gearing hastily divested himself of his thick shooting-jacket and wrapped it about his companion with an authoritative firmness which admitted of no question.

"I have four matches—and a half, to be ex-act," he said, after a careful search through his various pockets. "Luckily it hasn't rained long enough to wet the ground; if the fates aren't too unkind we'll have a camp-fire inside of five min-utes."

A flash, a sizzle, an impatient exclamation announced that match number one had weakly succumbed to the untoward influences of the place and hour. Two, three, and four followed with disheartening unanim-ity, during intervals plainly occupied in a frantic search for drier material.

"If you only had some paper," ventured a timid voice out of the darkness.

"Of course! Thank heaven you reminded me before I struck that last half-match!"

Another moment, and a score of closely written pages treating learnedly of the coleoptera and arachnida of the great northern wilderness were blazing merrily in the midst of a skilfully constructed pile of twigs and branches.

"Wasn't it fortunate you happened to have that paper?" observed Miss Terrill, as she leaned forward to warm her chilled fingers at the now thoroughly established fire.

"Fortunate!" echoed John Gearing, dropping his specimen-box as he stooped to lay another stick on the fire—whereat the scarlet-headed arachnid and the coleoptera, one and all, wriggled out and away with joyful haste. "It was by all odds the most fortunate thing I know of."

"Perhaps you will think me a coward," began the girl, after a prolonged pause which the raindrops filled with a soft, insistent murmur. "Do you think it would be very wrong for me—that is, for you—" She turned her head away from the searching firelight as she continued in so low a voice that John Gearing was forced to bend his tall head to listen—"if they find us? You said they would search for us?"

"They will search for us—certainly, and find us."

"If they know—that is, if you—if—I must tell them that I took the spool to—to find you, I could not face them—I could not bear it!"

"Ah, but the fact is that I found you!" said John Gearing in his deepest voice.

"Yes—but—the spools!"

The bug-hunter leaned forward and deliberately dropped a full half dozen of them into the red heart of the fire.

"There are no spools," he said calmly.

A more unpleasant spot than the virgin forest of the Adirondacks on a wet night it would be difficult to find. Mr. Percy Algernon Smith put this fact more forcibly; he said— But why repeat the words of a man who has forced his way through some six or eight miles of soaking coves, pursued all the way by jubilant throngs of mosquitoes—his energies being still further taxed by laborious and systematic performance on a big tin horn?

"I say, Jake," he bawled, pausing after a succession of ear-splitting blasts, "d'ye hear anything?"

The guide nodded. "To the west on us," he said, jerking his thumb over his shoulder. " 'Tain't fur, neither."

The sagacious reader has already divined that this is only the beginning of the story. Its ending was after the old, old fashion, of which wise people the world over never grow tired, and which in truth is the end—or the beginning—of every story that is at all worth the telling. In this place it must be set down in just four words—afterward they were married.

It was my good fortune, not many months later, to hear Mrs. John Gearing relate the above romantic circumstances, which she did with the prettiest smiles and blushes imaginable.

In closing she declared solemnly that never in all the course of her existence had such a welcome, glad, cheerful, happy, enlivening, and altogether delightful vision greeted her eyes as the round, freckled face of "Cinnamon" Smith as he burst through the dripping branches on that rainy August night.

But she never so much as mentioned the spools; it was their ashes that told the tale.

# EVERYBODY'S CHANCE

## BY JOHN HABBERTON

*John Habberton (born in Brooklyn, N. Y.,
February 24, 1842) achieved such an unprece-
dented success with his "Helen's Babies"
that his name is almost exclusively associated
in the public mind with lightsome humor and
dainty romance. Yet through the large body
of his work there runs a main artery of
altruism from which the pulse of the author's
personality must be taken. The present selection contains this heart-throb of helpful
purpose, and is in addition a love romance,
tender and true, as may be said of all Mr.
Habberton's love stories.*

2

# EVERYBODY'S CHANCE

## BY JOHN HABBERTON

### I—HOW THEY HEARD OF IT

BRUNDY was the deadest town in the United States; so all the residents of Brundy said. It had not even a railway station, although several other villages in the county had two each. It was natural, therefore, that manufacturers' capital avoided Brundy. There was a large woolen mill at Yarn City, eight miles to the westward, and Yarn City was growing so fast that some of the farmers on the outskirts of the town were selling off their estates in building lots at prices which justified the sellers in going to the city to end their days. At Magic Falls, five miles to the northward, there was water power and a hardwood forest, which between them made business for several manufacturers of wooden-ware, as well as markets, with good prices, for all farmers of the vicinity.

But Brundy had only land and people. The latter, according to themselves, were as good as the people anywhere, but the soil was so poor that no one could get a living out of it without very hard work. There was no chance of any kind for any of the natives. Young men were afraid to marry, and young women were afraid to marry them; for what girl wanted to go through the routine of drudgery in which she had pitied her own mother, and what lover wanted to ask his sweetheart to descend from the position of assistant at her old home to slave of all work in a new one?

The lack of a chance for any one had made itself manifest at Brundy many years before the date at which this story opens, so many of the natives had gone elsewhere to better their condition. The great majority of them had not been heard from afterward, so Brundy did not doubt that they had become too prosperous to think of their simple old friends and neighbors. Some, however, who had gone to great cities and the great West, had returned to the place of their birth to end their days, and they were so reserved as to how they had made their money, and how much they had made, that Brundy agreed that there were some great secrets of wealth to be discovered in the outside world, could the inhabitants of Brundy ever get away and search for it.

For instance, there was old Pruffett; he had gone to Chicago when barely twenty-one, remained there forty years, and been so busy all the while that he declared that he never had found time to look about him for a wife. He had made money, too; no one knew how much, and Pruffett never would tell, but as he paid cash for whatever he bought in the village and never haggled about prices, it seemed evident that he was very well off, for Squire Thomas, the richest native who had always remained at home, would never buy even a pound of butter until a penny or two of the price had been abated.

Sad though it be to relate, there were pretty and good young women in Brundy who would gladly have married old Pruffett for his money, and loving mothers who would have advised and helped them in that direction had old Pruffett given them any encouragement, but what could any one do with a millionaire—so they called him—who was satisfied to do his own work and do his own cooking in the cottage in which he was born, and which he had kept for years just as his mother left it when she died, and he had been too busy to hurry home to receive her dying blessing?

There was nothing mean about Pruffett; he contributed liberally to all church subscriptions, and when any neighbor chanced to fall into any trouble the old man was the first to offer counsel and substantial aid; still, why did he not be wholesouled and tell younger men how and where to find their chance in life—the chance which Brundy persistently denied every one?

One morning the entire village was thrown into a fever of excitement and sarcasm by the appearance of the following notice, which was posted on the bulletin-board in front of the town hall and on trees in the several streets:

*"Everybody has a Chance*

"A lecture on the above subject will be given at the town hall next Friday night. The lecturer has nothing to sell, nor any medicines or other goods to recommend, nor anything to advertise. It is to be a square talk by a square man, who can prove what he says.

No charge for admission; people who like the lecture may, if they desire, drop some small change into a box which will be at the door."

"Everybody has a chance, eh?" said the natives to one another. "That man doesn't know what sort of town he's coming to. If he is depending upon the collection at the door to help him to the next town he'll have to walk."

The more the lecturer's subject was discussed the more ridiculous it appeared, and as most people rather enjoy the spectacle of a man making a fool of himself the town hall was absolutely jammed on Friday night, half an hour before the usual time for the appearance on the platform of such strolling entertainers as did not know of the impecuniosity of the natives.

When the town clock struck eight the audience saw coming from the ante-room to the platform a middle-aged man with the garb and the eye of a well-to-do mechanic and the manner of a preacher, although he soon manifested an unpreacher-like disregard for grammatical rules. The lecture, too, although humorous enough at times to set every one laughing, was somewhat like a sermon in its general character.

"People talk about not havin' a chance," began the lecturer. "Why, if chances were eggs, none of you could move without steppin' on 'em. When a man says he hasn't got his chance in life he's talking about the particular chance he wants—that's all. What we

want most isn't always what we need most, my
friends, though few of us are honest enough and
smart enough to see it an' say so.

"I'd bet a dollar to a doughnut that the chance—
an' the only one—that every man in this room is
simply achin' for, so that he won't look at any other,
is the chance to make a lot of money! Did he ever see
anybody that had made a lot of money? Did the rich
man look any happier than other folks? If not, why
not? Can any of you tell the difference between the
rich and the poor by their faces? I can't, except that
generally the richest man looks most anxious and
most discontented."

By this time every one in the house was looking at
old Pruffett, who was looking at the back of the seat
in front of him, although the expression of his countenance did not imply that there was anything particularly cheerful and inspiring in the back of that seat.
The lecturer continued:

"An old book which all of you have in the house,
and which some of you profess to believe with all
your might, says that 'A man's life consisteth not in
the abundance of the things which he possesseth'; you
can read the passage for yourselves, and correct me
if I am wrong. That same old book tells of chances
that came to lots of people that hadn't a cent, either
before or after. There are just as good chances now,
and Brundy's as full of 'em as any other place, an'
the people that don't get 'em are the people who won't
see 'em, though if the chances were bears they'd bite
'em, they're so close. A man's best chance is what-

ever is closest to him; if it isn't also closest to his heart, that's the man's fault—not the chance's."

The lecturer went on in the same vein, and told of some of his own chances which he had missed, as well as of some in which he had, to use his own expression, "caught on"; and he told some stories of personal experience so well that he made a lot of people cry a little, and laugh much, and not a few were compelled to do some serious thinking.

When the talk ended there was quite a melodious jingling of coin in the box at the door; and several members of the audience who were nearest to old Pruffett told their neighbors for a week afterward that the old man actually dropped into the box a ten-dollar bill, forty times as much as would have paid the lecturer's stage fare to the next town.

"Got any small change about your clothes, Champ?" asked Charley Wurring, a smiling youth, of Champney Bruff, a serious-looking man of about thirty years, who was exploring his vest pocket. Charley had abundant reason for smiling, for by his side, where she had been throughout the lecture, was Luce Grew, the handsomest girl in the village. "I didn't bring any money, for I came only to laugh, but I found my chance during the lecture, and here she is, eh, Luce?"

Luce looked rather bashfully toward Champ with her great dark eyes and strong face, and then, for relief, smiled pleasantly at Charley. Champ flushed a little under his dark brown skin, but mechanically extended a coin toward Charley, who took it and dropped it into the box. Then he took Luce's hand, placed it on his arm, whispered something to the girl, which elicited a smile which Champ regarded fixedly, although the longer he looked the whiter and more fixed it became. Suddenly it appeared to him that old Pruffett was regarding him intently, and as he did not care to be looked at closely at that particular moment he abruptly left the hall and started homeward.

So Charley Wurring and Luce Grew had come to an understanding.

And Luce Grew was the one woman of Brundy whom Champney Bruff had ever thought he could love. Could love? Had he not loved her for years? He had not dared tell her so, for how could he? He was the oldest member of his father's family; his mother was dead, his father unfit for work; and the farm was one which required steady work and rigid economy if it was to support all of Champ's brothers and sisters. The farm would be better if he could clear and drain about twelve acres of marshy woodland that belonged to it, and to clear that land had been his special effort for two or three years; but after the usual farm routine had been gone through with, even in winter, he could find time to chop down only two or three trees a day, and after all the trees were gone there would still be the stumps, and after the stumps the ditching. When all this had been done, he would propose to Luce Grew, but now, evidently, his chance or his duty, which to the lecturer had seemed to mean the same thing, was the finishing of that clearing—while Luce Grew loved another man and would marry him.

He heard footsteps behind him, and in a moment old Pruffett joined him with:

"Not a bad lecture, Champ?"

"Not for those who found their chances while the lecture was going on," was the reply, in words that sounded as if each had been savagely bitten off. There was a moment of silence before the old man said:

"I guess I know what you mean. I'm very sorry, too—for you. Yet Luce herself seemed to be happy; I suppose that's what you've longed to see her? You'd have done anything to make her happy—eh?"

"Yes; anything in my power."

"Good. Now's your chance."

"What on earth do you mean, Mr. Pruffett?"

"Merely what I say. If you loved her, not yourself, or loved her more than you loved yourself, you can do a great deal to make her happy; far more than Charley Wurring can."

"I wish I knew what you were trying to say, Mr. Pruffett."

"Do you? Then I'll try to make myself understood. Charley is a well-meaning fellow, but nowhere near enough of a man to marry a girl like that. Splendid girls sometimes accept a husband of that kind after waiting a long time in vain for a better one; the range of choice in this town is rather small, you know. Charley's much the best of his family; indeed, he hasn't any bad habits of his own, and he has learned to hate all that he might have inherited, but you know his fix; a father who has drunk himself into incapacity for anything, and a mother who is utterly discouraged and bad-tempered. Luce will have many occasions for feeling sorry for her choice; and Charley will often have to feel desperate, for what chance can he see, at present, of marrying and supporting a wife?"

"Well!" exclaimed Champ, savagely.

"Well, you know what the lecturer said about chances? Yours is right at hand—right now. Why don't you put Charley into that wooded marshland of yours, to clear it? Give him the wood in payment; you'd not lose a cent by that. Get his father to help him; the weakest man has enough romance in him to want to help his son to a good wife. Work is the best cure for drunkenness, and the fellow daren't and can't drink while his son is with him all the while. By doing this you would be improving a chance to greatly benefit three people; such a chance seldom comes to any one."

"And I would also help another man to marry the woman whom—"

"Whom you love? Well, for what do you love her? For her sake or for your own?"

Champ remained silent; the old man went on:

"You don't seem to know. It's well, then, that you didn't chance to marry her."

"Mr. Pruffett," exclaimed Champ—he almost roared it—"do you know what you are saying? Are you human? Are you a man, like other men?"

"I am, my boy," replied the old man calmly. "I

don't mind telling you, in strict confidence, that I loved Luce's mother—God bless her!—forty years ago. I never loved any other woman—I tried to, but I couldn't. I had an awful fight with myself, after Grew won her, and I got the worst of it, for I was obliged, as an honest man, to admit to myself that I loved myself more than I loved her. To reform myself, I determined to go on loving her, but for her sake only, and the way I did it was to do just as I am advising you. I hadn't any marshland to clear, and there was nothing in Grew's family history for the young man to be ashamed of, but I put him into the one good chance which I had here, and I went away to shift for myself. I don't deny that I hoped that something would happen to break their engagement, but there didn't. I wish Luce were my daughter, for there's no one I would rather see her marry than you, but there are some things which one can't change— some chances which a man loses. Your chance is just as I'm putting it; I'm advising only what I did myself, and what I never had cause to regret. I know, though, it isn't the sort of thing to press on a young man too hard, and I'm sure that, while you're in your present frame of mind, you don't care to listen to any more of this kind of talk, so—good-night."

"Good-night," was the response, as sharp as the crack of a rifle.

"Shake hands with me, won't you, Champ?" said the old man softly. "No one else knows so well how to sympathize with you. Don't forget that I loved her mother—and lost her."

They shook hands as they parted, but Champ's head was in a whirl, and his heart was thumping angrily. What? Help the man who had just taken from him the prize toward which he had been struggling for years? Pruffett had probably told the truth, but—well, men were not all of the same clay. Love Luce for her own sake? Why, what else had he thought of but what he would do to make Luce happy? Had not his delay been entirely because of his doubts and fears for her? What was most in his mind whenever he thought of her—himself? Never! He thought only of her—her great, deep eyes, her noble face, her womanly composure, her strength of character—everything that was best in womanhood, so far as he knew women. He was sure that through his very admiration of all that was best in her, he knew best how to make her happy, while Charley, a mere good-natured, happy-go-lucky fellow, who had seemed to be in love with half-a-dozen other girls for no especial reason, would be utterly unable to comprehend the needs of so superior a nature.

Yet there was some truth in what old Pruffett had said about the ways in which Charley could be helped to become a more fit husband. If some one else could help him, well and good, but as to Champ—. He struggled hard with himself a few moments; then he suddenly stopped, bared his head, looked upward, and exclaimed:

"Heaven help me, I'll do it—for her sake! 'Tis my chance—but what a chance."

### II—IN THE CAMP OF THE ENEMY

Luce Grew told herself, after Charley had reluctantly gone home and she found herself alone with her thoughts, that she wondered how she had come to say "Yes" to the very pointed question which Charley Wurring had put to her during a certain point of the lecture. Charley had one of the sympathetic natures which are rare among men, or, perhaps, less rare than the willingness of their owners to manifest them, so Luce had always liked him. He was quick to see the application of an argument, or the inner and better sense of almost anything that might be said, so Luce had never failed to find him good company, although she regarded him very much as if he were a boy, although he was fully as old as she. She had been deeply interested in the lecture, and her better self approved all that the speaker said; so it pleased her greatly that when she looked at Charley for sympathy his face was frank and open, and he seemed to be of exactly her own way of thinking; while most of the young men about him were looking grim, or were sneering, or exchanging satirical winks with other young men.

So, when the lecturer told the hearers that their chances were all about them—nay, right at their side, waiting only to be accepted, Charley had whispered:

"Luce, don't you think you could make a personal application of that remark? I am right at your side; won't you accept me? I won't ask any other or grander chance than you while I live."

She felt like laughing at the boy, but he looked so earnest, so manly, yet at the same time so appealing, that she did what many another woman has done in similar circumstances—she began to wonder. Life was long; Brundy was a small place; there were other young men in the village, but very, very few whom she could by any possibility marry. She did not like the possibility of remaining single all her life. Charley was not the kind of man upon whom she had set her fancy, but young men were disappointing creatures; she had never been in love with one, but girls of her acquaintance had made dreadful mistakes in marrying men whom Luce herself had thought quite good. Charley was good—she never had heard a word against him; he was very attentive to his mother and kind to his sisters. He had nothing upon which to marry, but engagements generally were long in Brundy; perhaps if she were to accept him it might be the means of making him everything he now failed to be.

"Does it take you so long to make up your mind?" whispered Charley. "I know I'm not worthy of you, but, on the other hand, neither is any one else; I'll be anything you wish, if you'll think me good enough to begin with."

She looked down into his eyes; they were very honest eyes, and at that particular instant they were very earnest. Luce blushed slightly and dropped her own eyes, Charley's hand sought hers, pressed it, and received a gentle pressure in return; then he whispered:

"Thank you. God bless you."

On the way home she talked to him kindly, but not enthusiastically; she told him that his proposal had been a great surprise, and perhaps she had accepted it too hastily, for she really had never thought of loving him; but Charley was so grateful, and so willing to wait, and so astonished at his own temerity, and so overwhelmed by his new joy, that she could not help being deeply affected, so she made but a single condition; the affair must be a secret between them until both of them were certain that they were not mistaken. Charley promised willingly, for he was concerned, for Luce's sake, about what people would say should they know of what had occurred. Marriage was a serious matter in Brundy, from the dollar and cents point of view; and he knew that every one in the village knew that he had neither money nor prospects, and that his only employment, thus far, had been several months of school teaching, during the winter months, and such occasional work as he could find in the village and among the farmers during the summer. He well knew, too, what people would say about a woman like Luce entering a family such as the Wurring family had become, through the habits of the head of the house.

The next morning, therefore, Charley made haste to find Champ, the only man to whom he had betrayed his feelings, and beg that young man to keep the matter a profound secret.

He found Champ in the marshland forest, working as if he were determined to fell all the trees in a single day. Champ rested upon his axe and kept his eyes on the ground while the communication was made; then, without raising his eyes, he said:

"What have you to marry on?"

"Not a cent," was the reply, "though here's the half dollar you lent me last night."

"Keep that to start your fortune with," said Champ. "There's money here for you if you choose to work for it."

"Here? Where? How?"

"By cutting away these trees. If you'll do it, and keep at the job until it is done, you may have all of the wood. Good firewood brings three dollars a cord in town during the winter months, which aren't far off, and the supply is none too great. There's at least a couple of hundred dollars' worth here, and I want it out of the way, but I've not the time to do it myself."

"'Tis mine, then!" exclaimed Charley joyously. "I'll go home at once for my axe."

"You needn't take that trouble," said Champ, anxious to get away from the spectacle of a man so happy, and from such a cause. "You may use mine for the remainder of the day. When you come back after dinner, perhaps you can persuade your father to help you; I'm sure he would do it if he knew the reason. Two pairs of hands are better than one at such a job, for 'twill be no easy one, I assure you."

"Thank you," said Charley. "I'll be glad to have my father with me, for reasons which I needn't explain to you. But, Champ, I feel as if I could do the whole job myself, in a very short time. Oh, I feel like a giant."

"Indeed?" was the reply, given almost with a sneer.

"Yes, indeed. Oh, you may look that way if you like, but you don't understand the feeling. Just wait, though, until you are fairly in love yourself, an' —"

"Oh, don't talk to me in that way," exclaimed Champ, biting his lips and turning aside; he felt that if he did not quickly get away he would fly at the fellow and strangle him.

"But I must talk so," persisted Charley, "and you are the only man to whom I can do it, for no one else knows of my great fortune but you. To think that I am the only man in the village who is so richly blessed. There's no other girl in Brundy who can compare with Luce; honestly now, old fellow, is there?"

Champ took his knife from his pocket and began to shave the rough bark from the coat of a slippery-elm tree.

"I do believe you think there is," said Charley, looking curiously at his companion, "and that you're in love with her. Oh, you sly chap! You always were the quietest young man in the town, and have seldom paid attention to any of the girls, but I do believe I have found you out. Who is she? I won't tell anybody. I'd like to know that some other man is as happy as I. Has she said 'Yes'?"

"Will you kindly attend to your own business and leave mine to me?" asked Champ, suddenly turning on Charley a face like a thunder-cloud. The younger man exclaimed quickly:

"I beg a thousand pardons, Champ. I didn't mean to be impertinent. You never saw anything like that in me, did you?"

"Not until a few moments ago," was the reply. "But I don't want ever to see it again."

"You shan't, I assure you," said Charley in haste, as he began to tone down his excitement by attacking the largest tree near at hand. He worked vigorously several moments, but finally stopped to say:

"Let me talk of Luce, though. She is so grand, so good, so unlike all other girls. I've thought myself in love before, but I soon found out 'twas all fancy." Charley leaned on his axe and looked contemplatively at the ground a moment or two before he continued: "Other girls seemed to like me to make love to them, but it soon became an old story to both of us, for they seemed to have nothing in their minds but what was trifling and merely romantic, but Luce —why, there's something in the very tone of her voice that makes her seem different from every other young woman, and better. She's—she's—oh, she's thoroughly womanly, while the others are merely girlish. Don't you think that is the proper distinction, so far as you have observed her and other Brundy girls?"

As Charley asked this question he raised his eyes for the answer, but Champ was no longer standing before him. Charley looked slowly about him, but could see Champ nowhere; then he quickly peered between the trees, in every direction, and finally saw

Champ, some distance away, walking rapidly and with his fingers to his ears.

"I declare," exclaimed the young man to himself, yet softly, as if he feared that even the trees had ears, "I believe I've been making a fool of myself. I didn't suppose, though, that a man generally so kind and sympathetic as Champ could have been quite so rude. Did I really say anything that was dreadfully silly?"

He thought a little while about it, and this naturally set him to thinking about Luce, and the subject was so interesting that he could not give any attention to anything else, so he leaned against a tree and indulged in delightful day-dreaming for he knew not how long. Neither could he afterward imagine how long he might have continued at his congenial occupation had he not been startled by a footfall, and, looking about him, seen Champ returning with an axe in his hand. Champ at first looked sheepishly toward him and said:

"I thought I could spare half a day to help you." When, however, the big fellow cast his eyes about and saw not a tree had been felled since he made his escape he glared savagely at Charley, and exclaimed:

"You're a fine fellow to think of marrying, aren't you? You've not chopped a stroke since I left you. I had better have offered this wood to a better man, even if I had been obliged to look for one not in love. I suppose you would like me to do all the work for you, after giving you the trees—eh?"

Charley's face turned scarlet; he seized his axe and began to make chips fly rapidly. Champ also attacked a tree, and for a few moments no sound was heard but

that of the axes upon the tree-trunks.  Soon Charley
wanted to stop, for he was unaccustomed to the work,
and his hands had begun to blister, but after what
Champ had said the young man was resolved to suffer
anything rather than remain under the cruel imputa-
tion of being willing that Champ should earn the
money on which the younger man should wed Luce
Grew.  Suddenly, however, to his great relief,
Champ's tree fell, and the axeman stood aside for a
moment.

"I covet your strength," exclaimed Charley; "and
I'm going to have it, or something like it, if hard
work will get it for me.  A man who is to marry Luce
Grew should have as much muscle as heart."

"Talk is cheap," responded Champ.  After this
there was nothing for Charley to do but attack his tree
again.  Soon, however, the blisters in his right hand
began to break, and the pain was very like torture,
so he laid down his axe and began to blow upon the
palms of his hands.  Champ approached him, took his
hand roughly and looked at it.  Then he looked inquiringly into Charley's face, and said:

"You're more of a man than I thought you.  You
can't go on with such a hand.  Wait a moment."

He went to a hollow tree, and drew from it a pair
of old leather gloves and a small bottle of oil.

"Here; put some of this on your hands, and put
these gloves on.  Once in a while I'm afflicted in the
same way, after I've been out of axe practice a little
while.  Give the oil a few minutes in which to get in
its work."

Champ returned to his tree, lopping off the boughs as if they were twigs, cutting them into four-foot lengths and tossing them aside; then he cut the trunk itself into four-foot lengths. Charley looked on in admiration, but while the giant looked about for another foeman worthy of his steel the younger man exclaimed:

"What a magnificent specimen of manhood you are! It is a man like you whom Luce should marry. I suppose, however, she knows her own mind."

"Whether she does—or no—" said Champ, speaking between the strokes of his axe, "her mind is—the only one she—can go by—for the present." Then he stopped a moment and said, "Can't you possibly talk of something else? You ought to be thinking and talking about how much you will do in a day, and asking who is most likely to buy the wood and pay quickest, and where you can best put your money at interest as fast as you collect it. Talking about a girl never helped a man to marry her; 'tis work—nothing else—that makes a man worthy of the love he pretends to bear a woman."

"I guess you're right, Champ," sighed Charley, addressing himself once more to work, "but I wish I knew where you got so much sense. I won't ask you any more about it, as it seemed to worry you a few minutes ago, but whoever the girl is that you're fond of, why, she's going to be the happiest woman alive."

"Umph, I hope so, but—I shan't believe it—until I—see it."

"Come, now, old fellow, you shouldn't distrust

yourself in that stupid manner. 'Faint heart never won fair lady'—keep that saying close in mind. Why, it was the most daring thing in the world—my proposing to Luce; I had everything against me, and I knew it; I took my chances, though, and you know what came to pass. If you would only see yourself as you are, and as everybody else sees you, and as the girl herself can't help seeing, and—"

"Will you be quiet?" exclaimed Champ, suddenly turning with a threatening face and with his axe still uplifted.

"No, I won't," replied the younger man, with a calm but determined face. "You've done me a great favor this morning, and I want to do you one in return. You may think that I want to pry into your affairs, but I don't. I want to tell you, though, what the lecturer told all of us last night, that every man has his chance in life, that it is very close to him, and that only he is to blame if he won't see it. To be happily in love is the one thing you need to make you as happy as you are manly, and I'm sure that's saying a great deal. Instead of that you're belittling yourself. You're my friend; you've done more for me this morning than any other man ever did, and until I can do something equally good for you I want to ease my mind by giving you some good advice. You ought to do just what I have done, determining, as I did, that whatever else had to be done afterward I would do with all my might, or make a better man of myself while failing. Why don't you do it? Have you proposed yet?"

"No!"

"Doesn't the girl even know that you love her?"

"No. I don't see, at least, how she can know it."

"That's bad—for her. 'Twould make life a very different thing for any woman in this dead-and-alive town to know that a man like you cared for her. Women in Brundy—young women—have a pretty dismal outlook. I'm not going again to ask you who she is, but I do wish I knew, for I'd take the responsibility of telling her; after that she'd wait forever, and be happy in spite of anything, to know that there was such great good fortune in store for her."

"You'd tell her, would you?" snarled Champ. "I've a great mind to let you, just to see what a flunk you would make of it, you—"

"I dare you to do it," said Charley, meeting Champ's scowl without flinching. The older man glared furiously, and suddenly betook himself again to his axe, dashing at the tree as if it were his rival himself. But Charley's blood also was up, and he went on, shouting so that his words should not be drowned by the shower of axe-strokes.

"Yes, I dare you. I don't care a bit for your temper; you're a first-rate fellow in spite of it, and the woman who doesn't know that you love her shall know it at once if I can find out who she is."

Champ faced about, dropped his axe, controlled his face, and said, with manly dignity:

"She is Luce Grew."

"Luce!" exclaimed Charley, staggering backward.

"Yes, Luce. Now do you know why you won't tell

her? It is because I love her, and want her to be
happy, that I've thrown this job into your hands this
morning. She has accepted you; well, that is her own
business, and her own right, and no one else has the
slightest use for complaining. But mark my words,
young man. I never shall annoy her in any way, but
I shall never cease to love her. On the other hand,
if you fail to be to her everything that you've promised and everything that is in your power, you will
have me to reckon with. She's one of your chances;
this job of wood-chopping is another; if you don't
take as industriously to this as you do to the other,
don't ever speak to me again anywhere, in any circumstances, and be careful to keep out of my path.
Good-morning."

### III—"THEY SAY—"

Although Luce had enjoined secrecy upon Charley,
and protested against publicity being given by acts
and manners any more than by words, she found
Charley's society so pleasant that she had not the
heart to forbid him to call frequently. She discouraged all attempts at effusive love-making; but she could
not help being interested and cheered by the young
man's enthusiasm, for the people of Brundy seldom
found anything to be enthusiastic about, and as Luce
was a great-hearted creature her lover's irrepressible
spirits made good the lack of something which she
often felt.

But how can any one keep a secret in a town where
the people have only other people's affairs to occupy

their leisure moments? Within a week everybody
was telling everybody else that Charley Wurring had
been three times—some said four—to the Grews'
since the night of the lecture, and that it must mean
something; as Luce was the only adult girl in the
family, and there were no young men among her
brothers, public opinion was not long in determining
what the something was. Luce was not the kind of
girl of whom girls in general ask leading questions,
but it needs not direct statements to establish anything which a lot of gossips desire to believe, so that
in less than another week all Brundy, despite Charley's
evasions, regarded the couple as fully engaged, and discussed them accordingly at shops, the post-office, and
wherever else men and women chanced to meet.

"It seems too bad," said one of the village pastors
at a grocer's, where he chanced to meet old Pruffett.
"I am not given to romance—my calling forbids it,
through the stern realities which I am obliged to en-
counter in the experiences of my flock; but that girl
has always seemed to me to be worthy of far greater
opportunities than our village affords, yet now she
seems to have given herself to a young man who shows
as few signs of rising as any one whom I know, and
who has much, for which he is not responsible, to keep
him down. Two young people more utterly unlike in
nature I have seldom met."

"Ah, well," replied Pruffett, "let us hope that it is
according to the designs of Providence. If like were
always to marry like, the world would soon be full of
petrified cranks, Dominie."

"I suppose," said the minister cautiously, "that you are right, on general principles, but I confess that the present application distresses me."

"Every one owes something to the community in which he lives," continued Pruffett. "If there is anything in this story—which has no authority but common report—perhaps it accounts for the wonderful change that has come over the entire Wurring family. Charley is working as hard as any farmer in the county, and his father is working with him, and seems to be taking no liquor."

"Charley's mother looks happier than I have seen her for years," admitted the minister; "I noticed it from the pulpit only last Sunday, and it inspired me in both preaching and praying. All of her children were at church, too—an unusual occurrence."

"Wurring has picked up a good deal of manliness in some way," remarked the grocer. "I've had to refuse him credit very often of late years—I hated to do it, for he used to be a good customer of mine; still, a man can't conduct a grocery business on bygones if he expects to pay his own bills. The other day, though, when he bought a small bag of flour, I told him he might as well take a barrel, and pay me out of the wood that he and Charley are clearing from that marsh for Champ and his father, but Wurring flushed up and said rather grandly that he couldn't do it, for the wood belonged entirely to Charley. It wasn't so long ago that he used to beg me for small credits, to be paid when Charley got his pay from the school board."

"Luce herself certainly looks happier than she used to," said the minister.

"Then I guess that everybody ought to be happy," said old Pruffett, although he doubted his own words as he thought of Champney Bruff and his dismal secret. He could not help recalling the days, that strung out sadly into months and years, in which he himself had tried to live down his disappointment at losing Luce's mother.

As time went on, however, people began to whisper to one another that matters did not seem to be as they at first had been with Charley and Luce. The woodpiles multiplied rapidly on the Bruff marshland, and Charley himself grew more and more manly in appearance to those who saw him on his way to work in the morning or returning late at night. He went as often to the Grews', but Luce did not look as happy as usual when people chanced to see her. She certainly did not seem to have stopped liking Charley, for those church-goers who spent their time in looking at other people during service said that she had her eyes upon him almost all the while except during prayer time. Veteran gossips, experienced at cross-questioning in ways that would occasionally put the shrewdest and most self-contained natives off their guard, waylaid Luce's little brothers and sisters and asked many questions, but learned nothing; it was evident, therefore, that the young couple did not converse freely in the family circle. What could the matter be?

"Luce," Charley had said one evening, after the

girl had several times rallied him on his unusual solemnity, "you do love me, don't you? I don't ask you to say that you care as much for me as I for you, because there's not as much of me to care for, but—"

"Love you? Indeed I do," murmured Luce, "as much as I know how to. You must remember that it is something new to me, while you say you have loved me a long time. I've never been in love before, nor thought much about it, but you know I am very, very fond of you."

"So fond that no one else could take you away from me?"

"You silly boy," said the girl, with a merry laugh. "What a question to ask. Don't you think you had better drop it and the thought of it, until some one else shows some signs of asking me?"

Charley looked as if he were not entirely sure that the question would keep so long, and Luce succeeded in changing the subject; she had read of such forebodings of lovers—novels were full of them, and she detested most novels.

The next time he called, however, Charley reverted to the subject, and would not be diverted from it; by this time the girl's curiosity was aroused and she insisted upon knowing what the young man meant.

"Only this," was the reply. "There's a better man than I who has been in love with you a long time, and I don't believe he thinks of anything else."

"Then his mind might be better employed," promptly replied the girl. "But who is he?"

"His name is Champney Bruff," said Charley, looking keenly into Luce's eyes as he spoke. To his infinite relief, yet somewhat to his pain also, Luce burst into hearty laughter as she exclaimed:

"How ridiculous!"

"But it isn't ridiculous, my dear," replied Charley very gravely. "It's serious—very serious."

"Why, Charley," said Luce, after another laugh—a long, melodious laugh, with a little wonder in it— "Champ Bruff never spoke to me more than twenty words in any one day in all his life. Whenever he was near me I felt uncomfortable, for he always looked—why, really he looked as if he was afraid I would bite him, which I solemnly assure you I never once thought of doing."

"What strange creatures you girls are," said Charley, rather pettishly. "There are some of you at whom a man can't look more than half a minute before they suspect him of being in love with them, while others can't see anything but—but what isn't."

"But what reason have you to be angry about it, you silly boy?" asked Luce. "One would think, to hear you talk, that you would like me to be grateful to Champ Bruff, and fall in love with him in return. If you really insist upon it, I suppose I could—"

"Stop! Stop, please—at once!" exclaimed Charley hastily. "Still, I'm awfully sorry for Champ."

"Why should you be?" the girl asked merrily; she scarcely knew what she said or why she said it, for the disclosure had amazed her greatly, and she was not accustomed to being amazed. "Hasn't some poet

—a man poet, too, written, ' 'Tis better to have loved and lost than never to have loved at all'?"

"Has he? I didn't know it, and I don't exactly understand why he did it, but perhaps he had more experience than I in such matters. Don't make fun of Champ, though, please, because his disappointment has hurt him dreadfully."

"Disappointment? Why, he never said a word to me about anything of the kind, and if he had I—" Luce did not conclude the sentence, for she could not. Like all other women of the nobler order, she had not spent much time in dreaming about lovers and longing for them; she had supposed that some day, in the natural order of affairs, some man would propose to her, and she might love him and afterward marry him, but the idea of being loved by a man who, as she had said, had scarcely spoken to her except in the briefest manner, and with whom she had no interests in common—why, it seemed almost shocking. How could the man have come by so silly a fancy?

"How did you come to know all this?" she asked Charley. "You've been hearing some gossip at the shops or the post-office, I'll warrant—something said for the sole purpose of teasing you. Quite a lot of people are curious about us, and I'm rather uncomfortable about it. Who told you this ridiculous story?"

"Champ himself." replied Charley.

"What? Are you dreaming?"

"I never was wider awake in my life, dear girl; the thought of it frequently keeps me awake when I should be asleep."

"But you must have misunderstood him," insisted Luce, with the positive manner of an entirely honest and simple nature. "It is he who has given you the chance of work which you are improving so splendidly, according to every one. The best things I hear about you are always accompanied by the expression 'Champ says.' Any one would suppose that, if you were right, Champ must be crazy, for he seems to be doing just what a sane man wouldn't do if he were in love with the same woman as the man whom he is praising and helping. I've heard many strange things and read some others, but really, this is the most incomprehensible, nonsensical thing I ever heard of in my life."

"Do stop laughing!" exclaimed Charley. "Your laughter is the sweetest music in the world, but there's a time for everything, and no good man's troubles should be laughed at by a good woman."

"You're a noble-hearted fellow," exclaimed Luce, with the first look of hearty admiration which the young man had ever seen in her face. It pleased him greatly, but did not prevent what he wanted to say; so when Luce begged him to tell her what he knew, and how he learned it, and insisted upon hearing all the particulars, he told her everything which had happened between Champ and him. When he had finished Luce was silent a long time; finally she said:

"What a noble-hearted fellow he must be! Who would imagine, to look at that serious, matter-of-fact face of his, that there was a single spark of romance in him?"

"Romance?" echoed Charley. "The romance isn't

near so wonderful to me as his heroism. If you'd seen him standing there in the woods, his axe upraised, and his face looking as if he wanted to kill me— you wouldn't have thought there was anything romantic about him."

"And he is doing all this for me," said Luce, who had gone into a reverie.

"He certainly is," was the reply. "He certainly doesn't do it for me. He never speaks to me unless I compel him; he passes me in the street with the merest nod, and with a look as if he were charging me with the basest form of theft. In fact, he has succeeded in making me feel the same way a great deal of the time."

"I'm sure I don't see why," said Luce, roused by her sense of justice. "You can not have robbed him of what he never had, nor of what he had any good reason to believe he ever would have. The idea of my marrying Champney Bruff!"

"It really doesn't seem possible to you?" asked Charley eagerly and with an intent expression of face.

"Utterly impossible," the girl replied. "Don't you too go crazy. What a strange world this is!"

"But you will try to be polite to him hereafter, when you chance to meet him?"

"I shall not only try; I shall be so, for all that he has done for you, and also for what you say he has suffered. I wish, though, that I hadn't heard of it."

"Why so?"

"Because—oh, because I'm sorry to be the cause of unhappiness to any one, even if the fault is not at all

mine. The affair will appear like a nightmare to me;
I wish you hadn't told me of it."

"Then so do I; it seems to be my luck to say and
do things at unexpected times."

"Don't blame yourself, you poor boy!" exclaimed
Luce; then, for the first time in their acquaintanceship,
she kissed him, and the kiss took an immense load from
Charley's heart.

After that, however, there was a strange change in
the ways of the two young people; Charley never
again alluded voluntarily to Champney Bruff, but Luce
persisted in asking questions about the unhappy man.
Did he seem as solemn as ever? Did he still look
and act as if he had been robbed? Did he make any
more threats?

The subject finally became unspeakably unpleasant
to Charley, for Luce slowly lost the cheerful manner
which she had displayed toward him from the beginning of their engagement. She never had acted as
sweethearts did in the hundreds of romances Charley
had read, but she had made him feel entirely welcome,
and this seemed a promise of something better in
sweeter days to come. Now, however, she began to
greet him inquiringly and anxiously; she said she
was in constant fear of trouble between him and
Champ, and if there should be anything of the kind
she would wish she never had been born. She wished,
and said so without a blush, that they were able to
marry and go away—anywhere, to any degree of
poverty, if only she might not have to be in the same
town with a man who was feeling as Champ was said

to feel.   Charley had read somewhere of a malady called monomania; he knew the meaning of the word, and he felt sure that it described Luce's condition.  He tried to dispose of such wood as he had cut, that he might bravely marry on the proceeds; marriages at Brundy were simple and inexpensive affairs, and a wedding trip was an indulgence of which no happy couples dared to think.  But winter was still two or three months away; the natives had ample time in which to haggle and chaffer about the price of their winter supply of fuel, so Charley was obliged to delay.

And all the while he was so sorry for Luce.  She, the grandest-natured young woman in the village— she, who never had been subject to the "nerves" of which even young men were occasionally obliged to hear—became pale, timorous, and sometimes tearful. Her parents blamed Charley, but the girl declared that he was the dearest fellow in the world, and had never said an unkind word to her; if only she could feel at ease about his future she did not care what might become of her.   She no longer tried to keep secret her promise to Charley; she announced, almost defiantly, some sage women thought, that they were engaged to be married, and that he was the best man she ever had known or heard of.   The family physician was called in, but he could make nothing of the case; the family's pastor talked with her and prayed with her, but went home afterward in a most bewildered frame of mind.   Indeed, no one seemed able to give her any cheer but old Pruffett, who shrewdly timed a call upon her mother at an hour when he knew well the good

woman was not at home. He was as kind-hearted and
tender as he was shrewd, so, almost before she knew
what she was doing, Luce was unburdening her heart
to him.

"There will be no trouble between them; drop that
thought from your mind," said the old man; "but if
both of you are as anxious as you say that Charley
and he shall be separated, suppose I send Charley out
West for me on a little matter of business? It will
put some money into his pocket, and take a great load
from your heart. In the meantime I will talk to
Champ; I happen to be the only person besides Charley
who knows how the poor fellow is feeling, and perhaps I can comfort him a little. No one is fitter to
do it, for I've been through a similar experience
myself.

"You?" said the girl wonderingly. To her, all
love was the exclusive property of young people.

"Yes, I. It was a long time ago, but I shall never
forget it. Your mother may perhaps tell you something about it if you ask her."

The very next day all Brundy knew that Charley Wurring had taken the stage for the nearest
railway station, and what to make of it no one knew,
for Charley had bluntly told inquirers that it was nobody's business where he went or what he went for.
When Champ heard this his usual reticence deserted
him, and he used language so severe about the young
man that the town soon had it that Charley had borrowed a lot of money from Champ, and left town to
avoid paying it.

### IV—THE WAYS OF WOMAN—AND MEN

No business man, no matter how great his experience or how perfect his methods, ever finds his time entirely equal to all the demands upon it, so old Pruffett did not reach Champney Bruff until that very volcanic person had heard all that the village could tell him about the departure of Charley Wurring. Pruffett was going to break the news to him in a masterly manner, and then force upon Champ some counsel which he did not doubt would have the proper effect.

He found Champ in the marsh forest, and also in a state of wrath. No sooner did the younger man see who it was that was intruding upon the solitude which he had sought for himself than he roared:

"A nice end your advice has brought things to, hasn't it? Luce is miserable, and that young scoundrel gone to no one knows where, while I—"

"Excuse me a moment," interrupted the older man. "Some one knows where Charley is; it is I. Charley isn't a scoundrel either; he's far more a man than I supposed. Still more, Luce isn't miserable; I called there this morning, and found her looking and feeling better than at any time in the last two or three weeks. As to you—but I interrupted you."

"She's looking and feeling better?" asked Champ. "Are you sure?"

"I've the evidence of my own eyes and ears, and her mother is of my opinion."

"Thank heaven!" exclaimed Champ, smoothing his brow somewhat.

"You were saying something about yourself," persisted old Pruffett.

"Never mind about me, if the girl is feeling better," was the reply. "You know very well, if what you told me a few weeks ago about her mother was true, that I don't care what happens to me if she can be happy."

"You've really learned to feel that way, have you?" The old man accompanied his question with a look so keen, despite the age of his eyes, that Champ winced a bit; but he pulled himself together and looked very manly when he finally said:

"Yes! It's been an awful fight, and one that's by no means over. There isn't an unhappier man on the face of the earth than I; I've thought all manner of dreadful things toward that youngster Charley, but I've been true to the girl in my heart all the while. I shall be ready, all my life long, to do anything in my power that will make her happy in any way."

"Good boy! You'll get your reward for it, as I got mine. You may not believe it—I didn't for a long while—indeed, I didn't think such a thing possible; but 'twas none the less comforting when it came. But let's see; you said just now that you'd be willing to do anything to make her happy; well, now's your chance."

"Now! What do you mean?"

"I think it would comfort her greatly if you would call and have a chat with her about Charley."

"Call?" gasped Champ, turning pale. "Why, Mr.

Pruffett, I—really, I never made a call on a young woman in my life!"

"Indeed? That's an awful confession. I don't wonder you are in your present condition of mind. The best way to atone is to begin to make amends as soon as possible. That poor girl has been haunted by the fear that you had some dangerous designs against Charley, and I don't believe that any one but you can disabuse her mind of this very painful impression. Do you intend to allow her to go on suffering?"

"How can I? Do go to her and tell her from me—"

"Second-hand news is poor stuff to send to a woman you profess to regard so highly."

"Then I'll write to her—at once."

"A person can't say much in a letter, at best; he can say wretchedly little to one who wishes to hear a great deal—and has an undoubted right to."

Champ looked like a criminal being led to execution, but he finally gasped:

"I'll—call."

"Promise me," said Pruffett, "that you'll go this very evening."

"I—I promise."

"Good! Now, don't be a coward, Champ. Girls are not ogres, as a rule; even when they are, they have a fair share of manners when meeting respectable young men who they know have put them under obligations. She knows all that you have done for Charley, and she therefore thinks that you are one of the finest fellows in the world. There are thousands of

great men and brilliant ones who would be delighted
to call on such a woman, with such a welcome awaiting them.   Don't be afraid that you won't know what
to say; a girl can make any man talk, unless he chances
to have lost the use of his tongue.   Don't hurry, either;
talk all you can about Charley, and say all the good
you can of him; if there are some things about him
which you're not entirely sure about, give him the
benefit of the doubt; it will please her, and you'll feel
the better for it afterward."

Champ promised everything asked of him, but he
did it all with the manner of a man talking in a dream.
The agonies of his preparations for the call need not
be dwelt upon, for they were too serious to be laughed
over, although the reader could do nothing else.
Suffice it to say, that he received a cordial welcome,
for old Pruffett had sent the girl word that Champ was
to be expected, and that as the affair was very em-
barrassing to him womanly pity should see to it that
he should not be obliged to feel uncomfortable.

Within five minutes after entering the Grews' door
Champ felt quite as much at ease as if he were at
home, so he had little trouble in asking after Charley.

"He has gone out West, for a little while, on business for Mr. Pruffett," said Luce.

"I heartily hope there is as much money in it for
him as there was for Pruffett himself when he went
West," said Champ.   "I don't know of any one whom
I'd rather see make a fortune in a hurry than Charley.
There's splendid stuff in that young man, Miss Grew."

"Do you really think so?" the girl asked, with a

look from which she could not keep a sign of curiosity. Champ met it as coolly as if it were a man's glance about a matter of business, and continued:

"Indeed I do. I'm personally proud of it, too, for I have had a little to do with bringing it out."

"Indeed you have," replied Luce heartily. "He has told me of all you have done for him, and I want to thank you, myself, for your manly friendship."

"Oh, don't say that, please!" exclaimed Champ, shading his eyes to keep the girl from seeing some thoughts which he feared might betray themselves.

"Then you are not friends, despite what you say about each other?" asked Luce anxiously. The tone of her voice compelled him to drop his hand and say:

"Miss Grew, I would do more for that young man than for any other man on the face of the earth. Can I make that any stronger?"

"No," murmured Luce, although she looked as if there was something else she would like to know. Champ wondered what it was. He was not accustomed to study women's faces, but he was sure that he knew what was in Luce's mind, so he continued:

"If he doesn't come back as soon as you want him to, I'll beg Mr. Pruffett to hurry him home; I'll offer to go out there in his place, if the old man thinks I can do the work as well as he, I'll—"

"No, no, no!" exclaimed Luce. "I don't want him to come back—not at present, at least. He is—he doesn't exactly know how, and it is better for both of us that he should be away for the present—unless your work is suffering through his absence?"

"My work?" echoed Champ. This was a strange place in which to be reminded of that marshland forest! His work, indeed! What would Luce say if she knew how that work had come about? What a gulf there seemed between him and her, although they were sitting face to face, and not three feet apart! The strangeness of the situation affected Champ so strongly that he lapsed into absent-mindedness, and it took several questions to recall him.

After that the delicate subject was avoided for a little while, and Champ was so rejoiced to find that it really was not hard to talk to an intelligent young woman that he soon felt quite at ease—nay, proud of himself. Besides, as he told himself, he had earned the right to chat with Luce Grew. Well, the right had been accorded him, most unexpectedly, and he was going to enjoy it to the best of his ability. The evening should be one which he would remember for years, and the recollection of it would help him through many a lonesome hour. He would never forget her face either; it had been in his mind for years, but never as it appeared that evening—never so handsome, animated, so full of cheer and yet full of soul. What a fool he had been to have delayed his pleasure so long!

Had he been more of a "company man" earlier in life, he might at least have numbered Luce among his friends, and who knows what better might have happened if he had enjoyed the stimulus which her face, her eyes, her manner, her voice, her entire presence, now gave him? He tried to analyze it, but he succeeded only in informing himself that it was solely because she was Luce Grew.

Time flew rapidly, but Champ took no note of it. The old clock in the kitchen struck loudly, but Champ did not hear it. For the time being he was in Elysium; yet really they talked only of village affairs and church matters and the doings of the various farmers. How different common subjects did appear when there was such a person as Luce to talk them over with!

Suddenly one of the children entered and handed Luce a letter.

"How strange!" she exclaimed. Letters delivered by hand were as rare during Brundy evenings as snowflakes in May. Suddenly she turned pale and exclaimed:

"Why, it's from Charley!"

With trembling hands she tore the envelope; Champ frowned and arose to go. Even from a distance, and on this one evening of all evenings, that bane of his existence was still active in making trouble for him.

Luce took from the envelope two inclosures, looked at them, and said:

"Why, one of them is for you!"

"Ah, something about that wood-chopping, I suppose," said Champ, opening his letter. It did not take him long to read it, for Charley wrote a large, round, schoolboy hand. The letter ran thus:

"Dear Champ:—Marry Luce. She knows how you love her, for I had to tell her all about it. That isn't all; she loves you too; she couldn't help it after she knew all. That's why I have gone West. God bless you both.          Yours always,
                                        "CHARLEY."

Champ looked up, startled by a slight exclamation from Luce. The girl was leaning against the table, upon which she had dropped her letter. Champ did not mean to read it; but the letter itself was so short and the penmanship so large that he could not help getting its entire contents at a glance.

"Miss Grew," said he quickly, although his voice trembled, "I've accidentally seen your letter. It's only fair, therefore, that you should read mine."

He extended it toward her. She took it slowly, took a long, long time, it seemed to Champ, to read it, but finally she looked up, smiled timidly, and said:

"Well?"

"Luce!" exclaimed Champ, taking the girl's hands. What either of them said afterward was entirely their own affair.

"I saw how things were going pretty soon after they began to go wrong between Luce and Charley," said old Pruffett to Champ the next day; "and when the boy admitted to me that he had told her all about your confession to him, I made up my mind that it was all up with him, because—well, I knew her mother, and it's grand good stock. Eh? Then why didn't her mother take me? Because the other man was the better man, my boy, just as you are the better man than Charley. I doubted her being able— doubted Luce, I mean, being able—to give her heart entirely to a youth like Charley, though there are a lot of good points about him; and I hoped that it might turn out in time, as it has, that both he and she would learn their mistake, and that your chance would come. In the meantime, what I said to you, and you acted upon, was just what you needed to make you search your heart and find out for whom you really loved Luce—for yourself, or for her. That's something that the best men sometimes fail to find out until it is too late, my boy, and they have a world of unhappiness about it."

"But how did you come to send Charley away at just the right time?"

"How? Because the right time had come. I had been giving my own entire time to watching for it. I wonder if those two young people could possibly imagine how closely their affairs interested an old man who was supposed to do nothing but gossip about town and read the newspapers. Charley made a clean breast to me about his trouble. I went to see the girl's mother—I've already told you about her—and found things about as I supposed. Then I talked with the girl herself. The rest of it was easy enough."

"Yes, to a man who had business in the West; but suppose there had been no such help for me?"

"My dear boy," said the old man, "there's an old Western saying that may do you good to bear in mind: 'Never cross a stream until you reach it.' There was a man here to send Charley to the West, so you can afford to drop that part of the subject."

"But everything worked as well as if it had been managed by Heaven itself," said Champ.

"I don't for a moment doubt that it was," replied the old man, reverently dropping his head for a mo-

ment.  Such things usually are—when the parties
deserve special attention.

"I don't see, though, how Charley timed those letters to arrive just right," persisted Champ.  "He must
be a thousand miles away by this time.  He didn't
know that I would ever call at the Grews' in the course
of my life."

Old Pruffett looked embarrassed; then he said:

"I've heard that new-made lovers are very slow of
perception.  Why, you stupid fellow, Charley wrote
those letters and gave them to me before he left; he
did it, willingly enough, at my own suggestion.  I personally made you promise to call last night; then I
stood in the night air for nearly an hour, a few rods
from your house, to make sure that you did it, even
if I had to drag you out and carry you there.  Then I
followed you, hung about the Grews' for a while, with
my heart in my throat, for fear you'd come away soon
—you seemed so scared at the idea of going, you know.
Finally I slipped across the street into the yard—I'm
glad the Grews don't own one of those annoying small
dogs that bark at every one who ventures upon the
premises—I slipped into the yard, and peeped through
one of the windows.  Yes, sir, I did.  I know it wasn't
exactly mannerly, but business is business, and the
whole affair was very serious business to me, I can
tell you.  I saw you both getting along pretty well together, so I thought it would make matters all the
easier afterward to let you go on.  Finally the night
air began to make me so chilly that I had to hurry matters in self-defence, so I slipped round to the back

door and got one of the children to deliver the note, first making him promise not to tell who left it. Then I looked through the window again; I really didn't feel comfortable about doing it, Champ, but it was a matter of business with me. I hope your heart didn't thump as mine did while you two were reading those letters. I waited until I saw you take Luce's hand, and then—don't blush—then I went home, got down on my knees, and thanked God that I had known Luce's mother."

"And poor Charley!" said Champ, with a sigh.

"Ah, well, 'tis better for him to have lost Luce than not to have been in love with her. I loved her mother, and I know."

# PURPLE-EYES

## BY JOHN LUTHER LONG

*Certainly the West and the East have met, and at their extremes, in the sturdy name of the author of "Madame Butterfly," "Miss Cherry-Blossom of Tokyo," and "Purple-Eyes," and the dainty titles of his stories. Unlike other Western writers who have gone to Japan for inspiration, Mr. Long (born in Pennsylvania in 1861) has refused to merge himself, his native individuality, unreservedly into the fascinating soul of Nippon. Thereby he has strengthened rather than impaired his value as an interpreter of Japan to the Western world. This is especially true in the present instance—the story of an Eurasian, a geisha girl of mixed foreign and native blood, which is told with an exquisite human sympathy that is universal in its appeal.*

# PURPLE-EYES

## BY JOHN LUTHER LONG

### I—THE FEVER JAPONICA

GARLAND was charmed with his reception. Before he could open his head (in his own perhaps too picturesque phrase) the two girls had buried their delightful noses in the mats, and were bobbing vividly up and down, sibilating honorifics at him in the voice and manner used only to personages. The mother joined them an instant later, making a phalanx; and she was nearly as beautiful, and quite as graceful, as her daughters. So that at one moment he would have presented to him the napes of three pretty necks, and at the next, with a conjurer's quick change, three pairs of eyes that smiled always, and three mouths that did their best (which was very well indeed) to assist the eyes. At first, I say, he was charmed, then a little bewildered, then bewitched. And perhaps it was well that his conversation-book was the only thing about him that spoke Japanese; for Garland's vocabulary, even when it was fairly accurate, had grown indiscreet since coming to Japan.

He perceived, however, by a surreptitious glance at the conversation-book when the napes of the necks were in view, that they were addressing him as "Augustness" and "Excellency," and that the mother was

From "Madame Butterfly," copyright, 1898, by The Century Co.

insisting that he should take immediate possession of her "miserable" house and its contents. He wondered dreamily—and he drifted into dreams with the most curious ease—whether the girls would be included.

Finally he began to feel it his duty to be tired of this fawning, as his refluent American democracy insisted upon naming it—though, personally, he liked it—and all the clever pretences of the Japanese. He sat bolt upright and frowned. But the charming kotowing did not in the least abate. He had heard somewhere that the only way to stop this sort of thing short of apoplexy was to compete in it.

He tried to reach the mats with his own nose. It seemed easy, but it was a disaster. There is a trick in it. He plunged forward helplessly almost into the lap of one of his hostesses. Garland sat up, with their joint assistance, very red in the face, but quite cheerful; for though the mother looked greatly pained, the girls were smiling like two Japanese angels. (The phrase is again Garland's: there are no Japanese angels.) Garland had the instant intelligence to perceive that this had at once stopped the kotowing, and precipitated a piquant intimacy.

"I say," said he, idiomatically, "I nearly broke my neck trying to say howdy-do in your way. Now won't you kindly say it in mine, without the least danger to life and limb?"

He held out his hand invitingly, and the one on his right went into debate as to which one to give him. She knew there was some foreign etiquette in the matter.

"In doubt, shake both," said Garland, doing it.

The one on his left emulated her sister to the last particular (the mother had retired for refreshments), but he noticed that the hands she gave him were long and white. He glanced up, and found himself looking into a pair of blue eyes. He followed the forehead to the brassy hair above. Then he began furiously to turn the leaves of the conversation-book. The one on his right laughed a little, and said:

"What you lig as', please?"

Garland closed the book, and stared. He did not ask what he had meant to, because of something he saw in the questioner's face.

"Ah, if you lig more bedder for do so, speak the English," she said, with a quiet flourish that was lost upon Garland.

He flung the conversation-book into a corner. Black-Eyes, as he had mentally named her, in despair of her Japanese name, which was Meadowsweet, smiled ecstatically.

"Ah-h-h! You lig those—those English?"

"Like it? It's heavenly! I say, fancy, if you can —but you can't—depending upon a dictionary for your most sacred sentiments for three months."

Wherein it will be perceived that Garland had learned the whole art of Japanese politeness—gentle prevarication.

"*How* that is nize!" breathed the blue-eyed one, fervently.

Garland turned suddenly upon her, then questioned her with his eyes. She understood.

"Those — thing — you — speak-ing," she barely breathed once more, in explanation.

"Oh!" said Garland. But it meant more than print can express. "Tell me, if you please, what your name is."

It was Miss Purple-Wistaria; but the Japanese of this was quite as impossible as the other.

"Do you mind me calling you Blue-Eyes?" asked Garland. "When it comes to Japanese proper names —I have already taken the liberty of mentally calling your sister Black-Eyes, and if you don't mind—"

"You call those blue-eye?" asked Miss Meadow-sweet.

"Why, yes," said Garland. "What do you call them?"

"Purple-eye."

"Well, I like that better, anyhow. It shall be Purple-Eyes."

"She got other already English name," confided Black-Eyes, with the manner for her sister he did not like.

"Oh! What is it?"

"Sarann," laughed the dark one. "Tha' 's jus' joke her fadder. He all times joke upon her."

Garland did not quite understand. He decided that he did not wish to, for the blue-eyed one looked very uncomfortable.

"I shall call her Purple-Eyes," he said.

The disagreeableness of the other continued.

"Yaes; tha' 's good name—for her," she added, with an intention that was distinctly odious.

"In America that would be the most beautiful name a man could give a beautiful woman," said Garland, severely.

The dark one looked a bit frightened. The blonde one gave him the merest horizon of her eyes as she raised her head. Gratitude was in them.

"Now, won't you go on, and tell me how you knew me before I opened my blooming head?"

He had again addressed himself to Purple-Eyes, but Black-Eyes answered:

"What is that—open you' head, an' blooming you' head?"

Garland informed her.

"Oh-h-h!" laughed the dark one. *"Tha' 's* way know yo' 'fore open you' *bloom*-ing head!"

She suddenly reached into the bosom of the kimono of the blue-eyed one, and brought forth a photograph of Garland; whereat Garland got red again, and again the blue-eyed one drooped her head.

"Oh, I say," Garland began, without a very distinct idea of what he was going to say, "Brownie sent you that—aha, ha, ha!"—he had happily drifted into the very thing—"and wrote you that I would arrive with a letter from him; so that you would know me—you know; and of course when I arrived—of course when I arrived—why, of *course*—oh, hang it!"

They both waited breathlessly upon his words.

"Of course," echoed Black-Eyes, sympathetically—"of course—tha' 's correc', an' tha' 's also—*nize*. Of course—you arrive when you arrive."

Garland wondered whether she was guying him.

"Yes—why, of course," said he once more, and a laugh *en masse* cleared the air.

Garland, in a panic, was searching his pockets.

"What lot pockets!" sighed Black-Eyes, insidiously desiring to compose his nerves.

"Sixteen," admitted Garland. "I wish they were only one, just now. By Jove, I've lost that letter!"

The graceful mother arrived with the tobacco *bon* (there appeared to be no servant), and Garland, professing an ignorance which seems problematical after three months in Japan, desired to be initiated into the art and mystery of the Japanese pipe. The tender was made to Purple-Eyes, but Black-Eyes undertook it.

"*So*," she said, rolling a pellet of the tobacco, and putting it into the pipe; "an' *so*," as she fearlessly put a live coal upon it with her fingers; "*so*," as she put it to her own lips and sent out a tiny puff; "an'—an'—an' *so!*" as she laughed and put it to his. And yet Garland found himself wishing that the other one had done it, and believing that she could do it better! And this, you perceive, was already perilous business.

It was afternoon when Garland arrived, and the mother's actions, though covered by diplomatic entrances and exits, with a view to impressing him to the contrary, indicated to him that she was cooking. And presently Purple-Eyes got up and lighted the *andon.* Garland, who delighted in her grace of motion, had not yet learned that each movement was the result of much study and the practice of many stoical rules of decorum. However, he rose as far as his knees,

and said he must go. A glance of alarm passed between the girls, and both stiffened in consternation.

"Sa-ay—tha' 's not nize for us," accused the dark
one, with valor. "Brownie he write unto us that you
so kine with him, you give him you' las' pair boots,
an' go naked on you' both feet. Tha' 's way we got
do you. *But*—account you go'n' go 'way, we can not.
Hence we got be always 'shamed 'fore Brownie—an'
*aevery*body. Tha' 's not nize—for us." Garland had
not risen above his knees, and she came hopefully forward. "Please don' go 'way!" She turned to Purple-
Eyes in the peremptory way that Garland resented.
"Sa-ay—why *you* don' as' him stay among us? Sa-ay
—don' you wish?"

Garland's eyes followed. Unconsciously they be-
sought her.

"We *lig*—if you stay—among us," said Purple-
Eyes, haltingly.

But there was something else—just the timid lifting
of an eyelid. Garland answered this with a rift of
pleasure which shot across his face.

"Me? *I* lig also if you stay among us—I."

But now it was spoken to the mats. There was the
edge of a smile visible, nevertheless, and Garland felt
the courage it took for this.

"Well, if *you* like," said Garland—he laughed suddenly—"*I* like too."

"Thangs!"

They both said it at once; but some splendid reward
passed from Purple-Eyes to Garland.

So presently they had a feast, in which four litt'e

tables stood in a circle—one for each. There would
have been only three had not Garland insisted that the
mother should dine with them. He had not the least
idea how fearfully he had disarranged domestic matters, for the mother, of course, instantly did as he requested. And then the three of them served him, and
cunningly joined in engaging him while one or the
other prepared the viands. But finally it was a very
joyous meal; and only when the Osaka beer came on
did Garland at all suspect how much out of the ordinary it was for them. They had forgotten to be
taught how to open the bottles!

## II—THE SHADOW OF THE SHOJI

And he went to sleep that night, when sleep came,
on a floor that was as dainty as any bed, in a huge
wadded overcoat called a *futon*, on a wooden pillow
that rocked and screeched a little (as if afraid to
screech more) when he turned. An *andon* burned
dimly behind a screen, and he was aware of the slum-
berous aroma Japonica, as he characterized it. But
he could not sleep—of course not. For, less than six
feet away, behind the translucent walls of paper, he
could hear the melodious dithyrambics of the three
voices. He could catch a sleepy word now and then,
which he knew came from the blue-eyed one. They
were much fewer than those of the other two. Some
vague picture of those eyes, patiently sad, as he had
conceived them, kept itself between him and sleep, until
finally it was sudden morning, and the splendid light of
Japan, subdued by the *shoji,* was shining in his face.

He lay indolently awake for a long time. Presently
a noise not much greater than the alighting of a fly
upon a stretched screen drew his attention. He perceived a dampened finger slowly working against the
other side of the *shoji*, until presently the paper parted,
and the finger came through. It was very pink at the
tip. Slowly it reamed the hole larger, then disappeared, to be replaced by an eye. And the eye was
blue. Garland nearly laughed aloud, until he remembered that he was the objective of the eye. Then unconsciously he arranged his hair a little, and began to
pose. But the humor of it came down upon him again,
and he laughed. The eyes instantly disappeared, and
he could see the shadow of its owner gliding away.
In a panic of regret, Garland called out:

"Don't go, Purple-Eyes!"

The shadow hesitated, and then returned.

"How you know tha' 's Purple-Eyes?"

"By her own confession—now."

Her pretty laugh sifted through the *shoji*.

"You want me come unto you?" asked the voice
beyond. "Tha' 's what I dunno."

Garland was (in his own phrase again) quite paralyzed. He might have thought, but he did not, that
she was only tendering the offices of the servant they
did not have; but he called out, with a mixture of
bravado and trembling which alarmed them both:

"Yes; come in!"

The damaged *shoji* slid haltingly aside, and she
entered very slowly and softly, and he thought of the
pictures of the returning Sun-Goddess as she came

through the opening and down the burst of light it let in. As she prostrated herself Garland noticed that her hair had been newly dressed (an operation of several hours), and that she wore a dainty blue kimono, too gay for any but a geisha to wear. But it became her royally.

"You look more than ever like a picture on a fan," greeted Garland, with even more admiration in his eyes than in his voice.

Instead of being pleased, as any other Japanese girl would have been, Purple-Eyes slowly shook her head.

"Alas! you naever see no picture on fan lig unto me."

"But I have," insisted Garland.

She shook her head again.

"Well, then, if not, why not?"

"They got not those purple eye—an' pink face—an' flaming hair—"

She sighed, and looked askance at Garland. He seemed fully to agree with her. She changed her tone to one of resigned solicitude and ceremony.

"You sleeping well—all those night?"

"Well, by the great Jehovah and the Continental Congress, if I were a Japanese artist, that is the kind of eyes and face and hair they should all have! Yes, sir!—every blamed one of them!"

The girl caught her breath, and something flamed up her face and lighted her splendid eyes anew. She dared to look at him. It had all sounded quite true. Wistfully she dissembled—this at least was truly Japanese.

"You sleeping well all"—she lost her purpose for a moment—"all those night—all?"

"Blue eyes for me, every day in the week."

"You sleeping well?"  Joy was all too plainly in her voice now—irrepressible joy.

He laughed, and caught her hands rapturously.  She did not deny him, and he kissed them.

"Oh, you are delightful!" said he.

"Me?  *I* don' sleep—moach."

"You look as fresh as new porcelain."

"Yaes; I been fix up."

She consciously let him look her over.

"No; I didn't sleep at first.   I was listening to your voice," Garland confessed, quite without reservation.

The girl was confused a little.

"You don' lig be annoy with those voice?"

"Why, it is divine!"

A white shaft of fear crossed her face.

"Tha' 's—jus'—fun—I egspeg?"

"Tha' 's ver' earnest," he gayly mocked.

He was pleasing her now.  She even went with his mood a little way.  Joy was such a beautiful and tempting and elusive thing!

"Lig goddess, mebby?"

Garland nodded seriously.

"Tha' 's nize—for *me*."

"An' for *me*"—in quite her own manner.

"But not the goddesses?"

They laughed together, and she drew confidently a little closer to him.

"Listen; I go'n' tell you a thing. You *not* in fun --*not?*"

"I mean every word," declared Garland, "and more than I have words to mean."

"An' you lig be tell?"

"That is what I am waiting so impatiently for—to be tell."

"Tha' 's nize. Eijinsan 'most always fun. Nobody but you aever lig those hair an' eye. Aeverybody hate me. *Why?* Account they say I b'long pink-face people. Account my fadder he sei yo jin—a west-ocean mans. *I* di'n' do so unto those hair an' eye! I can *not* help. *Me?* When I see you got those purple eye lig unto me, an' also those yellow hairs, an' all pink in the face, I thing mebby you go'n' lig me liddle—lig I was brodder an' fadder with you. Also, I thing mebby you go'n' take me away with you—beyond those west-ocean, where pink-face people live. *Me?* Don' you thing those pink-face people lig me liddle if I come unto them?"

"God bless you—yes," said Garland, with something suspiciously tender in voice and eyes. He still had her hands, delighting in them, caressing them. The girl's face was irradiated. She poured out all her soul for him.

"*Me?* Listen 'nother time. Before I know you' eyes purple an' you' hair yellow lig unto me, I lig you? *Me?* Sa-ay—I lig jus' your *picture!*" She laughed, confused, and shifted a little closer. "You don' hate me account I doing those?"

"No," said Garland, guiltily—"no, I don't hate you."

"Sa-ay—you go'n' take me at those pink-face people?"

Garland was silent.

"*If* you don', I got go myself. *Me?* I *got* go!"

Garland nodded, and she understood him to have assented. This was wrong. But her joy was superb, and Garland had a very soft heart.

"Oh—*how* that is nize! *Me?* I got so. I dunno —all times seem lig I b'long 'cross west-ocean. Seem lig I different from *aevery*body else. *Me?* I got have somebody *lig* me—somebody *touch* me—hole my hands —*so—so—so!*" She illustrated fervidly.

Garland, alarmed at her dynamic emotion, released them. She returned them to him.

"*But*—nobody don' *wish*. Others—Japan people— they don' lig be ligued. But me? I *got* be—else I got pain in my heart an' am ill. You aever have those pain at you' heart—lig you all times falling down—down— down? Tha' 's mos' tarrible. Tha' 's lone-some-ness. *Me?* I thing I go'n' die sometime account that. Tha' 's lone-some-ness to cross west-ocean to pink-face people. Yaes; tha' 's why I *got* do those. Oku-Sama —tha' 's my modder—she saying 'most all times, 'Jus' lig pink-face people. Always got be lig by 'nother— touch by 'nother—speak sof' by 'nother.' An' tha' 's *you*—yaes! You lig me, an' you touch me, an' you speak sof' unto me the ver' first time I seeing you. *Me?* I *know,* those time I first seeing you, that you don' hate me account I got those pink face upon me."

"No," admitted Garland, seriously.

"*How* that is nize! It make something rest—go

'sleep inside me. I got that peace. Jus' when you
touch my hand at first I got some happiness. But *now*
—I got that peace."

She began regretfully to detach herself. Garland
detained her. She was very dainty and very confiding
—very wise. She had unconsciously got very close to
him. And Garland had vanquished his alarm of her.

"*Me?* I don' wish; but I got git you somethings
eat. Soon you starve. I *got.*"

But Garland would not let her go—and she was a
willing captive, though she dissembled an urgent
necessity.

"Where is Black-Eyes—and your mother?" asked
Garland.

The girl seemed reluctant, but told him that they all
worked in the neighboring silk-mill, the pulsations of
which he had heard in the night.

"Never mind. I'd rather famish," said the impul-
sive Garland, with a strange remorse. "Will you
assist?"

"Yaes," laughed the girl. "*Me?* I been famish—
many times."

"Heavens!" breathed Garland, inventorying all her
daintiness once more. "How much do your mother
and sister earn?"

The girl seemed quite indifferent as to this.

"Sometime fi' sen; sometime ten—fifteen; one times,
twenty-two."

"And you?"

"Me? Oh, jus' liddle."

She earned more than the other two.

"And what does it cost you to live?"

"Live? Half those fi'—ten—fifteen sen."

"And you save the rest? That is very prudent."

The girl looked bewildered; then she explained:

"Other half sen' Brownie."

He suddenly let her go. She leaned over him bewitchingly.

"Firs' some breakfas'; then I go'n' help you famish —all day! What you thing?"

She came back in a moment. The sleeves of her kimono were tucked out of the way, and there was rice-flour on her pretty arms.

"You go'n' to naever tell—'bout those fi'—ten— fifteen sen, an' all those?"

"No," said Garland; "I will never tell."

"Else they go'n' kill me," she threatened gayly.

"I prefer to have you live," he laughed, as brightly as he could.

"Tha' 's secret among jus' you an' me?"

"Yes," said Garland.

She started away, then came back.

"*Me?* I lig—I *lig*—have secret among jus' you an' me." With a radiant face she fled.

And here was Brownie's poor little skeleton stripped naked. He had lived at the university like a gentleman. He was still living in Philadelphia like a gentleman. Garland wondered whether it would make any difference in Philadelphia if it were known that it was the pitiful "fi'—ten—fifteen sen" that his mother and sisters earned each day that supported him. A great disgust for Brownie and a great pity for Purple-Eyes were the immediate postulates. And is not pity akin to love?

### III—THE DANCE OF THE RED MAPLE-LEAVES

The question of making one's toilet in the interior of Japan is still a serious one for the American who lives behind closed doors and cherishes his divine right of privacy. Garland had solved the vexation for all his contemporaries (according to Garland) by making his toilet as to half or quarter of his sacred person at a time (depending somewhat upon the danger of surprise), thus reducing the chances of exposure by one-half or three-quarters. Purple-Eyes brought him the requisites for his toilet, and the moment she was gone he bared his shoulders and chest, and plunged into the delightful water, perfumed, like everything else, with the aroma Japonica. But his pretty hostess reappeared through the movable walls at an unwatched place.

He abandoned a momentary impulse to scuttle behind the screen because of the admiration he saw in her eyes, and then he half turned that she might see the muscles of his back.

"*How* you are beau-ti-ful!" she said slowly, as her eyes traveled, quite without embarrassment, over his athletic uppers.

"Thanks," he laughed, with pleasure in the little incident.

Garland turned a little further, and raised his arms above his head in the way of athletes.

She handed him a towel he had dropped.

"I thing I come tell you we got large tub for bath," she said then.

"Where is it?" asked Garland, suspiciously.

"There."

She pointed.

"That's what I thought. You must excuse me. I can't perform that sacred rite in the fierce light that beats upon a front porch."

"Yaes? Eijinsan don' lig?" She did not understand.

"No," admitted Garland.

"Also, you lig for me go 'way liddle?"

Garland said yes, and she went.

When she returned, it was with a delightful breakfast of fish, rice, and persimmons. She put the little table between them, and on her knees, on the other side, taught him how to eat as a Japanese should. This is really not difficult, except the chopsticks; and with these she had to help him so often that their fingers were in almost constant contact. Alas! Garland made it as difficult as possible. And, alas! Garland was glad of the chopsticks!

Her joy overflowed the mouth and eyes which it seemed should know nothing but tears.

Afterward he helped her, with masculine joy of his own ineptitude, to reform the apartment, and secrete the things which had made it successively a reception-room, sleeping-chamber, and breakfast-room. You may judge whether or not this was delightful to a fellow like Garland, and also whether it was perilous.

It is not often that one has the felicity of ending
one's breakfast with a song, and then of ending the
song with a dance.   Purple-Eyes brought her samisen
quite without suggestion from Garland, and said with
naïveté:

"I go'n' sing you a song.   You lig me sing?"

"Try me!" challenged Garland, with an admiration
in his eyes which pleased her greatly.

"Long down behine the Suwanee River" was the
curious song she sang, in Japanese English.

Garland laughed.

"Don' you lig those?" she pouted.   "I learn it for
you."

He said it was lovely, and begged her to go on.

But his eyes wandered from the fingers on the
strings to those on the plectrum, and then away to the
lips above; and when she turned into the chorus he
joined her with his inconstant eyes still there.   It was
only an indifferent tenor, but the girl thought it full
of fervor.   It was only that it joined and mingled
with hers—as she fancied their spirits doing and might
always do.

"*How* that is nize!" she breathed in frank ecstasy.
"You got voice lig—lig—"

But there was nothing at hand to compare it with,
and she laughed confessingly.

"Nothing," said Garland.   "It's original."

"Yaes—nothing original," she admitted.

"Sing another," begged Garland, with enthusiasm.
She did—"When the swallows flying home"; and
then still another—" 'Tis the last rosebud summer."

"Where did you learn them?" asked he.

"That day when I got you' picture. *Me?* I thing you lig me sing, mebby. Well, I git those song; I make them United States' language, so you comprehend."

"God bless you!" said Garland.

The girl leaned forward with dewy eyes.

"Sa-ay—you lig me also dance—jus' one—liddle— dance—for *you?*"

She came bewitchingly nearer. Garland glanced again at her geisha-like costume. Had she thought all this out for his entertainment, he wondered.

"Yes," he said.

"But—you naev—*naever* go'n' tell?"

She raised her brows, and held up a finger archly.

"On my sacred honor!" laughed Garland.

"No one?"

"Not a soul."

"Tha' 's go'n' be 'nother secret among jus' you an' me foraever an' aever?"

"Forever and ever," announced Garland, as if it were the Service.

"Account if you aever do, they go'n' kill me!"

"What! Kill you?"

"Dade!" She nodded ominously.

"Who?"

"Black-Eyes an' those modder."

"Oh!" said Garland. He understood.

He was left to guess that this dainty flower had been taught the arts of a geisha to assist also in keeping up Brownie's state.

"I lig dance for *you*," confessed the girl, joyously. "Others? No; I do not lig. They as' me, 'Where you got those pink face?' *Me?* I don' lig those. I rather work in those mill. My modder an' my sister getting all times an-gery—account I don' dance. *But*—tha' 's in-sult upon me! I don't *lig* be insult. So! *Me?* I jus' don' dance for no one—but—but—but—jus'—*you!*"

She vanished through the *shoji*, and presently returned, a symphony in autumnal reds and browns.

"I go'n' dance for you that red maple-leaf dance. Me? I am that leaf."

"You look it," said Garland, more tenderly than he knew.

The girl spread her garments that he might inspect her.

"This is a forest," she went on; "an' you—sa-ay—you a *tree!* Aha, ha, ha!"

She laughed, made him a noble courtesy, and murmured a little tune to which she floated down from the top of a maple-tree. For a while she lay quite still, shivering a little. Then the wind stirred her, and she rose, and swept down upon Garland, then back and into a whirl of other leaves. Then hither and thither, merrily, like an autumn leaf, until she shivered down at his feet, with bowed head.

She was making it more and more perilous for Garland.

### IV—"*HOW* THAT IS NIZE!"

That night they had a gay little supper, with a tiny servant, who, Garland guessed, with entire accuracy, had been borrowed for the occasion.

"You got nize day?" asked Black-Eyes.

Garland caught a startled glance from Purple-Eyes, and answered discreetly that he had had—oh, yes; a very pleasant day, giving no damaging particulars.

But Black-Eyes fancied from the blankness of his countenance that he was indulging in the same kind of prevarication with which she would have met such a question. She devoted herself to him all the rest of the evening. As he retired for the night, the last thing she said to him, with a reproachful glance at Purple-Eyes, was:

"To-morrow you go'n' have mos' bes' nize times. *I* go'n' stay home with you!"

And she did, making it a very dreary day for Garland. He could not help thinking of Purple-Eyes at the factory, with her dainty hands begrimed.

But presently, when she returned, there was no grime upon her hands. She was dainty and smiling.

"You got nize day?" she asked, with her head coyly down. She knew he had not. And she purposely quoted her sister.

"No," he said savagely. "I'm glad it's over."

The flame was in her face again. But she kept it down.

"I thing Black-Eyes ver' be-witch-ing."

"But she is not—*you*," he said.

She looked slowly up. The little weariness which had been limned upon her face by the day's drudgery was gone, and in its stead was a vague glory reflected from within.

"*How* that is nize," she whispered—"for *me!*"

"For me," said Garland, approaching her threateningly. She did not retreat. She subsided a little toward him—just a little—that he might know she would never retreat from him. Her eyes smiled confidently.

He stopped where he was.

"Who is to be chatelaine to-morrow?"

"What is that chat—?" she asked.

"Who is to keep the house?"

"Me. Me one day, Black-Eyes next."

She saw his face lighten.

"You lig that?"

"I like half of it."

She thought a moment until she understood; then she lifted her shining face.

"Ah, Eijinsan, how be-witch-ing *you* are!"

### V—THE PLAINTIVE TEMPLE BELLS

The next day they went up to the temple on the mountain-side, the plaintive bells of which Garland had heard. Purple-Eyes was tall, and walked with less difficulty than most Japanese girls, so they walked. It was a day of dreams. Garland remembered afterward the smell of the incense, the voices of the chanting *bonzes*, that the tea-house on the mountain-side where they rested called itself the House of the Seven Golden Crystals; the rest was Purple-Eyes —and happiness. Japan had been growing upon him for three months, and now unhappiness made but little impression.

The day remained in his mind with the sum of his dreams—this lotus-eating, nectar-drinking, happy-go-lucky Garland!

Thus it curiously went on. One day it was Black-Eyes, and the true Japan, and the real Garland. The next it was Purple-Eyes, and the ideal Japan, and the lotus-eating Garland. What is more like lotus-eating than being adored? At first Garland used to smile at the strange dual life which circumstances had wrought out for him. Then he used to wonder which was better. Later he tried to decide only which he liked better. Now he no longer differentiated at all. His analytical edge was quite dulled. Still, he had heard that this fever of Japan always wore off. Some said it lasted as long as two years, some said five; no one had said ten. And what then?

"Why, then? *Me!*"

He had spoken the last three words aloud, and they had been answered by the laughing, dewy-eyed subject of them.

He looked at her.

"Well, one ought to be content," he laughed.

"An' you—content?" she smiled back.

He did not answer at once.

"Do you know that you have been growing more bewitching every day since—"

"Sinze *you*—an' *joy*—came at Japan?"

From the opened *shoji* she flung him the gay greeting he had taught her, and disappeared; for it was Black-Eyes' day, and she had yet to dress for her work.

That day he harbored madly the notion of marriage with Purple-Eyes and a residence in Japan. It had quite infected him before night, and was distinctly, but less and less strongly, in his mind for several days. But then came a letter from his elder brother, in answer to his own of a rather confessional and emotional sort, asking him what he meant by living upon three working-women. It told him to go away—to the devil—anywhere—but away from there. It was like a cold douche. The fever Japonica, as every one had said, was at last gone. So small a thing as his brother's letter had cured it. Now he smiled. He had meant to write to Miss Warburton, offering to release her.

## VI—"SAYONARA?"

I know not what he said to Purple-Eyes, but with her tears there was a certain buoyancy that had not been there but for some hope. And why not? For Garland was a very sweet and gentle fellow, who abhorred pain. The three went to see him off, and he tried desperately to be gay; but something was pulling at his heart-strings, and there were tears perilously near his eyes. Black-Eyes did not marvel at this. She had always understood that it was the way of west-ocean men. But they were only too evidently

ready to be answered by other tears in the dewy eyes
that were blue. And *this* was annoying to Black-
Eyes. She made her sister tremble by a look. So she
of the blue eyes could only grasp and hold Garland's
big hand in both her own exquisite ones when the
others looked away. When their eyes returned hers
looked off to the big funnels of the ship, though she
still held the hand. But when she looked at Garland
again he had his handkerchief to his eyes; something
inside had given way. Then hers came from her
sleeve, too. So at last it was quite a little tragedy.

Sad it is that one forgets that one has eaten of the
lotus; but thus it is with the lotus, and thus did
Garland.

That night, in bed, Black-Eyes undertook some
criticism of Garland. Her sister flared up in a way
that was new and superb.

"Tha' 's a lie! He's the mos' bes' nize gent in the
whole worl'." And she fell to sobbing.

"What is the matter?" asked the mother, who was
kinder than Black-Eyes.

"I got that lone-some-ness," sobbed the girl, in
answer.

"Poor little pink-face!" said the mother, touching
her cheek. "Always must be touch by some one!"

"*Me?*" said Purple-Eyes, with a power and assur-
ance which were startling. "I am glad I have that
pink face!" She laughed. "And I am glad I have
*not* that brown face! Aha!"

The mother asked in alarm:

"Has the Eijinsan told you strange things?"

"The strangest and most beautiful things in all the world!" breathed Purple-Eyes. "Not *told* them, but looked them—thought them—to me."

"And you believed?"

"I believed."

"That is very sad," said the mother. "It is the way of the west-ocean men."

"Ah, it *is* his way, thank Shaka! and it is *not* sad. It is very joyous."

"Shaka grant that it is not, my daughter. To the Eijinsan you are only a plaything, I fear."

"He may have me for a plaything," said the girl, defiantly. "Who has not playthings?"

"When a plaything becomes shabby—"

"But I am not, and I never shall be."

"In a little while we shall know," said the mother, finally.

"In a little while we shall know," repeated the girl, joyously.

### VII—"WHAT YOU BED?"

Later they found the letter—in the discarded conversation-book. It said that Garland was having his final outing before becoming a Benedick; and the missionary on the hill told them that that meant that he was to be married upon his return to America. Purple-Eyes drew a sharp breath, then faced the other two savagely. She was able to laugh presently; but it was a very piteous laugh.

"Tha' 's what I know! Aha, ha, ha! He—he—tell me all those." But the pitiful lie stuck in her throat, and her lips were dry. "He tell me *aevery-thing!* Yaes"—to a look of doubt from Black-Eyes—"he go'n' marry that other for jus' liddle—"

"Speak Japanese," said her mother, who was not so clever at English as her daughters; but the request fell like a lash upon Purple-Eyes' heart.

"I will not!" she flamed forth. "I will speak his language. He will come for me. If he do not come, I shall go to him. He go'n' marry that other—*if* he marry her—*if*—jus' liddle— *Me?* He go'n' marry me las' an' foraever!"

Suddenly she became aware that she had betrayed her secret.

"Oh, all the gods in the sky!" she cried in anguish. "Tha' 's lie. He *not* go'n' marry me. He *don'* say. Jus' I thing so—jus' I—" She had to debase herself still further, if she would be shriven. "He *not* go'n' come for me. I *not* go'n' go at him. *Me?* Tha' 's correc', Oku-San; I jus' his liddle plaything. He don' say nawthing. Jus' *I* thing so."

Her mother nodded.

"And when he tires of the plaything—"

She threw an imaginary something into the air.

"Yaes," whispered Purple-Eyes, humbly bowing her head; but when her face was down she smiled. It was all very sure to her. As she looked up she saw something like malevolence upon the face of her sister.

"*But*—also he not *go'n'* marry that other foraever!"

Her sister smiled unbelievingly.

"I bed you don'!"

"Ah! *what* you bed?" challenged Black-Eyes.

"That heart in my bosom!" answered Purple-Eyes.

### VIII—LONE-SOME-NESS

Garland did not reach the end of his ante-Benedick wanderings until a year later. Then he found, among other letters awaiting him, one in a long, dainty envelope addressed in English and Japanese. He knew it was from Purple-Eyes before he opened it. It was seven months old.

As he read, all her little tricks of inflection came back upon him. He knew that her long white hands were waving emphases at him—very gently. The questioning which her eyes had learned after his coming—as if she were not quite sure of something—was upon him out of the shadows beyond the lamp. The subtle aromas which always exhaled from her garments were distinct enough to startle him. He looked quickly back and about the room. Then he laughed softly. But his face had flushed, and gladness had lit his eyes. The fever Japonica was once more in his veins—and it was his own room—and America— with only her pictured face (fallen from the envelope) before him—herself on the other side of the world. Unconsciously he read aloud—in her voice and manner:

"That is ledder from me, Miss Purple-Eyes, unto you, Mister J. F. Garland. That is nize day in Japan. I lig if you hoarry soon coming at Japan 'nother time. You been 'way ver' long time. I lig if you

hoarry account aeverybody hating me more an' more.
I got those feeling again 'bout somethings I want an'
have not got it.  That is lone-some-ness.  That is to
cross west-ocean.  You have also got those?  Me?
I been that sad aever sinze you gone me away from.
I been that ill.  I thing mebby I go'n' die soon.
'Aexcep' you come?  Say you go'n' come, that I don'
die?  Black-Eye she all times make amusement 'bout
you don' come.  That is a liar.  She don' know you
who you are.  She don' know you that you go'n'
come  soon as you kin.  Mebby you go'n' marry
with those pink-face for liddle while?  Me?  I
study those conversation-book so I kin write unto you.
Also, I fine those ledder you lose when you first arrive
among us at Japan.  You desire those ledder?  Me?
I keep it upon my bosom among those photograph of
you.  Mister J. F. Garland, I don' keer you do marry
those other for liddle while.  Then you go'n' marry
me las' an' foraever.  Jus' hoarry.  Yit I am not gay.
I can not be gay until you come again.  That is sad
for me.  Also, you do not lig for me be gay, but
lig unto widow till you come.  Then, Mister J. F.
Garland, I shall be that happy.  Mebby you ill an' can
not come unto me?  Then I come unto you, if you
wish me.  What you thing?  That is a picture of me
lig I promise.  I fix up same lig those day you hol'
my hands.  How that was nize!  That is first time I
aever been my hands hol' so nize—so sof'.  Mister J.
F. Garland, that is you hol' my hands that sof'.  Me?
I don' let no one else do those unto my hands—lig
you wishing, mebby.  Jus' you.  Mister J. F. Gar-

land, you go'n' hol' my hands all times this after-while? Say, don' stay marry with that other so ver' long. Account those lone-some-ness. Please sen' me picture of those other you marry unto. If you marry unto them. I lig see how she is that beautiful. Please write me letter aevery day. Please come back that soon. So I kin be joyous. It is that sad for me."

Every laboriously formed letter, printed like the first copy of a child at school, told him what this had cost her; and the little flourishes at the end, where she had grown more certain, what pride she had in them! The picture was exquisitely colored, as only the Japanese can color them, and had been very costly to her. He set it before him, and with his head in his hands studied it. The eyes were very blue, but no bluer than her own. They looked into his half sadly, half gayly, tempting him again. The Japan fever had its way with him, and for a moment—ten—he lived that lotus life with her over again. Then came a great up-heaval inside which was yearning. He was tired. He had been tired ever since leaving Japan. In those eyes he saw again the invitation to rest. The hair, with its brassy lustre—he could see the sun on it again—smell its perfume—feel it under his hands. The lips were parted a little, as they nearly always were, and within showed the brilliant teeth.

"Oh," he cried out, as he rose, "get thee behind me —moon-goddess—get thee behind me!" He laughed wofully, and took up the picture again. "I thought it gone—the fever—the dreaming—the lotus-eating."

There was a knock on the door, and a messenger-boy handed in the answer to a note.

"Yes," it ran; "I shall be home at eight—*and so glad!*"

It was twenty minutes to eight.

Garland hurried into his evening clothes and hastened away, leaving the rest of the letters unopened. But he came back, from down the stairs, and again set the picture up before him. Then he strode softly up and down the apartment, a smile half sad, half gay, upon his face. The little clock chimed the few notes which told him it was a quarter past eight. He smiled —another kind of smile. He had forgotten—that she would be at home at eight and would be glad! He looked again briefly at the picture of Purple-Eyes. There was moisture in his own. Then softly, as if it were sentient, he turned it face down and went out.

# THE RUN OF THE YELLOW MAIL

## BY FRANK H. SPEARMAN

*When, at the age of twenty-nine, Frank Hamilton Spearman (born in Buffalo, N. Y.) became a bank president, he considered his business ambitions to be realized, and entered into the new career of authorship. He went back, as it were, with a diploma from the school of commerce to enter the academy of literature, selecting therein a special course in the fiction of business. With his fine equipment of practical experience it is no wonder that he took place at once as head of his class. His railroad stories, gathered together in the volume "Held for Orders," are especially notable. The present selection is one of these. It is packed with railroad personality, ranging from the powerful will of the magnate to the no less indomitable grit of the mechanic.*

# THE RUN OF THE YELLOW MAIL

## BY FRANK H. SPEARMAN

THERE wasn't another engineer on the division who dared talk to Doubleday the way Jimmie Bradshaw did.

But Jimmie had a grievance, and every time he thought about it, it made him nervous.

Ninety-six years. It seemed a good while to wait; yet in the regular course of events on the mountain division there appeared no earlier prospect of Jimmie's getting a passenger run.

"Got your rights, ain't you?" said Doubleday, when Jimmie complained.

"I have and I haven't," grumbled Jimmie, winking hard; "there's younger men than I am on the fast runs."

"They got in on the strike; you've been told that a hundred times. We can't get up another strike just to fix you out on a fast run. Hang on to your freight. There's better men than you in Ireland up to their belt in the bog, Jimmie."

"It's a pity they didn't leave you there, Double-day."

"You'd have been a good while hunting for a freight run if they had."

Then Jimmie would get mad and shake his finger

From "Held for Orders," copyright, 1901, by McClure, Phillips & Co.

and talk fast: "Just the same, I'll have a fast run here when you're dead."

"Maybe; but I'll be alive a good while yet, my son," the master mechanic would laugh.   Then Jimmie would walk off very warm, and when he got into private with himself he would wink furiously and say friction things about Doubleday which needn't now be printed, because it is different.   However, the talk always ended that way, and Jimmie Bradshaw knew it always would end that way.

The trouble was, no one on the division would take Jimmie seriously, and he felt that the ambition of his life would never be fulfilled; that he would go plugging to gray hairs and the grave on an old freight train; and that even when he got to the right side of the Jordan there would still be something like half a century between him and a fast run.   It was funny to hear him complaining about it, for everything, even his troubles, came funny to him, and in talking he had an odd way of stuttering with his eyes, which were red.   In fact, Jimmie was nearly all red; hair, face, hands—they said his teeth were freckled.

When the first rumors about the proposed Yellow Mail reached the mountains Jimmie was running a new ten-wheeler; breaking her in on a freight "for some fellow without a lick o' sense to use on a limited passenger run," as Jimmie observed bitterly.   The rumors about the mail came at first like stray mallards —opening signs of winter—and as the season advanced flew thicker and faster.   Washington never was very progressive in the matter of improving the transcontinental service, but they once put in a post-master-general down there, by mistake, who wouldn't take the old song. When the bureau fellows that put their brains up in curl papers told him it couldn't be done he smiled softly, but he sent for the managers of the crack lines across the continent, without suspecting how it bore incidentally on Jimmie Bradshaw's grievance against his master mechanic.

The postmaster-general called the managers of the big lines, and they had a dinner at Chamberlain's, and *they* told him the same thing. "It has been tried," they said in the old, tired way; "really it can't be done."

"California has been getting the worst of it for years on the mail service," persisted the postmaster-general moderately. "But Californians ought to have the best of it. We don't think anything about putting New York mail in Chicago in twenty hours. It ought to be simple to cut half a day across the continent and give San Francisco her mail a day earlier. Where's the fall-down?" he asked, like one refusing no for an answer.

The general managers looked at our representative sympathetically, and coughed cigar smoke his way to hide him.

"West of the Missouri," murmured a Pennsylvania swell, who pulled indifferently at a fifty-cent cigar. Everybody at the table took a drink on the *exposé*, except the general manager, who sat at that time for the Rocky Mountains.

The West End representative was unhappily accustomed to facing the finger of scorn on such occasions. It had become with our managers a tradition. There was never a conference of continental lines in which we were not scoffed at as the weak link in the chain of everything—mail, passenger, specials, what not— the trouble was invariably laid at our door.

But this time there was a new man sitting for the line at the Chamberlain dinner; a youngish man with a face that set like cement when the West End was trod upon.

The postmaster-general was inclined, from the reputation we had, to look on our chap as a man looks at a dog without a pedigree, or at a dray horse in a bunch of standard breeds. But something in the mouth of the West End man gave him pause; since the Rough Riders, it has been a bit different about verdicts on things Western. The postmaster-general suppressed a rising sarcasm with a sip of Chartreuse, for the dinner was ripening, and waited; nor did he mistake—the West Ender *was* about to speak.

"Why west of the Missouri?" he asked, with a lift of the face that was not altogether candid. The Pennsylvania man shrugged his brows; to explain might have seemed indelicate.

"If it is put through, how much of it do you pro-pose to take yourself?" inquired our man, looking evenly at the Alleghany official.

"Sixty-five miles, including stops from the New York post-office to Canal Street," replied the Pennsylvania man, and his words flowed with irritating smoothness and ease.

"What do you take?" continued the man with the jaw, turning to the Burlington representative, who was struggling, belated, with an artichoke.

"*About* seventy from Canal to Tenth and Mason. Say, seventy," repeated the "Q" manager, with the lordliness of a man who has miles to throw at almost anybody, and knows it.

"Then suppose we say sixty-five from Tenth and Mason to Ogden," suggested the West Ender. There was a well-bred stare the table round, a lifting of glasses to mask expressions that might give pain. Sixty-five miles an *hour?* Through the *Rockies?*

But the postmaster-general struck the table quickly and heavily; he didn't want to let it get away. "Why, hang it, Mr. Bucks," he exclaimed with emphasis, "if you will say sixty, the business is done. We don't ask you to do the Rockies in the time these fellows take to cut the Alleghanies. Do sixty, and I will put mail in 'Frisco a day earlier every week in the year."

"Nothing on the West End to keep you from doing it," said General Manager Bucks. He had been put up then only about six months. "But—"

Every one looked at the young manager. The Pennsylvania man looked with confidence, for he instantly suspected there must be a string to such a proposition, or that the new representative was "talking through his hat."

"But what?" asked the Cabinet member, uncomfortably apprehensive.

"But we are not putting on a sixty-five mile schedule just because we love our country, you understand, nor to lighten an already glorious reputation. Oh, no," smiled Bucks faintly, "we are doing it for 'the stuff.' You put up the money; we put up the speed. Not sixty miles; sixty-five—from the Missouri to the Sierras. No; no more wine. Yes, thank you, I will take a cigar."

The trade was on from that minute. Bucks said no more then; he was a good listener. But next day—when it came to talking money—he talked more money into the West End treasury for one year's running than was ever talked before on a mail contract for the best three years' work we ever did.

When they asked him how much time he wanted to get ready, and told him to take plenty, three months were stipulated. The contracts were drawn, and they were signed by our people without hesitation because they knew Bucks. But while the preparations for the fast schedule were being made, the Government weakened on signing. Nothing ever got through a Washington department without hitch, and they said our road had so often failed on like propositions that they wanted a test. There was a deal of wrangling, then a test run was agreed upon by all the roads concerned. If it proved successful—if the mail was put to the Golden Gate on the second of the schedule—public opinion and the interests in the Philippines, it was concluded, would justify the heavy premium asked for the service.

In this way the dickering and the figuring became, in a measure, public, and keyed up everybody interested to a high pitch. We said nothing for publication, but under Bucks' energy sawed wood for three whole months. Indeed, three months goes as a day getting a system into shape for an extraordinary schedule. Success meant with us prestige; but failure meant obloquy for the road and for our division chief who had been so lately called to handle it.

The real strain, it was clear, would come on his old—the mountain—division; and to carry out the point rested on the motive power of the mountain division; hence, concretely, on Doubleday, master mechanic of the hill country.

In thirty days Neighbor, superintendent of the motive power, called for reports from the division master mechanics on the preparations for the Yellow Mail run, and they reported progress. In sixty days he called again. The subordinates reported well except Doubleday. Doubleday said merely "Not ready"; he was busy tinkering with his engines. There was a third call in eighty days, and on the eighty-fifth a peremptory call. Everybody said ready except Doubleday. When Neighbor remonstrated sharply, he would say only that he would be ready in time. That was the most he would promise, though it was generally understood that if he failed to deliver the goods he would have to make way for somebody who could.

The plains division of the system was marked up for seventy miles an hour, and, if the truth were told, a little better; but, with all the help they could give us, it still left sixty for the mountains to take care of, and the Yellow Mail proposition was conceded to be the toughest affair the motive power at Medicine Bend

ever raced.  However, forty-eight hours before the
mail left the New York post-office Doubleday wired to
Neighbor, "Ready"; Neighbor to Bucks, "Ready";
and Bucks to Washington, "Ready"—and we were
ready from end to end.

Then the orders began to shoot through the mountains.  The test run was of especial importance, because the signing of the contract was believed to depend
on the success of it.  Once signed, accidents and delays might be explained; for the test run there must
be no delays.  Despatches were given the 11, which
meant Bucks; no lay-outs, no slows for the Yellow
Mail.  Road masters were notified: no track work in
front of the Yellow Mail.  Bridge gangs were warned,
yard masters instructed, section bosses cautioned, track
walkers spurred—the system was polished like a bar-
keeper's diamond, and swept like a parlor car for the
test flight of the Yellow Mail.

Doubleday, working like a boiler washer, spent all
day Thursday and all Thursday night in the roundhouse.  He had personally gone over the engines that
were to take the racket in the mountains.  Ten-
wheelers they were, the 1012 and the 1014, with fifty-
six-inch drivers and cylinders big enough to sit up and
eat breakfast in.  Spick and span both of them, just long
enough out of the shops to run smoothly to the work;
and on Friday Oliver Sollers, who, when he opened
a throttle, blew miles over the tender like feathers,
took the 1012, groomed as you'd groom a Wilkes
mare, down to Piedmont for the run up to the Bend.

Now Oliver Sollers was a runner in a thousand.

and steady as a clock; but he had a fireman who couldn't stand prosperity, Steve Horigan, a cousin of Johnnie's. The glory was too great for Steve, and he spent Friday night in Gallagher's place celebrating, telling the boys what the 1012 would do to the Yellow Mail. Not a thing, Steve claimed after five drinks, but pull the stamps clean off the letters the minute they struck the foothills. But when Steve showed up at five A. M. to superintend the movement, he was seasick. The instant Sollers set eyes on him he objected to taking him out. Mr. Sollers was not looking for any unnecessary chances on one of Bucks' personal matters, and for the general manager the Yellow Mail test had become exceedingly personal. Practically everybody East and West had said it would fail; Bucks said no.

Neighbor himself was on the Piedmont platform that morning, watching things. The McCloud despatchers had promised the train to our division on time, and her smoke was due with the rise of the sun. The big superintendent of motive power, watching anxiously for her arrival, and planning anxiously for her outgoing, glared at the bunged fireman in front of him, and, when Sollers protested, Neighbor turned on the swollen Steve with sorely bitter words. Steve swore mightily he was fit and could do the trick—but what's the word of a railroad man that drinks? Neighbor spoke wicked words, and while they poured on the guilty Steve's crop there was a shout down the platform. In the east the sun was breaking over the sand-hills, and below it a haze of black thickened the horizon. It was McTerza with the 808 and the Yellow Mail. Neighbor looked at his watch; she was, if anything, a minute to the good, and before the car tinks could hustle across the yard, a streak of gold cut the sea of purple alfalfa in the lower valley, and the narrows began to smoke with the dust of the race for the platform.

When McTerza blocked the big drivers at the west end of the depot, every eye was on the new equipment. Three standard railway mail cars, done in varnished buttercup, strung out behind the sizzling engine, and they looked pretty as cowslips. While Neighbor vaguely meditated on their beauty and on his boozing fireman, Jimmie Bradshaw, just in from a night run down from the Bend, walked across the yard. He had just seen Steve Horigan making a "sneak" for the bath-house, and from the yard gossip Jimmie had guessed the rest.

"What are you looking for, Neighbor?" asked Jimmie Bradshaw.

"A man to fire for Sollers—up. Do you want it?"

Neighbor threw it at him across and carelessly, not having any idea Jimmie was looking for trouble. But Jimmie surprised him; Jimmie did want it.

"Sure, I want it. Put me on. Tired? No. I'm fresh as rainwater. Put me on, Neighbor; I'll never get fast any other way. Doubleday wouldn't give me a fast run in a hundred years. Neighbor," exclaimed Jimmie, greatly wrought, "put me on, and I'll plant sunflowers on your grave."

There wasn't much time to look around; the 1012

was being coupled on to the mail for the hardest run on the line.

"Get in there, you blamed idiot," roared Neighbor presently at Jimmie. "Get in and fire her; and if you don't give Sollers 210 pounds every inch of the way I'll set you back wiping."

Jimmie winked furiously at the proposition while it was being hurled at him, but he lost no time climbing in. The 1012 was drumming then at her gauge with better than 200 pounds. Adam Shafer, conductor for the run, ran backward and forward a minute examining the air. At the final word from his brakeman he lifted two fingers at Sollers; Oliver opened a notch, and Jimmie Bradshaw stuck his head out of the gangway. Slowly, but with swiftly rising speed, the yellow string began to move out through the long lines of freight cars that blocked the spurs; and those who watched that morning from the Piedmont platform thought a smoother equipment than Bucks' mail train never drew out of the mountain yards.

Jimmie Bradshaw jumped at the work in front of him. He had never in his life lifted a pick in as swell a cab as that. The hind end of the 1012 was as big as a private car; Jimmie had never seen so much play for a shovel in his life, and he knew the trick of his business better than most men even in West End cabs —the trick of holding the high pressure every minute, of feeling the draughts before they left the throttle; and as Oliver let the engine out very, very fast, Jimmie Bradshaw sprinkled the grate bars craftily and blinked at the shivering pointer, as much as to say, "It's you and me now for the Yellow Mail, and nobody else on earth."

There was a long reach of smooth track in front of the foothills. It was there the big start had to be made, and in two minutes the bark of the big machine had deepened to a chest tone full as thunder. It was all fun for an hour, for two hours. It was that long before the ambitious fireman realized what the new speed meant: the sickening slew, the lurch on lurch so fast the engine never righted, the shortened breath along the tangent, the giddy roll to the elevation and the sudden shock of the curve, the roar of the flight on the ear, and, above and over it all, the booming purr of the maddened steel. The canoe in the heart of the rapids, the bridge of a liner at sea, the gun in the heat of the fight, take something of this—the cab of the mail takes it all.

When they struck the foothills, Sollers and Jimmie Bradshaw looked at their watches and looked at each other, but like men who had turned their backs on every mountain record. There was a stop for water —speed drinks so hard—an oil round, an anxious touch on the journals; then the Yellow Mail drew reeling into the hills. Oliver eased her just a bit for the heavier curves, but for all that the train writhed frantically as it cut the segments, and the men thought, in spite of themselves, of the mountain curves ahead. The worst of the run lay ahead of the pilot, because the art in mountain running is not alone or so much in getting up hill; it is in getting down hill. But by the way the Yellow Mail got that day up hill and down, it seemed as if Steve Horigan's dream would be realized, and that the 1012 actually would pull the stamps off the letters. Before they knew it they were through the gateway, out into the desert country, up along the crested buttes, and then, sudden as eternity, the wheelbase of the 1012 struck a tight curve, a pent-down rail sprang out like a knitting-needle, and the Yellow Mail shot staggering off the track into a gray borrow-pit.

There was a crunching of truck and frame, a crashing splinter of varnished cars, a scream from the wounded engine, a cloud of gray ash in the burning sun, and a ruin of human effort in the ditch. In the twinkle of an eye the mail train lay spilled on the alkali; for a minute it looked desperately bad for the general manager's test.

It was hardly more than a minute, though; then like ants from out a trampled hill men began crawling from the yellow wreck. There was more—there was groaning and worse, yet little for so frightful a shock. And first on his feet, with no more than scratches, and quickest back under the cab after his engineer, was Jimmie Bradshaw, the fireman.

Sollers, barely conscious, lay wedged between the tank and the footboard. Jimmie, all by himself, eased him away from the boiler. The conductor stood with a broken arm directing his brakeman how to chop a crew out of the head mail car, and the hind crews were getting out themselves. There was a quick calling back and forth, and the cry, "Nobody killed!" But the engineer and the conductor were put out of action.

There was, in fact, but one West End man unhurt; yet that was enough—for it was Jimmie Bradshaw.

The first wreck of the fast mail—there have been worse since—took place just east of Crockett's siding. A west-bound freight lay at that moment on the passing track waiting for the mail. Jimmie Bradshaw cast up the possibilities of the situation the minute he righted himself.

Before the freight crew had reached the wreck, Jimmie was hustling ahead to tell them what he wanted. The freight conductor demurred; and when they discussed it with the freight engineer, Kingsley, he objected. "My engine won't never stand it; it'll pound her to pieces," he argued. "I reckon the safest thing to do is to get orders."

"Get orders!" stormed Jimmie Bradshaw, pointing at the wreck. "Get orders! Are you running an engine on this line and don't know the orders for those mail bags? The orders is to move 'em! That's orders enough. Move 'em! Uncouple three of those empty box-cars and hustle 'em back. By the Great United States! any man that interferes with the moving of this mail will get his time—that's what he'll get. That's Doubleday, and don't you forget it. The thing is to move the mail—not stand here chewing about it!"

"Bucks wants the stuff hustled," put in the freight conductor, weakening before Jimmie's eloquence. "Everybody knows that."

"Uncouple there!" cried Jimmie, climbing into the Mogul cab. "I'll pull the bags, Kingsley; you needn't take any chances. Come back there, every mother's son of you, and help on the transfer."

He carried his points with a gale. He was conductor and engineer and general manager all in one. He backed the boxes to the curve below the spill, and set every man at work piling the mail from the wrecked train to the freight cars. The wounded cared for the wounded, and the dead might have buried the dead; Jimmie moved the mail. Only one thing turned his hair gray; the transfer was so slow, it looked as if it would defeat his plan. As he stood fermenting, a stray party of Sioux bucks on a vagrant hunt rose out of the desert passes, and halted to survey the confusion. It was Jimmie Bradshaw's opportunity. He had the blanket men in council in a trice. They talked for one minute, in two he had them regularly sworn in and carrying second-class. The registered stuff was jealously guarded by those of the mail clerks who could still hobble—and who, head for head, leg for leg, and arm for arm, can stand the wrecking that a mail clerk can stand? The mail crews took the registered matter; the freight crews and Jimmie, dripping sweat and anxiety, handled the letter bags; but second and third class were temporarily hustled for the Great White Father by his irreverent children of the Rockies.

Before the disabled men could credit their senses the business was done, themselves made as comfortable as possible, and with the promise of speedy aid back to the injured, the Yellow Mail, somewhat disfigured, was again heading westward in the box-cars.

This time Jimmie Bradshaw, like a dog with a bone, had the throttle. Jimmie Bradshaw for once in his life had the coveted fast run, and till he sighted Fort Rucker he never for a minute let up.

Meantime there was a desperate crowd around the despatcher at Medicine Bend. It was an hour and twenty minutes after Ponca Station reported the Yellow Mail out, before Fort Rucker, eighteen miles farther west, reported the box-cars and Jimmie Bradshaw in, and followed with a wreck report from the Crockett siding. When that end of it began to tumble into the Wickiup office Doubleday's face went very hard—fate was against him, the contract was gone glimmering, he didn't feel at all sure his own head and the roadmaster's wouldn't follow it. Then the Rucker operator began again to talk about Jimmie Bradshaw, and "Who's Bradshaw?" asked somebody; and Rucker went on excitedly with the story of the Mogul and of three box-cars, and of a war party of Sioux squatting on the brake-wheels; it came so mixed that Medicine Bend thought everybody at Rucker Station had gone mad.

While they fumed, Jimmie Bradshaw was speeding the mail through the mountains. He had Kingsley's fireman, big as an ox and full of his own enthusiasm. In no time they were flying across the flats of the Spider Water, threading the curves of the Peace River, and hitting the rails of the Painted Desert, with the Mogul sprinting like a Texas steer, and the box-cars leaping like yearlings at the points. It was no case of scientific running, no case of favoring the roadbed, of easing the strain on the equipment; it was simply a case of galloping to a Broadway fire with a Silsby rotary on a 4—11 call.  Up hill and down, curve and tangent, it was all one.  There was speed made on the plains with that mail, and there was speed made in the foothills with the fancy equipment, but never the speed that Jimmie Bradshaw made when he ran the mail through the gorges in three box-cars; and frightened operators and paralyzed station-agents all the way up the line watched the fearful and wonderful train jump the switches with Bradshaw's red head sticking out of the cab window.

Medicine Bend couldn't get the straight of it over the wires.  There was an electric storm in the mountains, and the wires went bad in the midst of the confusion.  They knew there was a wreck, and supposed there was mail in the ditch, and, with Doubleday frantic, the despatchers were trying to get the track to run a train down to Crockett's.  But Jimmie Bradshaw had asked at Rucker for rights to the Bend, and in an unguarded moment they had been given; after that it was all off.  Nobody could get action on Jimmie Bradshaw to head him off.  He took the rights, and stayed not for stake and stopped not for stone. In thirty minutes the operating department was ready to kill him, but he was making such time it was concluded better to humor the lunatic than to try to hold him up anywhere for a parley.  When this was decided Jimmie and his war party were already reported past Bad Axe, fifteen miles below the Bend, with every truck on the box-cars smoking.

The Bad Axe run to the Bend was never done in less than fourteen minutes until Bradshaw that day brought up the mail. Between those two points the line is modeled on the curves of a ram's horn, but Jimmie with the Mogul found every twist on the right of way in eleven minutes; that particular record is good yet. Indeed, before Doubleday, then in a frenzied condition, got his cohorts fairly on the platform to look for Jimmie, the hollow scream of the big freight engine echoed through the mountains. Shouts from below brought the operators to the upper windows; down the Bend they saw a monster locomotive flying from a trailing horn of smoke. As the stubby string of freight cars slewed quartering into the lower yard, the startled officials saw them from the Wickiup windows wrapped in a stream of flame. Every journal was afire, and the blaze from the boxes, rolling into the steam from the stack, curled hotly around a bevy of Sioux Indians, who clung sternly to the footboards and brake-wheels on top of the box-cars. It was a ride for the red men that is told around the council fires yet. But they do not always add in their traditions that they were hanging on, not only for life, but also for a butt of plug tobacco promised for their timely help at Crockett siding.

By the time Jimmie slowed up his amazing equipment the fire brigade was on the run from the roundhouse. The Sioux warriors climbed hastily down the fire escapes, a force of bruised and bareheaded mail clerks shoved back the box-car doors, the car tinks tackled the conflagration, and Jimmie Bradshaw, dropping from the cab with the swing of a man who has done it, waited at the gangway for the questions to come to him, and for a minute they came hot.

"What the blazes do you mean by bringing in an engine in that condition?" yelled Doubleday, pointing to the blown machine.

"I thought you wanted the mail," winked Jimmie.

"How the devil are we to get the mail with you blocking the track for two hours?" demanded Calahan insanely.

"Why, the mail's here—in these box-cars," responded Jimmie Bradshaw, pointing to his bobtail train. "Now don't look daffy like that; every sack is right here. I thought the best way to get the mail here was to bring it. Hm! We're forty minutes late, ain't we?"

Doubleday waited to hear no more. Orders flew like curlews from the superintendent and the master mechanic. They saw there was a life for it yet. A string of new mail cars was backed down beside the train before the fire brigade had done with the trucks. The relieving mail crews waiting at the Bend took hold like cats at a pudding, and a dozen extra men helped them sling the pouches. The 1014, blowing porpoisewise, was backed up just as Benedict Morgan's train pulled down for Crockett's siding, and the Yellow Mail, rehabilitated, rejuvenated, and exultant, started up the gorge for Bear Dance, only fifty-three minutes late, with Hanksworth in the cab.

"And if you can't make that up, Frank, you're no good on earth," spluttered Doubleday at the engineer he had put in for that especial endeavor. And Frank Hawksworth did make it up, and the Yellow Mail went on and off the West End on the test, and into the Sierras for the coast, *on time*.

"There's a butt of plug tobacco and transportation to Crockett's coming to these bucks, Mr. Doubleday," winked Jimmie Bradshaw uncertainly, for with the wearing off of the strain came the idea to Jimmie that he might have to pay for it himself. "I promised them that," he added, "for helping with the transfer. If it hadn't been for the blankets we wouldn't have got off for another hour. They chew Tomahawk—rough and ready preferred—Mr. Doubleday. Hm!"

Doubleday was looking off into the mountains.

"You've been on a freight run some time, Jimmie," said he tentatively after a while.

The Indian detachment was crowding in pretty close on the red-headed engineer. He blushed. "If you'll take care of my tobacco contract, Doubleday, we'll call the other matter square. I'm not looking for a fast run as much as I was."

"If we get the mail contract," resumed Doubleday reflectively, "and it won't be your fault if we don't—hm!—we may need you on one of the runs. Looks to me like you ought to have one."

Jimmie shook his head. "I don't want one—don't mind me; just fix these gentlemen out with some tobacco before they scalp me, will you?"

The Indians got their leaf, and Bucks got his contract, and Jimmie Bradshaw got the pick of the runs on the Yellow Mail, and ever since he's been kicking

to get back on a freight.  But they don't call him
Bradshaw any more.  No man in the mountains can
pace him on a dare-devil run.  And when the head
brave of the hunting party received the butt of tobacco on behalf of his company, he looked at Doubleday with dignity, pointed to the sandy engineer, and
spoke freckled words in the Sioux.

That's the way it came about.  Bradshaw holds the
belt for the run from Bad Axe to Medicine Bend; but
he never goes by the name of Bradshaw any more.
West of McCloud, everywhere up and down the
mountains, they give him the name that the Sioux
gave him that day—Jimmie the Wind.

# FRICTIONAL ELECTRICITY

## BY MAX ADELER

*About thirty years ago, when humorous stories bearing the signature of "Max Adeler" all at once ceased to appear, it was generally taken for granted that their author, Charles Heber Clark (born in Berlin, Md., July 11, 1841) had ungenerously sneaked "Out of the Hurly-Burly" of mundane existence without poetic notice of his demise through the obituary column—which his genius had made the official bulletin of the mirthful muse. But "Mr. Adeler" had only hidden his identity under the alias of Clark, a writer of economic literature, proverbially the antipodes of mirth and the Muses. Five years ago the sudden return of the old Max Adeler affected his readers with a shock of joy scarcely less than the man must have felt to whom Mark Twain telegraphed: "Reports of my death greatly exaggerated." The present selection is one of Max Adeler's new stories. Were it not in the author's vein of thirty years ago, it would be taken for an imitation of W. W. Jacobs.*

# FRICTIONAL ELECTRICITY

## BY MAX ADELER

I HAPPENED to visit the accident ward of St.
Paracelsus' Hospital because a friend of mine
who is interested in the Flower Mission asked
me to stop there during my afternoon walk and give
a few flowers to the sufferers.

When I had arranged the last half-dozen of the
roses in a vase upon the little stand by the bedside of
one bruised and battered patient, he looked at me gratefully, and said:

"Oh, thank you, sir! And would you mind, sir,
stopping for a bit of talk? I'm so lonely and
miserable."

I sat upon the chair by the bed and with my hand
smoothed the counterpane, while the patient asked
me:

"Do I really look like a burglar, sir, do you think?"

I hesitated to reply as I examined his face. It
was really covered with bandages, but his nose
seemed swollen and there were bruises about both
eyes.

"I don't wonder you don't like to speak your mind
when you see me here a broken wreck, smashed all
up and not looking a bit like myself, sir. But if you

Reprinted by permission of the author, Charles Heber Clark, from "The Saturday
Evening Post."

would see me well and strong and all fixed up for going to church you'd say right off that I don't favor no
burglar in looks."

I asked the unfortunate man his name.

"Mordecai Barnes, sir, and I'm a journeyman plumber, sir, with a good character and don't take no second
place in that business with no man. How did I get
here? What banged me all up into a shame and a
disgrace like this? Well, I'll tell you, sir, if you have
the patience to listen, for it does me good to talk who
has been used so hard, and can get no attention from
the nurses or nobody in this here asylum. Do you
understand about frictional electricity, sir? No? I
thought not; and well had it been for me, for this
shattered hulk that you see a-lying here, if I had
never heard of it neither! I'll tell you how it was,
sir. My mate, George Watkins, and there ain't no
better man nowheres if you go clear round the globe—
George Watkins is one of these men with inquiring
minds, always a-hungering for knowledge, and so
George off he goes week after week to the lectures up
at the Huxley Institute. You know it; in that yallow
building over by Nonpareil Square. And George
often he told me about the wonderful things he learned
there, and among others he was fond of explaining to me about frictional electricity.

"It seems, sir, for you may not know it any more'n
I knowed it until George explained it to me, that
there's three different kinds of electricity. There's
the kind you make with a steam engine, and the kind
you make with acid, and the kind you make with

friction.    Well, sir, would you believe—or, let me say first, have you ever rubbed a black cat on the back in a dark room and seen the sparks fly?  Of course, and, sir, I know it's almost beyond belief, but, positive, they told George Watkins, my mate, up at the Huxley Institute, that them sparks and the aurora borealis that you see sometimes a-lighting up the heavens is one and the same thing!  Wonderful, isn't it, sir, that Science should discover that a black cat is some kind of kin to the aurora borealis?   But George says that's what they said, for the aurora borealis is caused by the earth a-rolling around and rubbing the air just as the sparks is caused by stroking the cat's back.

"And George he says that this here frictional electricity is the only kind that'll cure pain.   The steam-engine kind won't do it, and the acid kind won't do it, but the frictional kind'll do it every time if you only know how to apply it.

"Well, sir, now I pass to the sorrerful part of my story.    There is a girl named Bella Dougherty that does housework for a man named Muffitt, and a mighty nice girl she is; or, I used to think her nice.   Maybe you know where Mr. Muffitt lives, on 149th Street, just above Parvin Street, the third house on the left with white shutters.

"Anyhow, I got to be fond of Bella and often used to set and talk with her in the evenings in Mr. Muffitt's kitchen, and maybe have two or three other girls come in sometimes, with a few men; though I never cared, sir, for much flocking together at such times, for Bella Dougherty she was good enough company for me, just her and I by ourselves.

"Howsomdever, there was another man that had a kind of fancy for Bella Dougherty, although in my opinion he isn't fit to wipe her feet on, and his name is William Jones.

"This yer William Jones used to come intruding around there in Mr. Muffitt's kitchen when he wasn't wanted and when he seen that me and Bella would rather be a-setting there by ourselves. And so, sir, one night, just to kill the time till he'd quit and go, I begun to tell them what George Watkins said to me about the Huxley Institute and frictional electricity being a sure cure for pain.

"And William Jones, a-winking at Bella Dougherty, as much as to say, sir, that he'd be having the laugh on me, said he had a pain that minute in his head from neuralgia and he'd bet me a quarter no frictional electricity would drive it out. I know now what was the matter with the head of William Jones. Not neuralgia, nor nothing of the sort, sir. It was vacuum. My mate, George Watkins, tells me that at the Institute they say that vacuum always produces pain, and that was the only thing the matter with this William Jones I'm a-telling you about.

"I never take no dare, not from no man of that kind, anyways, sir, so I bet him a quarter I'd cure him, and cure him with frictional electricity, too. So he set down on the chair a-laughing and a-winking at Bella Dougherty, who set over by the range holding the quarters; and I begun to rub William Jones's eyebrows with my two thumbs; just gently, but right along just like stroking a cat; keeping it up, a-rubbing and a-rubbing, until at last I asked him how he felt now; and, you can imagine my supprise, sir, when I seen that William Jones was fast asleep! I was skeered at first; but in a minute I seen that I had hypnertized him unbeknown to myself, and there set William Jones 's if he was froze stiff.

"I wa'n't so very sorry, sir, when I found out how things was a-going, although if I could have seen what was the consequences of this strange occurrence I'd 'a' seized my hat and bid Bella Dougherty good-by and started straight for home.

"But, sir, of course I acted like a fool, for I'd read in the papers how a man who hypnertizes another man can make him believe anything and do anything, and so I thought I'd have some fun with William Jones and enjoy a lovely, quiet evening with Bella Dougherty.

"So I says to William Jones:

"'Now, William, you're a little school-scholar oncet again and you've missed your lesson, and so you just go over there in that corner by the china closet and stand with your face to the wall and say over and over your multiplication table till you know it right.'

"And so, to the supprise of Bella Dougherty, William Jones went right over in the corner, like I told him, and there he stood, saying: 'Six sixes is thirty-six, six sevens is forty-two,' and so on, whilst I set over with Bella Dougherty peacefully enjoying ourselves just exactly 's if William Jones wasn't any-wheres about.

"And so, sir, it went on until Mrs. Muffitt she come down and said to Bella Dougherty it was time to shut the house up, and then I bid her good-night and told William to go home and go straight to bed, which he did, and a-saying the multiplication table all the way down the street. He would have said it all night, sir, I do believe, if I hadn't ordered him to stop and to begin saying his prayers when I passed him in at his front door.

"You may believe me, sir, that I had William Jones on my mind all night and was a-worrying a little about him too, for fear maybe he'd never come to. So around I goes the first thing in the morning to his boarding-house, and his landlady tells me he had been a-saying his prayers all mixed up like with the multi-plication table ever since he come home the night be-fore. She was a bit troubled about it, sir, as you may imagine, for William Jones was a good boarder and it 'd 'a' been money out of her pocket if he had lost his mind.

"So, then, I seen William Jones and knowed at oncet that the hypnertizing still had hold of him. Very well; I had no idea how to get him out of it and it didn't hurt him nohow, so I just commanded William Jones to drop the multiplication table and his prayers and to fix all his intellect in the regular way on plumbing; and William Jones at oncet calmed down and seemed his old self again.

"Then a wicked thought flashed into my mind.

You know how it is yourself, sir; you are tempted and you are weak and you fall, and then the first thing you know, to be sure your sin'll find you out and there you are! Here I am, a shattered hulk. It suddenly occurred to me, sir, that if I could control William Jones, why not turn his affections away from Bella Dougherty, who might take a fancy to him? who knows? women are so queer! and direct his thoughts toward my own Aunt Maggie, who is a middle-aged widder and not so bad-looking, and far too good for such a man as William Jones, although to speak the plain truth I had no objections to having him for an uncle by marriage.

"Therefore I did so, sir, and before the week was out I heard that William Jones was plumbing in the most supprising manner, plumbing here and plumbing there, and paying attentions vigorously, so to speak, to Aunt Maggie every evening.

"In the meantime, sir, believe me, I did not lose time in my suit with Bella Dougherty, who seemed real mad at William Jones when people began to talk about his courting Aunt Maggie, so that in less than two weeks, when Bella Dougherty heard that William Jones and Aunt Maggie had agreed to marry, I got Bella Dougherty about as good as to say, although she never quite said it square, that she would have me.

"I never knowed how it happened, sir, whether somebody waked William Jones up or he just come to by himself, but, sir, anyhow, William Jones about that time dropped hypnertism and was himself again.

Imagine, sir, how things stood! There never was a man as mad as William Jones; mad with me, and mad with Aunt Maggie, to whom he sent a cruel message that he wa'n't marrying no grandmas, and that made Aunt Maggie mad; and then William Jones set down and wrote me a letter to the general effect that whenever he met me my course in this life would be short.

"Naturally, sir, as you may believe, I kept out of William Jones's way, for I am not fond of quarreling, and besides, William Jones is forty pounds heavier, sir, than I am.

"But one night while I was setting in the kitchen at Muffitt's, having some uplifting conversation with Bella Dougherty, there was a sudden knock on the side door, and up she jumps, pale and skeered, and says: 'I do believe that is William Jones. He said he might call, maybe, this evening!' So, of course, as I never hunt trouble, I raised the window sash over by the kitchen table at the back and went out just as William Jones come in the side door. He kept the door open a-watching for me, and so as I couldn't get to the gate I climbed over the high fence into the next yard.

"I ought to have gone right home, sir, without stopping, but I hated to leave William Jones there with Bella Dougherty, and me just driven out; so, as it was raining hard and I had on my Sunday suit, what does I do but try the latch on the kitchen door of the house next to Mr. Muffitt's, and finding the door opened, in I walked and set down in a chair to await what was going to happen.   That was a bad job for me, sir!   It isn't safe to take one false step.

"For the next minute the inside door from the dining-room springs open and a man jumps out and grabs me and says: 'I've got thee at last, have I!'   He was a Quaker, sir; a big man and with a grip like iron.   I never knowed a man with a grip like that. Did you ever, sir, have your fingers in the crack of a door and somebody a-leaning hard on the door?   That was the way this Quaker held me.   Then he calls out 'Amelia!   Amelia!' and in a minute a sweet old Quaker lady comes out with a candle, and he says to her: 'I've caught that burglar, Amelia; thee get the clothes line.' "

"So the lady she gets the clothes line and that man he ties my hands and my arms behind my back, good and tight, and then he made me set down and he ties me to the chair, and at last he gives the rope two or three turns around the leg of the kitchen table and says to me: 'Friend, thee can just set there while I go to get an officer!'   Gave me no chance to explain. Took it all for granted; whereas if he would have listened to me I could have cleared up the whole mystery in two minutes.

"So then, sir, out he goes for a policeman, and the old lady sets down in a chair not far from me and said she was sorry I was so wicked and asked me about my mother, and if I ever went to First-Day school, and a whole lot of things.   Then a thought seemed to strike her and she went into the next room and came back with a book in her hand, and she said she would read a good book to me while we waited for justice to take its course.

"She was lovely to look at, sir, with her tidy brown frock and the crape handkerchief folded acrost her bosom and her cap and the smile on her face; a sweet face, sir; an angel face; yes, sir, but sweet faces often has cruel dispositions behind them. For then she told me that the book was called Barclay's Apology for the People called Quakers, or something like that, and she begun to read it to me.

"Have you ever read that book, sir? It is dedicated, I think, to Charles the Second, and it begins with Fifteen Propositions, and she read every one of them Propositions from first to last. Then she turned to the section, sir, about Salutations and Recreations, and she read and read and read until, sir, actually it made my head swim.

"Do you know, sir, is Barclay still alive—the man who wrote that book? Is there no way of getting even with him?

"I couldn't get away. I might have walked out somehow with the chair fastened to me; but I couldn't go, could I, sir, with the table tied to my leg, and particularly if I had to climb the fence? So I had to set there and be regarded as a burglar.

"But at last I *would* be heard, and I told her I was no burglar but an innercent man; and then she looked in the index to find if Barclay had anything interesting to say about the wickedness of telling falsehoods. And then I said I was a member of the Baptist Society, and she said at once she would read Barclay on

the errors of that sect; but I insisted on being heard,
and I explained to her that I got into this trouble by
trying to cure William Jones by frictional electricity,
and she said: 'Thee has an ingenious and fruitful mind
to invent such a story  Oh, that it had been turned
to better devices than following a life of evil!'

"'And it seems hard, too,' I said, 'that a perfectly
respectable Baptist plumber should be arrested as a
burglar simply because he tried to relieve the pain of
William Jones by a scientific method invented by the
Huxley Institute.'

"'Where is thy friend William Jones?' she asked.

"Do you know, sir, at that very moment you could
hear through the partition William Jones and Bella
Dougherty laughing next door!  It seemed like mockery to me, a-setting there in chains, so to speak.

"'He is next door, ma'am,' I said, 'a-courting the
hired girl.'

"'I will prove if thee is telling the truth,' she said,
and she got up and moved toward the door.

"'No, ma'am, no!' I said; 'please don't do that!
William mustn't know that I am here'; and so she
comes back and sets down again, and picks up Barclay, and looks sorrerful at me, and says:

"'It is wicked for thee to have such vain imaginations.  Why does thee persist in pretending that there
is a William Jones?'  And then she started to look
through Barclay to find if he had anything that would
fit the William Jones part of the case.

"What could I do?  I daresn't call in William
Jones to prove my innercence; he was mad all over at

me and a bigger man, too, and here I was tied; and I couldn't call Bella Dougherty without William Jones knowing it. It was hard, sir, for a man as innercent as a little babe to set there with that sweet and smooth old lady considering him a shameless story-teller and firing Barclay at him, now wasn't it, sir? Would you have called William Jones, sir, under them there circumstances, and his laughter and Bella Dougherty's still a-resounding through the partition?

"Well, sir, that policeman was a long time a-coming with the old Quaker. I never knowed why; but Friend Amelia she set down again and turned over the leaves of Barclay and begun oncet more to read about Salutations and Recreations while, strange as it may seem to you, sir, I felt that I'd ruther see the policeman and be locked up in a dungeon than to hear more of it.

"But, howsomdever, after a while in comes the Quaker and the officer with him, and the very first minute the officer seen me he says:

" 'I reckernize him as an old offender.'

" 'No you don't!' says I; 'I'm no old offender nor a young offender. I'm a perfeckly honest Baptist plumber, and I kin prove it, too.'

" 'How kin you prove it?' says the officer.

" 'By William Jones,' says I, 'who is a-setting in that kitchen right next door, a-wooing the hired girl.'

"I was bold about it, sir, because I knowed William Jones daresn't strike at me while the officer was there.

" 'We'll see about that,' says the officer, and in he goes to Mr. Muffitt's yard next door and comes back with William Jones. I have no use for a man like William Jones. What do you think he does, sir? Why, he looks me over, from head to foot, in a blank sort of a way, and then, turning to the policeman, he says: 'I don't know the man, officer; never seen him before'; then that low-down plumber walks out and leaves me there and goes back, and in a minute I hear him and Bella Dougherty a-laughing worse than ever.

" 'I thought not,' says the officer, slipping the handcuffs on me, 'and so now you come right along.' And Friend Amelia looked mournful at me and says to me she would come around regular and read Barclay to me in my cell after I was convicted.

"And so, sir, to make a long story short, I was took up before the magistrate and held for burglary, and my mate, George Watkins, went my bail and so I was let go.

"I might stop here, sir, but I must tell you that the following Thursday I met William Jones up a kind of a blind alley where I was working, while he was working in a house on the opposite side. He had me in a corner where there was no chance to run, so I put on a bold face and went right up to him and says:

" 'William, there's been some differences betwixt us, but I'm not the man to bear grudges and I forgive you."

" 'What's that?' says he, savage.

" 'Why,' says I, 'the whole thing is just one of them unpleasant misunderstandings'; and then I started to explain to him about the Huxley Institute theory of frictional electricity and the aurora borealis.

"I can't tell what he said, sir, in reply, with reference to the aurora borealis, because I'm a decent man and never use no low language; but suddenly he jumped on me, and the first thing I knowed I was being lifted in the ambulance and fetched to this yer hospital. Was it right, sir, do you think, for William Jones to strike me foul, like that, while I was trying to state my case to him? No, sir. But that's not the worst of it. Last Tuesday word came to me that Bella Dougherty had throwed me over and is going to marry William Jones on Decoration Day! Think of that, sir!" and Mordecai Barnes turned his head upon his pillow and moaned.

Turning again toward me, he was about to resume his statement, when suddenly he exclaimed:

"Why, there's Aunt Maggie."

A woman of fifty years, nicely clad, came to the bedside and said to him coldly: -

"Is that you, Mordecai Barnes?"

"Yes, Aunt Maggie."

"I'm ashamed of you, Mordecai Barnes," said she; "ashamed of you. It served you right. You got just what was comin' to you. I wish William had banged you worse."

Mordecai Barnes groaned.

"And more than that," continued Aunt Maggie, glaring at him through her spectacles, "I've torn up my old will which named you my sole heir and made a new one and left all my property to this yer very hospital."

With these words Aunt Maggie walked away and left the room.

Mordecai Barnes could not speak for a few minutes. He looked as if death would be welcome. Then, pulling the bedclothes up under his chin and closing his eyes wearily, he said:

"Curse the day, say I, when George Watkins first went to the Huxley Institute and heard about frictional electricity."

# IN THE WAKE OF WAR

## BY HALLIE ERMINIE RIVES

*Miss Rives (born in Christian County, Kentucky, May 2, 1876) has disciplined herself more arduously than most of the popular novelists in that training school of style, short story writing. The book of hers which first attracted general attention, "A Furnace of Earth," was in form and spirit a short story. Its very title is suggestive of the severe process of refinement that it underwent in the manuscript: it was rewritten seven times. "In the Wake of War," a Southern story, has been selected for the present series by the author herself as representative of her recent work in brief fiction.*

# IN THE WAKE OF WAR

BY HALLIE ERMINIE RIVES

THERE is nothing so elusive yet so fascinating as a chance resemblance. We walk a street crowded with thousands of human atoms like ourselves, yet each meaningless, unindividual. The mass has the consistency of a stream of water parted by a stone. Suddenly one of these atoms acquires form, color, substance, and character; its individuality strikes a chord in the brain. A thousand disassociate fragments — memory-worn strands of time and place—struggle to coalesce, to reweave themselves into a pattern we once knew. Our thoughts give aid. Recollection puzzles itself, finds itself impotent, rages at its own powerlessness. At such a moment the mind recurs again and again with painful insistence to the problem, and the chance resemblance, by reason of aggravation, acquires an importance wholly disproportionate. The man who pursues such a will-o'-the-wisp memory does so protesting, in spite of himself.

It was in some such frame of mind that Brent Maxwell stood looking out across the desolate hillside. The landscape still mourned, in blackened stone walls and thinned forests, the devastation of Sherman's march to the sea. The bare unpromise of the scene

(1681)

was in his soul. He knew the gaunt poverty that follows in the wake of war. He had fought loyally for the Union. And now, after fifteen years of reconstruction, he had learned that Appomattox had dawned only upon the first chapter of defeat. The fierce patriotism which had led him, a youth of enthusiasm and dreams of the glory of sacrifice, to leave his place and portion in the North when the first call sounded, and the earnestness of intention with which he had flung himself into the newly breathing industrial life of a Southern city, had had time to cool and sober. In spite of success the very intensity of the struggle against adverse conditions had bred in him a resentment against the necessity which made green fields a desert, plantation a waste, and a smiling country a cemetery of unmarked graves. Something of the dogged sadness which hung on the people among whom he elected to dwell had centred into him. He had lived down the hatred and the sneer, but the process had made him bitter against the circumstances which had given this hatred rise.

On this early morning his thoughts, which had been busy estimating the possibilities of the farm, whose deeds he had in his pocket, and whose foreclosure had brought him from his own city, had been suddenly arrested and turned from their channel. A rattling vehicle had passed him, containing two figures—a man and a woman. The faces of both interested him. The woman's was sad and sober-sweet, surmounted by pearl gray hair. There was a little color in her cheeks. The man had dead white hair and beard, with face

blue-tinged and shifting eyes of yellow. He wore a
heavy butternut overcoat and a knitted nubia of child-
ishly bright colors.

There was something in this last face that started
reverberating echoes in Maxwell's brain. An intan-
gible hand was at work tying together loose ends of
recollection. He knew and yet he did not know.
Wherever he looked, as he plodded over the farm land,
he saw this blue face and dodging gaze. It came before him with an absurd incongruity and yet with a
reiterate malevolence.

The sun was high as he walked back toward the
village, past the great, gray-columned house whose
shambling porticoes pointed to a past of wealth and
grandeur. As he neared the gate a sudden cry made
him quicken his steps. A repeating scream—a man's,
yet wolf-like, rising and falling with monotonous in-
flections—filled all the hollows with sound. Its note
had a quality of the animal that thickened the hearer's
blood. It came from the house. Maxwell broke into
a run, burst open the gate and rushed toward the
porch.

Rounding a clump of evergreens he saw a strange
spectacle. Seated on the ground was the blue-faced
man, his fingers clutching the stubble, his lips emitting
the beast-like screams which had brought Maxwell
from the roadway. Bending over him, with her back
toward the gate, was the lady of the sad face and the
pearl-gray hair. She was smoothing the thin fringe
from the sunken temples, bending now and then to lay
her lips caressingly and sobbingly upon his head.

From under her arm the yellow eyes looked out straight toward Maxwell. He felt them pass shiftily across his face with a sense of shrinking repulsion. The volume of screams showed no abatement.

The tones with which the woman sought to soothe this outburst were exquisitely tender. "Poor Victor!" she was saying; "poor, poor boy!"

Maxwell had stopped short at the mad lustre of those yellow eyes; the woman had not heard his approach. With a strange tightening of the throat he shrank behind a bush and retreated to the road, looking fearfully back over his shoulder. Throughout the long walk back to the village hotel, at every turning, this picture started before him—a slight, gray-gowned figure with hands whose trembling motions suggested the settling of a dove to guard its young, and from under whose caress gleamed out topaz eyes in which lurked the devil of madness.

He stared over the table of the low-ceiled, smoky-beamed dining-room, unheeding the conversation, his mind pursuing the vagrant resemblance of the morning. He came to himself with a sort of shock to hear his neighbor say: "That's the first time I've seen ole Vic Brockman for two years. Miss Ma'y Ann took him drivin' this mornin'—you ought to seen 'em. The ole fellow had on a nubia that had as many colors as a peacock's tail. Queer how he hangs onto life all these years," he continued reflectively. "It'd be a blessin' if he'd shuffle off. Speakin' of women—there's a woman for you! Job Stacker, when he lived on the next farm, used to say that she cared for that idiot brother of hers ever since the war like a baby.  If he'd got killed out and out, instead of comin' home with no top to his head and no sense in it, it'd been better for her.  Then she could have married that sweetheart of hers and had troubles of her own."

He turned to Maxwell.  "I was talkin'," he said, "of Miss Brockman, who owns the Pool place—that big white house over the hill.  It's a pity the mortgage changed hands.  I suppose Miss Ma'y Ann is going to be sold out.  It's hard.  Old Squire Pool, her grandfather, was the biggest man in four counties, and befo' the war her ma was the high-headest girl you ever saw.  Wonder who got that mortgage?"

In the evening, as Maxwell and the village lawyer, who was Justice of the Peace, Conveyancer, and Notary Public all in one, walked in the fading light up the hill toward the property which was so soon to be sent to the hammer, there was small conversation between them.  The papers requiring the final signature protruded from Maxwell's great-coat pocket.  His mind was wandering through a labyrinth of recollection, pursuing the phantom of a blue face, surmounted by rough, white hair, and two eyes shot with feline yellow, which met his and wavered away in ferret uneasiness.  The likeness clung to him with a wilful persistence, and he swept his hand impatiently across his eyes as if to banish the thing that baffled him.

.    .    .    .    .    .    .    .    .

As the two men seated themselves in the lamplight of the great room, which yet bore the inextinguishable marks of aristocracy, Maxwell became unpleasantly aware of a huddled object on a sofa, which seemed to create in itself a centre of attraction. The errand was not a pleasant one, though relieved by the serene face and low tones that belong to the gentlewoman; but in the lax face of old Victor Brockman was another element—an element of arrested progress, of piteous recoil—the genius of unconscious despair. It drew Maxwell while it repelled him. He found himself turning his head to gaze upon it.

He realized in the midst of a genial sentence that the yellow eyes had ceased their roving, and had settled, fixed and stealthy, upon his face. The aggravating resemblance again caught his attention.

Thereafter he ceased to be himself—ceased in some inexplicable way to feel his will and intention master of the situation. The idiot's gaze had got upon his nerves. He found himself shifting in his seat, pushing his chair back by slow degrees to bring the sofa between him and it. Now and then he turned his eyes unwillingly to meet that look: the yellow eyes had ceased to twitch, and now rested with, it seemed to him, a quiet, dreamy hatred upon his own. The gaze affected him strangely; it angered him. He felt himself put out by this meaningless persistence. His smooth sentences flowed with less ease, and he felt a nervous contraction in the muscles of his throat.

Miss Mary Ann had drawn nearer to the squat occupant of the sofa, and her hand, trembling unwontedly, he thought, reached out now and then to touch the frayed sleeve. And surely the lawyer was looking at him closely. Maxwell felt himself sweating, and yet internally scoffing at this strange mood that had smitten him.

The situation was a simple one, and yet it had suddenly become impossible to him. He, Brent Maxwell, landowner, dealer in farm properties, had come to present an official paper for signature. He had done it scores of times, and yet the usual conversation with which custom softens the unpleasant alternatives of business failure into kindly and courteous agreement had become suddenly a way of pain—a chapter of indefinable reproach. A look of vacant, yellow eyes, grown steadfast, was making this hour one of loathing and horror.

As the last words were spoken and the necessary signatures were affixed, he snatched the papers from the lawyer's hands, crushed them into his pocket, and in sudden revulsion, his tense nerves released, sprang to his feet.

The effect upon the huddled figure opposite him was instantaneous and terrible. It cringed backward, with a shrinking gesture of fear and agony. Its palsied arms, shaking and uncertain, wavered before its face. A shriek came from its lips, but this time not the monotonous, wordless wail of habit, but an articulate cry: "My God! My head! Don't strike me again!"

Maxwell dimly heard the sobbing cry with which the sister's arms went round the cowering, abject figure, and the lawyer's abrupt ejaculation of astonishment and reassurance, as he rushed to the door and flung himself out into the frosty evening. His breath was coming heavily, and his fingers worked nervously in and out of clinched fists. As the sky opened before him, a vision hurled itself with the appalling directness of a thunderbolt before him—a vision of an acre of bloody, trampled sward, iron-sown, and blue with pungent wreaths of smoke. In the foreground a dismantled gun, prone upon whose stock a figure lay, with blackened face and tattered gray uniform, and over it a second figure swinging a clubbed musket, remorselessly cruel with the lust of war. The crest of that spattered knoll strewn with quiet forms—these two alone fiercely erect. Then the clubbed weapon descended. From the limp figure stretched across the gun rose two protesting arms; two hazel eyes looked from beneath the bloody mat of hair, and a voice shrill and terrifying: "My God! My head! don't strike me again!"

The vision blurred. Gusts of smoke came in between. Did the blue figure strike again? Did it? *Did it?*

Maxwell threw his hands toward the night sky that flared with that quick rose of condemnation and died again, as though appealing and inviting doom. The vision had scarce faded into the dim of the early night sky when the lawyer came down the steps. It was as though he had approached, black-robed and grotesque, from the corner of the dimming picture—a vengeance witnessing and impeaching, binding him, the Brent Maxwell of that savage battery charge, to the Brent Maxwell of this day, a strong man flying from the piteous pallor of a shrunken and deranged wreck.

The one upon whom this sudden panic of soul had crashed like a falling tower gripped him fiercely by the arms. "The man in there," he said hoarsely, "the man with the blue face and yellow eyes—the man that looked at me! Did you see him look at me?"

The other shrank back half fearfully. "Why, Maxwell," he said, "what's the matter? It was merely a fit of some sort. I thought you knew he was crazy. Why, man, you're shaking! Come along and we'll get something to warm us up."

"Did you see him put up his hands?"

The lawyer drew away his arm, almost angrily. "Heavens!" he said, "you're almost as bad as the old man himself. He's crazy, I tell you, plumb crazy, and has been ever since they brought him home from the war. He was struck in the head by a shell or something."

"Yes, yes. Where? Where was it? What battle was it?"

"I've always heard it was at Missionary Ridge." The match he struck against his boot-heel burned, sputtering, as he bit the end from a cigar."

Maxwell suddenly drew from his pocket the packet of papers; the parchment crackled as he reached forward and held a curling corner to the flame. While the lawyer stood in a maze Maxwell waved it, a flaming funnel, around his head until it scorched his fingers. As he dropped it to the ground, a mass of slowly blackening embers, a white shadow sprang out of the surrounding circle of blackness. It was Miss Mary Ann.

"Miss Ma'y Ann," cried the lawyer, "do you see what he's doing? He's burned up the mortgage! He's burned it up! That's all that's left of it there on the ground!"

Miss Mary Ann stepped forward half fearfully, her fascinated eyes on the glowing firebrand between them. She clasped her hands together. "Sir," she said, painfully, "sir"—then she stopped.

An overmastering desire seized Maxwell to take upon himself the act of that dead day—to shout to them both that he, *he,* had been asked mercy and had denied it. It was the right of war, but now, after all these years, it had recoiled upon him in shame. Circumstance had again put in his hand the weapon; the lust of acquisition called upon him to strike, but as he stood face to face with this new victim, out of that red mist of the stained past that cry had sounded, and his hand dropped nerveless before the same helpless, accusing eyes. He would have shouted that it was not charity, not kindness, that spared that roof, but self-accusation—a yearning for atonement and for absolution.

He received her broken words of gratitude with a sense of shame upon his soul, and the lawyer's bluff comments upon his benefaction pierced him like swords of searing.

. . . . . . . . . .

As Maxwell turned again toward the village, he rested his gaze upon the hillside, sleeping under the early stars. Field and knoll were covered silvery with the sheen of hoar-frost lances. It seemed the dwarf symbol of buried armies—thousands upon thousands of the dead, who died with upthrust bayonets still standing to guard in death the integrity of homes. And standing thus, with the sorrow of his thought upon him, Maxwell cried to his own soul, no less than to his land, to glory, to power, to war, and to victory:

"What have you done?  What have you done?"

# WHILE THE AUTOMOBILE RAN DOWN

## BY CHARLES BATTELL LOOMIS

*The position which Mr. Loomis (born in Brooklyn, N. Y., September 16, 1861) holds among American humorists is indicated by the fact that Jerome K. Jerome, the leading humorist of England, has recently taken him on as a partner to make a lecturing tour of America and England. "While the Automobile Ran Down" has been selected by Mr. Loomis as his favorite of the "Cheerful Americans" stories. Certainly the equanimity and resourcefulness displayed by the hero under the very trying circumstances in which the author has placed him, admirably fit in with the general title of the collection.*

# WHILE THE AUTOMOBILE RAN DOWN

### A CHRISTMAS EXTRAVAGANZA

## BY CHARLES BATTELL LOOMIS

IT was a letter to encourage a hesitating lover, and certainly Orville Thornton, author of "Thoughts for Non-Thinkers," came under that head. He received it on a Tuesday, and immediately made up his mind to declare his intentions to Miss Annette Badeau that evening.

But perhaps the contents of the letter will help the reader to a better understanding of the case.

"DEAR ORVILLE: Miss Badeau sails unexpectedly for Paris on the day after Christmas, her aunt Madge having cabled her to come and visit her. Won't you come to Christmas dinner? I've invited the Joe Burtons, and of course Mr. Marten will be there, but no others—except Miss Badeau.

"Dinner will be at sharp seven. Don't be late, although I know you won't, you human time-table.

"I do hope that Annette will not fall in love in Paris. I wish that she would marry some nice New Yorker and settle near me. I've always thought that you have neglected marriage shamefully.

"Remember to-morrow night, and Annette sails on Thursday. Wishing you a Merry Christmas, I am,
"Your old friend,
"HENRIETTA MARTEN."

Annette Badeau had come across the line of Orville's vision three months before. She was Mrs. Marten's niece, and had come from the West to live

From "Cheerful Americans," published 1903, by Henry Holt & Co. This story originally appeared in "The Century Magazine," in 1901, and was copyrighted at that time by the Century Co.

with her aunt at just about the time that the success of Thornton's book made him think of marriage.

She was pretty and bright and expansive in a Western way, and when Thornton met her at one of the few afternoon teas that he ever attended he fell in love with her.  When he learned that she was the niece of his lifelong friend, Mrs. Marten, he suddenly discovered various reasons why he should call at the Marten house once or twice a week.

But a strange habit he had of putting off delightful moments in order to enjoy anticipation to its fullest extent had caused him to refrain from disclosing the state of his heart to Miss Badeau, and so that young woman, who had fallen in love with him even before she knew that he was the gifted author of "Thoughts for Non-Thinkers," often wished to herself that she could in some way give him a hint of the state of *her* heart.

Orville received Mrs. Marten's letter on Christmas Eve, and its contents made him plan a schedule for the next evening's running.  No power on earth could keep him away from that dinner, and he immediately sent a telegram of regret to the Bell-wether of the Wolves' Club, although he had been anticipating the Christmas gorge for a month.

He also sent a messenger with a note of acceptance to Mrs. Marten.  .  .  .

Then he joined the crowd of persons who always wait until Christmas Eve before buying the presents that stern and unpleasant duty makes it necessary to get.

It would impart a characteristic Christmas flavor if it were possible to cover the ground with snow, and to make the air merry with the sound of flashing belts of silvery sleighbells on prancing horses; but although Christmases in stories are always snowy and frosty, and sparkling with ice-crystals, Christmases in real life are apt to be damp and humid. Let us be thankful that this Christmas was merely such a one as would not give a ghost of a reason for a trip to Florida. The mercury stood at 58, and even light overcoats were not things to be put on without thought.

Orville knew what he wished to get and where it was sold, and so he had an advantage over ninety-nine out of a hundred of the anxious-looking shoppers who were scuttling from shop to shop, burdened with bundles, and making the evening the worst in the year for tired sales girls and men.

Orville's present was not exactly Christmassy, but he hoped that Miss Badeau would like it, and it was certainly the finest one on the velvet tray. Orville, it will be seen, was of a sanguine disposition.

He did not hang up his stocking; he had not done that for several years; but he did dream that Santa Claus brought him a beautiful doll from Paris, and just as he was saying, "There must be some mistake," the doll turned into Miss Badeau and said: "No, I'm for you. Merry Christmas!" Then he woke up and thought how foolish and yet how fascinating dreams are.

Christmas morning was spent in polishing up an

old essay on "The Value of the Summer as an Invigorator." It had long been a habit of his to work over old stuff on his holidays, and if he was about to marry he would need to sell everything he had—of a literary-marketable nature. But this morning a vision of a lovely girl who on the morrow was going to sail thousands of miles away came between him and the page, and at last he tossed the manuscript into a drawer and went out for a walk.

It was the draggiest Christmas he had ever known, and the warmest. He dropped in at the club, but there was hardly any one there; still, he did manage to play a few games of billiards, and at last the clock announced that it was time to go home and dress for the Christmas dinner.

It was half-past five when he left the club. It was twenty minutes to six when he slipped on a piece of orange-peel and measured his length on the sidewalk. He was able to rise and hobble up the steps on one foot, but the hall-boy had to help him to the elevator and thence to his room. He dropped upon his bed, feeling white about the gills.

Orville was a most methodical man. He planned his doings days ahead and seldom changed his schedule. But it seemed likely that, unless he was built of sterner stuff than most of the machines called men, he would not run out of the roundhouse to-night. His fall had given his foot a nasty wrench.

Some engineers, to change the simile, would have argued that the engine was off the track, and that therefore the train was not in running condition; but

Orville merely changed engines. His own steam having been cut off, he ordered an automobile for twenty minutes to seven; and after he had bathed and bandaged his ankle he determined, with a grit worthy of the cause that brought it forth, to attend that dinner even if he paid for it in the hospital, with Annette as special nurse.

Old Mr. Nickerson, who lived across the hall, had heard of his misfortune, and called to proffer his services.

"Shall I help you get to bed?" said he.

"I am not due in bed, Mr. Nickerson, for many hours; but if you will give me a few fingers of your excellent old Scotch, with the bouquet of smoked herring, I will go on dressing for dinner."

"Dear boy," said the old gentleman, almost tearfully, "it is impossible for you to venture on your foot with such a sprain. It is badly swollen."

"Mr. Nickerson, my heart has received a worse wrench than my foot has, therefore I go out to dine." At sound of which enigmatical declaration Mr. Nickerson hurried off for the old Scotch, and in a few minutes Orville's faintness had passed off, and with help from the amiable old man he got into his evening clothes—with the exception of his left foot, which was incased in a flowered slipper of sunset red.

"Now, my dear Mr. Nickerson, I'm a thousand times obliged to you, and if I can get you to help me hop downstairs I will wait for the automobile on the front stoop." (Orville had been born in Brooklyn, where they still have "stoops.")    "I'm on time so far."

But if Orville was on time, the automobile was not, the driver not being a methodical man; and when it did come, it was all the motorman could do to stop it. It seemed restive.

"You ought to shut off on the oats," said Orville gayly, from his seat on the lowest step of the "stoop."

The picture of a gentleman in immaculate evening clothes, with the exception of a somewhat rococo carpet slipper, seemed to amuse some street children who were passing. If they could have followed the "auto" they would have been even more diverted, but such was not to be their fortune. Mr. Nickerson helped his friend into the vehicle, and the driver started at a lively rate for Fifth Avenue.

Orville lived in Seventeenth Street, near Fifth Avenue; Mrs. Marten lived on Fifth Avenue, near Fortieth Street. Thirty-eighth Street and Thirty-ninth Street were reached and passed without further incident than the fact that Orville's ankle pained him almost beyond the bearing point; but, as it is not the history of a sprained ankle that I am writing, if the vehicle had stopped at Mrs. Marten's my pen would not have been set to paper.

But the motor wagon did not even pause. It kept on as if the Harlem River were to be its next stop.

Orville had stated the number of his destination with distinctness and he now rang the annunciator and asked the driver why he did not stop.

Calmly, in the even tones that clear-headed persons

use when they wish to inspire confidence, the chauffeur said: "Don't be alarmed, sir, but I can't stop. There's something out of kilter, and I may have to run some time before I can get the hang of it. There's no danger as long as I can steer."

"Can't you slacken up in front of the house, so that I can jump?"

"With that foot, sir? Impossible, and, anyway, I can't slacken up. I think we'll stop soon. I don't know when it was charged, but a gentleman had it before I was sent out with it. It won't be long, I think. I'll run around the block, and maybe I can stop the next time."

Orville groaned for a twofold reason: his ankle was jumping with pain, and he would lose the pleasure of taking Miss Badeau in to dinner, for it was a minute past seven.

He sat and gazed at his carpet slipper, and thought of the daintily shod feet of the adorable Annette as the horseless carriage wound around the block. As they approached the house again, Orville imagined that they were slackening up, and he opened the door to be ready. It was now three minutes past seven, and dinner had begun beyond a doubt. The driver saw the door swing open, and said: "Don't jump, sir. I can't stop yet. I'm afraid there's a good deal of run in the machine."

Orville looked up at the brownstone front of the house with an agonized stare, as if he would pull Mrs. Marten to the window by the power of his eyes. But Mrs. Marten was not in the habit of pressing her

nose against the pane in an anxious search for tardy
guests. In fact, it may be asserted with confidence
that it is not a Fifth Avenue custom.

At that moment the purée was being served to Mrs.
Marten's guests, and to pretty Annette Badeau, who
really looked disconsolate with the vacant chair beside her.

"Something has happened to Orville," said Mrs.
Marten, looking over her shoulder toward the hall
door, "for he is punctuality itself."

Mr. Joe Burton was a short, red-faced little man,
with black mutton-chop whiskers of the style of '76,
and a way of looking in the most cheerful manner
upon the dark side of things. "Dessay he's been run
over," said he choppily. "Wonder any one escapes.
Steam, gasoline, electric, horse-flesh, man-propelled
juggernauts. Ought to be prohibited."

Annette could not repress a shudder. Her aunt
saw it, and said:

"Orville will never be run over. He's too wide-
awake. But it is very singular."

"He may have been detained by an order for a
story," said Mr. Marten, also with the amiable purpose of consoling Annette. For both of the Martens
knew how she felt toward Mr. Thornton.

"Maybe he's lying on the front sidewalk, hit by a
sign or bitten by a dog. Dogs ought not to be allowed in the city; they only add to the dangers of
metropolitan existence," jerked out Mr. Burton, in
blithe tones, totally unaware that his remarks might
worry Annette.

"Dear me! I wish you'd send some one out to see, Aunt Henrietta."

"Nonsense, Annette. Mr. Burton is always an alarmist. But, Marie, you might step to the front door and look down the avenue. Mr. Thornton is always so punctual that it is peculiar."

Marie went to the front door and looked down the street just as Thornton, gesticulating wildly, disappeared around the corner of Fortieth Street.

"Oh, why didn't she come sooner!" said he aloud to himself. "At least they would know why I'm late. And she'll be gone before I come round again. Was there ever such luck? Oh, for a good old horse that could stop, a dear old nag that would pause and not go round and round like a blamed carrousel! Say, driver, isn't there any way of stopping this cursed thing? Can't you run into a fence or a house? I'll take the risk."

"But *I* won't, sir. These automobiles are very powerful, and one of them turned over a news stand not long since and upset the stove in it, and nearly burned up the newsman. But there's plenty of time for it to stop. I don't have to hurry back."

"That's lucky," said Orville. "I thought maybe you'd have to leave me alone with the thing. But, say, she may run all night. Here I am due at a dinner. I'm tired of riding. This is no way to spend Christmas. Slacken up, and I'll jump when I get around there again."

"I tell you I can't slacken up, and she's going ten

miles an hour. You'll break your leg if you jump, and then where'll you be?"

"I might be on their sidewalk, and then you could ring their bell, and they'd take me in."

"And have you suing the company for damages? Oh, no, sir. I'm sorry, but it can't be helped. The company won't charge you for the extra time."

"No, I don't think it will," said Thornton savagely, the more so as his foot gave a twinge of pain just then.

"There was no one in sight, ma'am," said Marie when she returned.

"Probably he had an order for a story and got absorbed in it and forgot us," said Mr. Marten; but this conjecture did not seem to suit Annette, for it did not fit what she knew of his character.

"Possibly he was dropped in an elevator," said Mr. Burton. "Strain on elevators, particularly these electrical ones, is tremendous. Some of 'em have got to drop. And a dropping elevator is no respecter of persons. You and I may be in one when it drops. Probably he was. Sure, I hope not, but as he is known to be the soul of punctuality, we must put forward some accident to account for his lateness. People aren't always killed in elevator accidents. Are they, my dear?"

"Mr. Burton," said his wife, "I wish you would give your morbid thoughts a rest. Don't you see that Annette is sensitive?"

"Sensitive—with some one dying every minute? It's merely because she happens to know Orville that his death would be unpleasant. If a man in the Klondike were to read of it in the paper he wouldn't remember it five minutes. But I don't say he was in an elevator. Maybe some one sent him an infernal machine for a Christmas present. May have been blown up in a manhole or jumped from his window to avoid flames. Why, there are a million ways to account for his absence."

Marie had opened the parlor windows a moment before, as the house was warm, and now there came the humming of a rapidly moving automobile. Mingled with it they heard distinctly, although faintly, "Mr. Marten, here I go."

It gave them all an uncanny feeling. The fish was left untouched, and for a moment silence reigned. Then Mr. Marten sprang from the table and ran to the front door. He got there just in time to see an automobile dashing around a corner and to hear a distinctly articulated imprecation in the well-known voice of Orville Thornton.

In evening clothes and bareheaded, Mr. Marten ran to Fortieth Street, and saw the vehicle approaching Sixth Avenue, its occupant still hurling strong language upon the evening air. Mr. Marten is something of a sprinter, although he has passed the fifty mark, and he resolved to solve the mystery. But before he had covered a third of the block in Fortieth Street he saw that he could not hope to overtake the runaway automobile, so he turned and ran back to the house, rightly surmising that the driver would circle the block.

When he reached his own doorstep, badly winded, he saw the automobile coming full tilt up the avenue from Thirty-ninth Street.

The rest of the diners were on the steps. "I think he's coming," he panted. "The driver must be intoxicated."

A moment later they were treated to the spectacle of Orville, still hurling imprecations as he wildly gesticulated with both arms. Several boys were trying to keep up with the vehicle, but the pace was too swift. No policeman had yet discovered its rotary course.

As Orville came near the Marten mansion he cried, "Ah-h-h!" in the relieved tones of one who has been falling for half an hour, and at last sees ground in sight.

"What's the matter?" shouted Mr. Marten wonderingly, as the carriage, instead of stopping, sped along the roadway.

"Sprained foot. Can't walk. Auto out of order. Can't stop. Good-by till I come round again. Awful hungry. Merry Christmas!"

"Ah ha!" said Joe Burton. "I told you that it was an accident. Sprained his foot and lost power over vehicle. I don't see the connection, but let us be thankful that he isn't under the wheels, with a broken neck, or winding round and round the axle."

"But what's to be done?" said Mrs. Marten. "He says he's hungry."

"Tell you what!" said Mr. Burton, in his explosive way. "Put some food on a plate, and when the carriage comes round again I'll jump aboard, and he can eat as he travels."

"He loves purée of celery," said Mrs. Marten.

"Very well. Put some in a clean lard-pail or a milk-pail. Little out of the ordinary, but so is the accident, and he can't help his hunger. Hunger is no disgrace. I didn't think he'd ever eat soup again, to tell the truth. I was making up my mind whether a wreath or a harp would be better."

"Oh, you are so morbid, Mr. Burton," said his wife, while Mr. Marten told the maid to get a pail and put some purée into it.

When Thornton came around again he met Mr. Marten near Thirty-ninth Street.

"Open the door, Orville, and Joe Burton will get aboard with some soup. You must be starved."

"There's nothing like exercise for getting up an appetite. I'll be ready for Burton," said Orville. "Awfully sorry I can't stop and talk; but I'll see you again in a minute or two."

He opened the door as he spoke, and then, to the great delight of at least a score of people who had realized that the automobile was running away, the rubicund and stout Joe Burton, a pail of purée in one hand and some table cutlery and silverware and a napkin in the other, made a dash at the vehicle, and with help from Orville effected an entrance.

"Merry Christmas!" said Orville.

"Merry Christmas! Awfully sorry, old man, but it might be worse. Better drink it out of the pail.

They gave me a knife and fork, but they neglected to put in a spoon or a dish. I thought that you were probably killed, but I never imagined this. Miss Badeau was terribly worked up. I think that she had decided on white carnations. Nice girl. You could easily jump, old man, if you hadn't sprained your foot. Hurt much?"

"Like the devil; but I'm glad it worried Miss Badeau. No, I don't mean that. But you know."

"Yes, I know," said Burton, with a sociable smile. "Mrs. Marten told me. Nice girl. Let her in next time. Unusual thing, you know. People are very apt to jump *from* a runaway vehicle, but it seldom takes up passengers. Let her get in, and you can explain matters to her. You see, she sails early in the morning, and you haven't much time. You can tell her what a nice fellow you are, you know, and I'm sure you'll have Mrs. Marten's blessing. Here's where I get out."

With an agility admirable in one of his stoutness, Mr. Burton leaped to the street and ran up the steps to speak to Miss Badeau. Orville could see her blush, but there was no time for her to become a passenger that trip, and the young man once more made the circuit of the block, quite alone, but strangely happy. He had never ridden with Annette, except once on the elevated road, and then both Mr. and Mrs. Marten were of the company.

Round sped the motor, and when the Martens' appeared in sight, Annette was on the sidewalk with a covered dish in her hand and a look of excited expectancy on her face that added a hundredfold to its charms.

"Here you are—only ten cents a ride. Merry Christmas!" shouted Orville gayly, and leaned half out of the automobile to catch her. It was a daring, almost an impossible jump, yet Annette made it without accident, and, flushed and excited, sat down in front of Mr. Thornton without spilling her burden, which proved to be sweetbreads.

"Miss Badeau—Annette, I hadn't expected it to turn out this way, but of course your aunt doesn't care, or she wouldn't have let you come. We're really in no danger. This driver has had more experience dodging teams in this last hour than he'd get in an ordinary year. They tell me you're going to Europe early to-morrow, to leave all your friends. Now, I've something very important to say to you before you go. No, thanks, I don't want anything more. That purée was very filling. I've sprained my ankle, and I need to be very quiet for a week or two, perhaps until this machine runs down, but at the end of that time would you—"

Orville hesitated, and Annette blushed sweetly. She set the sweetbreads down upon the seat beside her. Orville had never looked so handsome before to her eyes.

He hesitated. "Go on," said she.

"Would you be willing to go to Paris on a bridal trip?"

Annette's answer was drowned in the hurrah of the

driver as the automobile, gradually slackening, came to a full stop in front of the Martens'.

But Orville read her lips, and as he handed his untouched sweetbreads to Mrs. Burton, and his sweetheart to her uncle, his face wore a seraphically happy expression; and when Mr. Marten and the driver helped him up the steps at precisely eight o'clock, Annette's hand sought his, and it was a jolly party that sat down to a big though somewhat dried-up Rhode Island turkey.

"Marriage also is an accident," said Mr. Burton.

# "MANY WATERS"

## BY MARGARET DELAND

*Margaretta Wade Campbell (born in Allegheny, Pa., February 23, 1857: married to Lorin F. Deland in 1880) wrote as her first novel a work of unusual psychological strength—"John Ward, Preacher." With every subsequent book her insight into character has become more penetrating, until there is now no novelist in England or America who stands higher as a psychologist. "Many Waters" received the second prize in the recent short story contest conducted by COLLIER'S WEEKLY. One of the three judges, William Allen White, gave it his vote for first place, "because," he said, "it handled a big universal theme in a strong way, with the dramatic power well in hand, and with the artistic quality always in the foreground."*

N

# "MANY WATERS"

## BY MARGARET DELAND

### I

"WELL?"

"True bill; I'm awfully sorry."

Thomas Fleming took his cigar out of his mouth, and contemplated the lighted end. He did not speak. The other man, his lawyer, who had brought him the unwelcome news, began to make the best of it.

"Of course, it's an annoyance; but—"

"Well, yes. It's an annoyance," Fleming said, dryly.

Bates chuckled. "It strikes me, Tom, considering the difference between this and the *real thing,* that 'annoyance' is just the right word to use!"

Fleming leaned over and knocked off the ashes from his cigar into his waste basket. He was silent.

"As for Hammond, he won't have a leg to stand on. I don't know what Ellis & Grew meant by letting him take the case before the Grand Jury. He won't have a leg to stand on!"

"Give me a light, will you, Bates? This cigar has gone out again."

"What has Hammond got, anyhow?" Bates continued, pulling a box of wax matches out of his waist-coat pocket; "what's he got to support his opinion that you pinched $3,000 from the Hammond estate? His memory of something somebody said twelve years ago, and an old check. Well, we won't do a thing to 'em!"

Fleming got up and began to pull down his desk top with a slow clatter. "Hammond's a fool," he said; "and you'll punch a hole in his evidence in five minutes. But it's—well, as you say, it's 'annoying.'"

The lawyer rose briskly and reached for his hat. "What we want now is to get the case up near the head of the list as soon as we can. Get it over! Get it over! Then, if you want revenge, we can turn round and hit back with 'malicious prosecution'!" He laughed, good-naturedly, and shrugged himself into his overcoat.

His client stood absently locking and unlocking his desk. "I suppose it will be in the evening papers?" he said.

"Oh, I guess so," the younger man said, easily; "the findings of the Grand Jury were reported at eleven this morning. Plenty of time for the first editions."

"Then I'll take an early train home," Thomas Fleming said, quickly; "my wife—" he paused.

"Doesn't Mrs. Fleming know about it?" the lawyer said, with a surprised look.

"No," the other man said, gloomily; "I didn't want her to worry over it, so I didn't say anything. But, of course, now she's got to know."

"Yes," Bates said, sympathetically; "but after all,

Fleming, it's a small matter, except for the nuisance of it. You tell her I say it's a sure thing."

Fleming let his key-ring drop, jingling, into his pocket. Except for the occasional faint clangor of cars far down in the streets, the room, high up in the big office building, was quiet; but its quiet was the muffled, inarticulate, never-ending roar of living, rising from below. Fleming sighed, and, turning his back to his lawyer, stared absently out of the window. Before him, in the afternoon dusk, lay the struggling, panting city. Far off to the south he could see the water, and ferryboats crawling like beetles back and forth. Below, the deep canyons of the streets were blurred with creeping yellow fog; but higher up, above the crowding roofs and chimneys and occasional spires, the air was clearer; it was full of tumultuous movement—sudden jets of white steam ballooning from hundreds of escape pipes; shuffling, shifting coils of black smoke; here and there the straining quiver of flags, whipping out from their masts. Fleming, his hands in his pockets, stood staring and listening—with unseeing eyes, unhearing ears. The lawyer behind him, at the office door, hesitated.

"Fleming, really, it isn't going to amount to anything. Of course, I know how you feel about Mrs. Fleming, but—"

The man at the window turned round. "Rather than have her disturbed, I'd compromise on it. I'd pay him. I'd—"

The lawyer raised his eyebrows. "This time, I think, Hammond is honest. I guess he really believes he has a case; but Ellis & Grew are sharks, and you'd be encouraging blackmail to compromise. Anyway, you couldn't do it. Grew volunteered the information that their man 'couldn't be bought off'; he meant to put it through, Grew said. I told him they'd got the wrong pig by the ear. I told him that Thomas Fleming wasn't the kind of man who purchases peace at the cost of principle. They're shysters, and I gave 'em plain talk. Now, don't let Mrs. Fleming take it to heart. Tell her I say it will be a triumph!"

He went off, laughing; and a minute later Fleming heard his step in the corridor, and then the clang of the elevator door. He took up his black cloth bag and poked about in it among some papers; then unlocked his desk and found what he had been looking for—a box of candy for his wife. He slipped it into his bag, and a minute or two later he was down in the muddy dusk of the street. As he moved along with the steady surge of the homeward-bound crowd, he looked doubtfully into the flower stores; he wished he had bought violets for Amy instead of candy; he had taken her candy last Saturday. He debated whether he had not better get the violets too, but decided against them, because Amy was stern with him when he was extravagant for her sake. She never saw extravagance in any purchase he made on his own account! He smiled to himself at the thought of her sweet severity.

"Amy keeps me in order," he used to say, whimsically; "she insists that I shall be *her* best; it appears that my own best isn't good enough for her!" This she would always deny, indignantly, and indeed justly; for Thomas Fleming stood on his own legs, morally, in his community. But in the ten years of their married life no doubt her ideals, in small matters, had created his. With his indolent good-nature, he had found it easier to agree with Amy's delicate austerities of thought than to dispute them. Her hair-splitting in matters of conscience always amused him, and sometimes touched him, but he accepted her standards of duty with real tenderness—which, for all practical purposes, was as good as conviction. Gradually, too, she pushed him, gently, before he knew it, into civic affairs; not in any very large way; perhaps hardly more than in a readiness to do his part as a citizen; but such readiness was sincere, and had given him a reputation for public-spiritedness in which Amy took a quiet pride. He had never had time, though he had had opportunity, to hold office, because his business demanded his entire energy; and, in fact, he had to be energetic, for he had hardly any capital, his income being almost entirely dependent upon his earnings; so he was not at all a rich man—except, indeed, as he was rich in the honor and respect of the community, and the love of a woman like Amy.

But then, if they were not rich in this world's goods, neither were they poor. There had been happy, anxious years, when they were first married, when they had ridiculously little to live on; but in those days Amy had steered their housekeeping bark between all rocks of hardship, as well as past breakers of extravagance. Even now, when things were easier each year, Amy was still prudent and economical, at least where she herself was concerned.

So Fleming, smiling, forbore to add a bunch of violets to his box of candy. After all, it was his thought that would bring the delicate and happy color up into her face, not the gift itself. They were very happy, these two; perhaps because they were only two. There had been a baby, but it had only lived long enough to draw them very close together, and not, as sometimes happens, to push them apart again; and there were many friends. But they were alone in their household and in the real heart of life. Naturally, all the thwarted maternity of the woman was added to the wife's love; and the paternal instinct of the man (which is, for the most part, only amusement, and the sense of protecting and giving joy) was centred in his wife. So it was no wonder that that night, going home on the train, he winced at the thought of telling her that that "fool Hammond," who "would not have a leg to stand on," had prosecuted him criminally for misappropriation of funds as trustee of old Mrs. Hammond's estate. The trusts had been closed at her death a month or two before, and the estate handed over to her son—this same Hammond who "thought he remembered" hearing old Smith say, twelve years before, that he, Smith, had paid the Hammond estate $17,400 for a parcel of land; whereas Fleming's trustee account put the sum received at $14,400.

Amy's husband set his teeth as he sat there in the train, planning how he should tell her. Her incredulous anger he foresaw; and her anxiety—the anxiety of the woman unversed in legal matters. He damned Hammond in his heart; and pulled out his evening paper. There it was, in all the shamelessness of the flaring headline: "A Leading Citizen Indicted!" and so on. The big black letters were like a blow in the face. Fleming felt that every commuter on the train was looking over the top of his newspaper at him. He found himself glancing furtively across the aisle to see what page of the paper another passenger was reading; he thanked God that none of the men he knew well were on the five o'clock, so he would not have to listen to friendly assurances of astonishment at Hammond's impudence. His skin was prickly over his whole body; his ears were hot. And he had to tell Amy! He sank his head down between his shoulders and pulled his hat over his eyes, in pretence of a nap; then, suddenly, sat bolt upright. The fact was, Thomas Fleming had no experience in disgrace, and did not know how to conduct himself. When the door banged open at his station, he swung off on to the rainy platform, and plodded slowly up the lane in the darkness to his own house. It seemed to him as though his very feet hung back! As the gate closed behind him, he saw an instant crack of light at the front door; and when his foot touched the lowest step of the porch, the door opened wide, and Amy stood there—it was rarely Jane who let him in or even his own latchkey!

"Go right into the house! You'll take cold," he commanded.

But she drew him inside with eager welcome. "Why, how *did* you manage to get the five o'clock? I heard the gate shut, and could hardly believe my ears! Oh, your coat is damp; has it begun to rain? Hurry! take it off. Then come into the library and get warm." She possessed herself of one of his hands, so that he had to dive into his bag as best he could with the other, to fish out her box of candy. She took it, smiling, with gay pretence of scolding, and then checked herself. "You look tired, Tom. When you've had your dinner (we have a good dinner to-night; I wish you had brought some man home with you!) you'll feel better."

He dropped down into his chair by the fire in silence, frowning slightly, and drawing impatiently away from her. Thomas Fleming did not always like to be fussed over; there were times when, perhaps, he endured it with a mildly obvious patience. Every tender woman knows this patience of a good and bored man. Amy Fleming knew it, and smiled to herself, quite unoffended. Something had bothered him? Well, he should not be talked to! But she looked at him once or twice. In her soft gray dress, with her gray eyes, and the sweet color in her cheeks, she brooded over him like a dove. At dinner his silence continued. Amy, being wise beyond her sex, fell into a silence of her own—the blessed, comprehending silence of love. When they came back from the dining-room to the library fireside, she let him smoke uninterruptedly, while she sewed. Sometimes her eyes rested on him, quietly content with his mere presence. But she asked no question. Suddenly, with a half-embarrassed cough, he said:

"Ah, Amy—"

"Yes? Tell me; I knew you hadn't had a good day."

.     .     .     .     .     .     .     .     .

When he had told her, she sat dumb before him. Her face was white, and her eyes terror-stricken. But that was only for the first moment. Almost instantly there was the relief of anger. She stood up, her delicate face red, her voice strained.

"To accuse you! *You!*"

It was just what Bates had said. The first thought everywhere would be of the absurdity of such a charge against Thomas Fleming.

"It's blackmail," Amy said, trembling very much.

"Of course we shall have no difficulty in throwing them down," he said. "They bring their case, really, on Smith's old check to me for $17,400."

"I don't understand?" Amy said. It had always been a joke between them that Amy did not know anything about business, so she tried to smile when she asked him to explain.

"Oh," he said, impatiently, "it's simple enough. L. H. Smith owed me $3,000—a personal matter. I once sold him some stock; he gave me his note; had to renew two or three times; thing sort of hung fire. You wouldn't understand it, Amy. But when he bought this Hammond property for $14,400, he made out the check for $17,400;—he'd had a windfall, so

he could pay me what he owed me, see? I got my
money. Understand?"

"Perfectly," she said; "what a rascal Hammond is!"

"Oh, well, I suppose this time he really thinks he
has a case; though on general principles I believe he's
equal to blackmail! But he has succeeded in getting
from the Smith heirs that old check for the total
amount, and I suppose he thinks he has me. He'll
find himself mistaken. But it's a nasty business," he
ended, moodily; "there will always be people who will
think—"

"What do we care what such people think?" she
said, passionately.

Her husband was silent. Amy's knees were shaking under her. "Oh, I could kill that man, I could
kill him!"

Well as he knew her, he looked at her with astonishment—this mild creature to speak with such
deadly, vindictive passion! She came and knelt
down beside him; he felt her heart pounding in
her side.

"Oh," she said, brokenly, "I know—"

"You know what?"

She spoke very softly. "I know how they felt;
those women, 'looking on, afar off.' "

"Looking on?" he said, vaguely. And Amy, her
face still hidden on his breast, said in a whisper:

"It must have been easier for—for Him, on the
cross, than for them to see Him there."

He moved abruptly in his chair; then, with a faint
impatience, said she mustn't talk that way. "It's fool-

ish!" he said, irritably. She kissed him, silently; and went back to her seat by the fire.

"I'll get out of it all right," Fleming said; "Bates says so. It's annoying"—he found himself falling back on Bates's word—"but there's nothing to it. You mustn't worry. Bates says Hammond is crazy to undertake it; Smith being dead, and—" Then he stopped.

"I don't worry; in the sense of being afraid that—" she could not even put into words the fear that she did not have. "But to have your name mixed up with anything dishonorable—even though it will come out clear and shining as heaven!"

He made no answer. The fatigue of the day was showing in his face—a heavy, handsome face, with a somewhat hard mouth. His wife, looking at him, said, quietly:

"Don't let's talk about it, dearest, any more to-night. It's only on the surface; it isn't a real trouble."

He nodded, gratefully; and they did not speak of it again.

But that night Amy Fleming, lying motionless in her bed, stared into the darkness until the glimmering oblong of the window told her that dawn had come.

## II

"Trouble shows us our friends," Amy said, smiling. And indeed it did, in the Flemings' case. When the news of the indictment of Thomas Fleming fell

upon his community, there was a moment of stunned
astonishment; then of protest and disbelief.

"Hammond is up against it," men said to each
other; "Fleming? What nonsense!"

The first day or two, while it was still a nine days'
wonder, public confidence was almost an ovation.
The small house behind the trim hedges was crowded
with Amy's women friends, coming and going, and
quoting (after the fashion of women friends) what
their respective husbands said:

"*Of course* Mr. Hammond has no case, Amy, dar-
ling! My Tom—or Dick or Harry—says so."

Amy did not need such assurances. She knew her
husband! So she held her head proudly, and with
certainty. Not certainty of the outcome of the trial—
because, secretly, she had the unreasoning terror of
most women of sheltered lives for the very word *law;*
it meant power; wicked power, even! The opportunity
of evil to get the better of goodness. But her pride
and certainty were for Thomas Fleming's honor,
and goodness, and courage. She was a little cold
when these tender women friends tried to reassure
her, quoting the opinion of their menfolk; she did
not want, by eager agreement, to imply that she
needed reassurance. She said, with gentle dignity,
that she was sorry Mr. Hammond was so—foolish.
Tom had been trustee of the Hammond estate for
nearly twenty years, and he had given time and
service—"service," she said, the coloring rising
faintly in her face, "that money could not have paid
for." And to have the Hammonds turn upon him

now!—"Though, of course, it is only Mr. Hammond," Amy corrected herself, carefully just; "the rest of the family are nice people. His mother was such an honorable woman. And his wife—I am sorry for his wife." Amy thought a great deal about this wife. "She must know what he is, poor soul!" she said to herself. And knowing, she could not respect him. And without respect, love must have crumbled away. She said something like this to her most intimate friend, almost in a whisper, because expression was not easy to Amy. "When Mrs. Hammond realizes that he is a blackmailer, what *will* she do!"

"Poor thing!" said the other woman; "but, Amy, I suppose she is fond of him? He has been a good husband, they say."

"A good husband? How do you mean? Kind? A good provider?" Amy said, with a droop of her lip.

"Well, my dear, at least the man has been faithful to her; among all the horrid things that have been said about him, nobody has said—*that*."

"They had better have said 'that'!" Amy said. "Oh, Helen, faithful to her with his body; but what about his mind? Don't you suppose a good woman could forgive the poor, sinful body? But the mind, the sinful mind! It is so much worse."

Her friend looked doubtful. "I suppose it is," she said; "but I think most wives could forgive the sinful mind more easily than—other things. And she **is** fond of him," she repeated.

"Fond of him! when she can't respect him? Oh, no, no!"

"Perhaps she doesn't know how bad he is," the other said, thoughtfully.

"What!" said Amy, "when she has lived with him for fifteen years? Of course she knows him. And I truly pity her," she ended simply.

So in spite of her deep resentment at Hammond, Amy felt something like tenderness for Hammond's wife—losing both respect and love, poor soul!

As the weeks passed before the day set for the trial, Amy grew perceptibly thinner and whiter. For beneath all her certainties, the fear of the Law remained. She brooded over instances of goodness suspected, of innocent men condemned, of the blunders and mistakes of Justice. It was not until three or four days before the trial that Bates realized what even Thomas Fleming had not understood, that she was consumed with *fear*. Fear of prison walls, of unmerited disgrace, of her house left unto her desolate. When the lawyer penetrated the tense cheerfulness with which she held herself in Tom's presence, and saw the fright below, he roared with laughter; which, though ill-mannered, was the best thing he could have done.

"You think I'm a fool?" she said, with a quivering smile.

"My dear lady, it would not be polite for me to use such a word; but certainly you—well, you are mistaken."

"Oh, *say* I am a fool," she pleaded; "I would like

to think I was a fool! But, Mr. Bates, the Law can be made to do such dreadful things. Innocent people have been put into jail; oh, you know they have," she said, her face trembling; "and at night I lie awake and think—" He saw her hands grip each other to keep steady.

"Now let me explain it to you," he said kindly; "and then you won't be frightened; why, you'll be so sure you'll send out invitations for a dinner party on the 19th, so we can celebrate! And mind you have plenty of champagne."

Then, very explicitly, he laid before her the grounds of his confidence. Hammond, to start with, was a fool. "He always has been a cheap fellow; a sort of smart Aleck, you know; but this time he's just a fool." He had fallen into the hands of a shyster firm, who were milking him—"If you'll forgive the slang."

"Oh, go on, go on!" she entreated.

Hammond, being a fool, and having this vague idea about the price paid by Smith for the land, and having secured the old check to prove (as he thinks) that such a price was paid, falls into the hands of these sharks. "They know there is nothing to it, but they think they can pull out a plum somehow," said Mr. Bates. Then, carefully, he told her the story point by point. Briefly, it was, that while there was no question that $17,400 had been paid to Thomas Fleming, Hammond could not disprove Fleming's defence that only $14,400 of it was to go to the Trust; and that the remaining

$3,000 was in payment of Smith's debt to him. "See?" said Bates, kindly. As he spoke, the drawn look in her face lessened, and she drew one or two long breaths; and then, suddenly, she put her hands over her eyes, and he knew she wept. This sobered the rather voluble man. He protested, with friendly vociferation, that she must promise him not to give the matter another thought. And she, still trembling a little, looked up, smiling, and promised.

And, such being her temperament, she kept her promise. Perhaps it was the rebound from having gone down to the depths of fear; but certainly there was almost bravado in the reaction. She made up her mind to have the dinner party! Tom would come home, cleared, crowned with the vindication of his own integrity; and he would find love, and friendship, and respect ready to exult with him. Tom, however, objected to her project.

"It's all right," he said; "it's perfectly safe, as far as the verdict goes; but—" he stopped and frowned. It was evident that the plan did not please him. But for the once Amy did not consult his pleasure. She had her own views; and she did actually invite a party of old friends to dine with them on the evening when it was expected that the verdict would be given.

### III

Amy, in her dove-colored dress, entered the court-room with her husband. During the trial, very quietly, and with a beautiful serenity, she kept her place at his side. If the proceedings troubled her, there was no indication of it. She looked a little tired, and once or twice a little amused. Sometimes she smiled at Thomas Fleming, and sometimes exchanged a word or two with Mr. Bates. But for the most part she was silent; and her repose was a spot of refreshment and beauty in the dingy court-room. Bates looked at her occasionally, with rather jovial encouragement; but she displayed no need of encouragement, and returned his smile cheerfully. Once he leaned over and said:

"You make me think of a poem I read somewhere; now, what was the name of it? I can only remember two lines:

> " 'In the fell clutch of circumstance,
>     I have not winced or cried aloud!'

That's as far as I can go; but that's what you make me think of."

She turned, smiling, and finished the verse. "It's Henley's 'I am the captain of my soul,' " she said. "I have it somewhere: I copied it once, because I cared so much for it. I'll read it to you to-night, after dinner."

"Do!" Bates said heartily, and turned away to listen to Fleming, who was on the stand. Fleming's evidence was as straightforward as the man himself. Yes, Smith (now deceased) had paid him in March, 1887, the sum of $17,400. Of this, $3,000 was on a personal account; $14,400 was for a parcel of land belonging to the Hammond estate. The check was made to his order; he deposited it in his own bank account and immediately drew against it a check for $14,400 to the order of the Trust.    Then followed a very clear and definite statement of that money Smith owed him; a debt which he was unable to corroborate by his books, for the simple reason that his books had been burned in the great fire of that year. Over and over, back and forth, round and round, the prosecution went, gaining not an inch.

Indeed, the end was obvious from the beginning. To assert that Thomas Fleming was an honest man was, so Bates told the jury, to utter a commonplace. He was so cheerful and kindly, in his reference to the unfortunate Mr. Hammond, that the jury grinned. The verdict, Bates declared, was a foregone conclusion.    And so, in fact, it was, being rendered fifteen minutes after the jury had been charged.

"And now," said the good Bates, shaking hands with his client, "let's go and get something to eat! Come, Mrs. Fleming, you'll go with us?    You look like an army with banners!"

But Amy, with proud eyes, said no; she must go home.    "You will come out with Tom this evening?" she said.    "Dinner is at half-past seven; you can dress at our house; and, of course, you must stay all night." Bates promised, and Fleming silently squeezed his wife's hand.    Amy's heart was beating so that her words were a little breathless, but her eyes spoke to him.

She did not want to lunch with the two men; she had it in mind to go into a church which was near the court-house, and there, alone, in the silence and

sacred dusk, return thanks upon her knees. And
deep human experience gives the soul a chance to see
God; and when Amy came out afterward into the
roar of the street, her face shone like the face of one
who has touched the garment hem of the Eternal, and
bears back the Tables of Law. . . .

The joyous and beautiful day passed; the afternoon was gay with congratulations; but the succession of friendly calls was fatiguing, and at half-past
five she said, courageously, "Now, dear friends, I'll
have to leave you! It's delightful to hear all these
nice things about Tom, but I must go and lie down,
or I shall go to sleep at dinner." So there was more
handshaking and gayety, and then, at last, she had
the house to herself. She reflected that it would be
well to have a little nap, so that she might be bright
and rested for the jubilant evening;—oh, that poem
Mr. Bates wanted to see! She had forgotten all about
it; she must find it before she went upstairs. But
she must first look into the dining-room to be sure
about the candles and flowers and wine-glasses; three
kinds of wine to-night! Generally Tom had just his
glass of sherry; but to-night—! The economical Amy
would have broached the tun of malmsey if she had
been able to secure it. The dinner, she knew, would
be good. She had picked out the partridges herself,
knowing well, under her calm exterior, that her mar-
ket man, looking at her with sidewise, curious eyes,
was thinking to himself, "My! and her husband to be
tried for a State's prison offence!" The partridges
were superb; and the salmon—Amy's eyes sparkled

with joy at the thought of such extravagance—salmon in February! the salmon was perfect; and the salad, the ices, the coffee—well, they would be worthy of the occasion!

The dining-room was satisfactory, with its ten friendly chairs drawn up about the sparkling table. And her best dress was upstairs spread out on the bed, with her slippers and gloves; her flowers—Tom would bring her her flowers! She thought to herself that she would wear them, and then put them away with her wedding bouquet, that had been lying, dry and fragrant, for all these years, with her wedding dress and veil. Sighing with the joy of it all, she climbed wearily half-way upstairs; then remembered Mr. Bates's poem again, and went back to the library, with an uneasy look at the hall clock. She would not get much of a nap! And the chances of the nap lessened still more, because she could not at once find her Commonplace Book, in which she had copied the poem. Taking out one book after another, she shook her head and looked at her hands—these shelves were very dusty; that told a housekeeping story that was disgraceful, she said to herself, gayly. Well, she would look after Jane, now that she could think and breathe again! So, poking about, pulling out one flexible, leather-covered volume after another, her fate fell upon her. . . .

The book looked like her own Commonplace Book; Tom had more than once given her blank-books just like his own—bound in red morocco, with mottled edges, and stamped, "*Diary,* 18—." There was a whole row of these books on one of the bottom shelves of the bookcase that ran round three sides of the room, and she had been looking at them, one by one, hurriedly, for she knew she needed that rest upstairs before the company came. She pulled the books out, impatiently, fluttering the leaves over, and putting them back. One or two were her own note-books; but the rest were Tom's memoranda—accounts, notes, etc., etc., back to— "Why, dear me!" said Amy to herself, "they go back to before we were married!"

There was one date that caught her eye; she had heard it repeated and repeated in the last few weeks; she had heard it that very morning in court, when Thomas Fleming had said: "In March, 1887, L. F. Smith paid me in one check $17,400; $14,400 for a piece of land belonging to the Hammond estate, and $3,000 which he owed my personal account."

The flexible, red-covered diary marked 1887 drew her hand with the fascination which comes with remembered pain. Ah! how she had suffered every time that date fell like a scalding drop of fear upon her heart! It is not true of spiritual pain that one remembereth no more the anguish for joy that a blessing has been born into the soul! She shivered as she opened the book. It occurred to her, with vague surprise, that this book would probably have settled the whole matter, if Tom had only remembered it. He had shown in court that records of that year had been among certain office books burned in the great March fire, when the building in which he had his office had been destroyed. Yes, this book might have cleared the whole matter up, easily and quickly, for, as she saw at a glance, here were entries about the Hammond Trust. She forgot her fatigue, and the nap she ought to have; she forgot the poem altogether; she sat down on the floor, running the pages over eagerly. It occurred to her, as a climax of the successful day, that she would bring this book out at dinner (if she could only find something about the $14,400) and show it as her final triumph. Then her eyes fell on the figures $17,000.

"Received from L. H. Smith, to-day, $17,400 for Hammond property, in Linden Hill." Then the comment, "A whacking good price. I hardly expected to get so much." The significance of this brief statement did not penetrate her joy. She began eagerly to look again for the other figures—and then turned back, perplexed. $17,400 for the Hammond property? Suddenly her eye caught another familiar sum—$3,000. Ah, now she would find it! Yes, verily, so she did. . . . "Borrowed $3,000 from Hammond Estate to pay back money borrowed from Ropes Estate."

Suddenly it seemed to this poor woman, sitting on the floor in the dark corner of the library, her fingers dusty, her whole slender body tingling with fatigue— it seemed as if something fell, shuddering, down and down, and down in her breast. Strangely enough, this physical recognition informed her soul. She heard herself speak, as one falling into the unconsciousness of an anæsthetic, hears, with vague astonishment, words faltering unbidden from the lips. "No. No. No," came the body's frightened denial.

"Then, in silence, the Soul: "He—did it. He did it."

It was characteristic of Amy that she sought no loophole of escape. It never occurred to her that there could be an explanation. There were the figures; and the figures meant the facts. *"A certain man named Ananias"* (so, suddenly, the words ran in her mind) *"sold a possession . . . and kept back part of the price."*

Out in the hall the half-hour struck, muffled and mellow. Then silence.

"God, if he did it, I can't live—can't live. *God?*"

Suddenly the happenings of the day seemed to blur and run together, and there was a moment, not of unconsciousness, but of profound indifference. Her capacity for feeling snapped. But when she tried to rise, her whole being was sick; so sick that again the soul forgot or did not understand, and heard, with dull curiosity, the body saying, "No. No." She steadied herself by holding on to the bookshelves; and then, somehow, she got upstairs. It was the sight of the soft, gray dress, with its pretty laces, that stung her awake. That dress: was it hers? Was she to put it on? Was she to go and sit at the head of that shining table down in the dining-room?

"But, you know, I—*can't,*" she said aloud, her voice hoarse and falling.

.   .   .   .   .   .   .   .   .

But she did.

By the time Fleming and his counsel came tramping up from the gate, at a quarter past seven, and stopped hilariously, to kick the snow off their boots before entering the hall, Amy Fleming had arisen to meet the summons of Life. She called Jane to fasten her dress, and when the woman, startled and shocked at the shrunken face, cried out:

"Oh, good land! what's wrong wi' ye, Mrs. Fleming?" she was able to say, quietly:

"Jane, when Mr. Fleming comes in, tell him I've had to go down to the kitchen to see about some things. And say I put his dress suit out on the sofa in my room. Tell him the studs are in his shirt."

Jane, silenced, went back to the kitchen. "Say, Mary Ann," she said, "look a-here; there's something the matter upstairs." The presence of the accommodating waitress checked further confidences; but, indeed, when Amy Fleming, ghastly, in her pretty dinner dress, sought refuge in the kitchen (the one spot where her husband would not be apt to pursue her), and stood listening to the voices of the two men going upstairs, Mary Ann needed no information that there was "something the matter."

"She looks like she was dead," the frightened women told each other.

"Jane," her mistress said, "I wish you would open a bottle of champagne; one of the pints, not one of the big bottles, and give—me—a glass;" her voice was faint. Jane obeyed hurriedly, and as the cork popped one man upstairs called out gayly to the other, "Hullo! has it begun already?"

Amy drank the wine and handed the glass back to

the anxious woman. "I was feeling faint, Jane. I am all right now, thank you. Oh, there's the door bell! I'll go into the library." And when the two rather early comers had taken off their wraps and made their way downstairs again, they found their hostess smiling whitely at them from the hearthrug.

"Oh, Amy *dear!*" the wife said, dismayed, "what is the matter?" And the husband protested in a friendly way that he was afraid Mrs. Fleming was tired out. "Of course it has been a wearing week for you, in spite of its triumph," he said, delicately.

Then Thomas Fleming and his lawyer came downstairs, and there was more handshaking and congratulations, and it was not until he looked at his wife at dinner that Fleming really saw her face; its haggard pallor struck him dumb in the midst of some gay story to the pretty neighbor on his right. He had been dull, just at first, and his gayety was a little forced, but after his first glass of champagne he brightened up very much, and had begun to tell a funny story. "And so the automobilist," he was saying—and broke off, staring blankly at Amy. "I'm afraid my wife is not well," he said, anxiously. But the pretty neighbor reassured him.

"Oh, it's the reaction, Mr. Fleming. Amy has been perfectly splendid; but now, naturally, she feels the reaction."

Somehow or other, with its gayety and good fellowship, that dreadful evening passed. When the friendly folk streamed out into the starry winter night, there was some anxious comment.

"How badly she looked!"

"My dear, can you wonder? Think what she's been through!"

But one woman, on her husband's arm, murmured a question: "You don't suppose he *could* have—done anything?"

"Twelve good men and true have said he didn't; your remark is out of order."

"But tell me, honestly, do you suppose it is possible that—that?"

"I don't know anything about it, Helen. I would bank on Tom Fleming as soon as on any man I know. But I don't know any man (myself included) who is not human. So, if you ask about 'possibilities'—but no! honestly, as you say, I'm sure Fleming is all right. And his wife is a noble woman. I've always admired Mrs. Fleming."

"She is the best woman in the world!" Amy's friend said, warmly. But in her own heart she was thinking that if it came to possibilities, she knew *one* man to whom wrongdoing was impossible! And, happily, she squeezed his arm, and brushed her cold, rosy cheek against his shoulder.

## IV

When Fleming closed the door upon the last lingering guest, he turned anxiously to his wife. "Amy, I haven't had a chance to speak to you! You are worn out. Bates, look at her—she's worn out!"

Bates, lounging in the library doorway, agreed. "Indeed she is; Mrs. Fleming, you ought not to have attempted a dinner party. I believe it's all my fault, because I suggested it."

"It's your fault because you got me off," Fleming said, jocosely. The dulness of the first part of the evening had quite disappeared; he was rather flushed and inclined to laugh buoyantly at everything; but his face was anxious when he looked at his wife. "Amy, you must go right straight to bed!"

"I am going now," she said, pulling and straightening the fingers of her long gloves. "Good-night, Mr. Bates. I—will copy that poem for you—sometime," she ended faintly.

Her husband put his arm about her to help her upstairs, but she drew away. "No; stay down and smoke with Mr. Bates." Then, as he insisted on coming up with her, she stopped on the first landing, and pushed his arm away, sharply. "Please—*don't!* My head aches. Please—go away."

Thomas Fleming, dumfounded, could not find his wits for a reply before she had slipped away from him, and he heard the door of their bedroom close behind her. He stood blankly upon the stairs for a moment, and then went back to Bates.

"I never knew Amy so upset," he said, stupidly. And, indeed, there are few things more bewildering than sudden irrational irritation in a sweet and reasonable soul.

"It's been a hard week for her," Bates explained, easily. But Fleming smoked morosely; he was plainly relieved when his guest said he thought he would go to bed. He suggested, in a perfunctory way, a last

visit to the dining-room for a drink of whiskey, and
when this was declined, arose with alacrity to conduct
the sleepy lawyer to the spare-room door.

"We'll take the eight-fifteen in the morning, Bates,"
he said; and Bates, yawning, agreed.

Fleming went softly into his own room, and was
half disappointed, half relieved, to find his wife lying
motionless, with closed eyes. "A good night's sleep
will set her up," he thought, tenderly. For himself, he
stopped in the process of pulling off his boots, and,
shutting his lips hard together, stared at the floor.
. . . After a while he drew a long breath;—"Well,
thank the eternal Powers," he said; and pulled off his
boots softly—Amy must have a good night's sleep.
Fleming himself had a good night's sleep. That
Amy's eyes opened painfully to the dark, when all
the house had sunk into silence, of course he did
not know. She seemed to be sleeping soundly when
he awoke the next morning; and again he crept about,
not even daring to kiss her, lest she might be disturbed. Just before he and Bates made a dash for the
eight-fifteen, he told Jane to ask Mrs. Fleming to
call him up on the telephone when she came downstairs, so he might know how she was.

As for Amy, when she heard the front door close
behind the two hurrying men, she got up and sat
wearily on the side of the bed.

"Now, I've got time to think," she said. There
was a certain relief in the consciousness of silence and
of time. She could think all day; she could think
until half-past six; how many hours? Ten! Ten

hours—in which to take up a new life. Ten hours in which to become acquainted with her husband.

"I have never known him," she said feebly to herself. Well, now she must think. . . . No doubt he had loved her; she was not questioning that. She was dully indifferent to the whole matter of love. The question was, what was she going to do? After restitution was made, what was she going to do? How were they to go on living? Mere restitution—(which must be made on Monday. No, Monday was a holiday; they would have to wait until Tuesday. Oh, how could she bear the delay?) Well, on Tuesday, then, the money would be given to Mr. Hammond. But mere restitution would not change the fact of what he was. She dropped back against her pillows, hiding her face. "I never knew him."

Oh, this would *not* do! She must think.

Poor soul! She had no thoughts but that one. Over and over the words repeated themselves, until her very mind was sore. But she did her best; the habit of common-sense was a great help. She had some coffee, and dressed and went down to the library —recoiling, involuntarily, at the sight of that corner where the books were still in some slight disorder. She even called Jane and bade her bring her duster. When the dusting was done, she told the woman that she would not see any one, all day. "I have a headache," she explained; "don't let any one in." And when Jane left her, she drew her little chair up to the hearth; "Now, I'll think," she said. But her eye caught the flash of sunlight on a crystal ball on the mantelpiece, and it seemed as if her mind broke into a glimmering kaleidoscope: those partridges had been a little overcooked last night . . . the gilt on the narrow, old-fashioned mirror over the mantel was tarnishing . . . the $3,000 had been "borrowed" from one Trust to pay another. . . . Borrowing from Peter to pay Paul. . . . How clear the crystal was. . . . Two thefts. . . . Jane must dust those shelves better. . . . Then she started with dismay —she was not thinking! Well, restitution, first of all; —on Tuesday. They would sell a bond, and take some money out of the bank. But after restitution they must go on living. She must try to understand him, to help him to be good, to be patient with him. "But I don't know him," came over and over the dreadful refrain, checked by the instant determination: "Oh, I *must* think!"

So the day passed. She told Jane to telephone her husband that she was up and feeling better; and he sent back some anxious message—she must rest, she must not overdo. He could not, unfortunately, come out on an early train, as he had hoped to do, being detained by some business matters, so he would have to dine in town. He would come out on the eight-thirty. She grasped at the delay with passionate relief; two hours more to think. Then it came over her that she was glad not to see him. What did that mean? She wondered, vaguely, if she had stopped loving him? Not that it made any difference whether she loved him or not. Love had no meaning to her. "Perhaps this is the way people who are dead feel about us," she

thought. Then she wondered if she hated him, this
stranger, this—thief? No, she did not hate him either.
But when respect, upon which love is built, is wrenched
away, what happens? There is no love, of course.
She thought, vaguely, that she had pitied Mrs. Hammond. And yet she herself did not care, apparently.
How strange not to care! Pulling her wedding-ring
off, slipping it on, pulling it off again, she said to herself, numbly, that she did not understand why she did
not care. However, she could not go into this question of love and hate. Neither mattered. She beat
her poor mind back to its task of "thinking."

The long, sunny winter afternoon faded into the
dusk; a gleam of sunset broke yellow across the pleasant room, and catching with a glimmering flash on the
crystal, melted into a bloom of gray, with the fire, like
the spark of an opal, shifting and winking on the
hearth.

When Fleming came hurriedly up the garden path
to his own door, he had to pull out his latchkey to
let himself into the house. This slight happening
made him frown; so she was not well enough to come
down? He took off his coat and started immediately
upstairs, then he caught sight of her in the library,
standing motionless, her back to the door, one hand
resting on the mantelpiece, the other drooping at her
side, the fingers between the pages of a book. He
came in quickly, with a gayly derisive laugh.

"You didn't hear me!" Then, as she did not turn,
he sobered. "Amy, what is it? Why, Amy! Is
there anything the matter? Is anything wrong?"

His face was keenly disturbed, and he put his hand
on her shoulder to make her look at him, but she lifted
it away, gently, still keeping her eyes fastened on the
fire.

"Yes. There is something—wrong."

"Amy!" he said, now thoroughly alarmed, "what is
the matter? Tell me!"

"I will tell you. Sit down. There: at the library
table. I will—show you."

He sat down, blankly, his lower-lip falling open
with perplexity. She sighed once, and brushed her
hand over her eyes; then came, quietly, away from the
hearth, and, going round the table, stood behind him
and laid the book down beside him. She pressed it
open, and in silence ran her finger down the page.

## V

The fire sputtered a little; then everything was still.
She had left him, and had gone back to the hearthrug,
and stood as before, one hand on the mantelpiece, the
other, listless, at her side. The silence was horrible.

Then, suddenly, Thomas Fleming ripped and tore
the pages out of the book, and threw them on the logs:
the quick leap of the flames shone on his white face
and his furious eyes. A minute afterward he spoke.
. . . Under that storm of outrageous words she bent
and shrunk a little, silently. Once she looked at him
with a sort of curiosity. So this was her husband?
Then she looked at the fire.

When, choking with anger, he paused, she said,
briefly, that she had been hunting for her Common-

place Book, down on that lower shelf, and had found
—this.

"What the devil were my diaries doing on your
lower shelf? One of those damned women of yours
poking—"

"When we moved they were put there. They had
been in your old desk in the other house. They were
locked up there. I suppose you forgot to lock them
up here," she ended, simply.

That next hour left its permanent mark on those
two faces; agony and shame were cut into the wincing
flesh, as by some mighty die. At first Fleming was
all rage; then rage turned into sullenness, and sullenness to explanation and excuse. But as he calmed
down, shame, an old, old shame, that he had loathed
and lived with for a dozen years, a shame that, except
when Amy was too tenderly proud of him, he was
sometimes able for days, or even weeks, to forget—
this old shame reared its deadly head, and looked out
of his abased and shifting eyes. Yet he had his glib
excuses and explanations. Amy, in the midst of them,
sat down in her little low chair by the fire. She did
not speak. She had her handkerchief in her hand, and
kept pulling it out on her knee; smoothing it; then
folding it; and a minute later, spreading it out again.
At last, after a labored statement—how he had only
borrowed it; how it had been at a time when he had
been horribly pressed; how he had always meant to return it, of course; how, in fact, he had returned it by
giving an enormous amount of work for which he had
never had any credit, or any money, either! (though,

as it happened, he had never been in a position to pay
it back in actual cash); after this miserable and futile
explanation had been repeated and repeated, he stopped
to get his breath; and then, still pulling the hem of
her handkerchief straight on her knee, his wife said,
in a lifeless voice:

"Need we talk about it any more? On Tuesday
we will send it back. (Monday is a holiday. You
can't send it until Tuesday.) Then we will never talk
about it any more."

"Send what back?"

"The money. To Mr. Hammond!"

"Are you out of your senses?" he said roughly.

She looked up, confusedly. "You can't send it until
Tuesday," she repeated, mechanically.

He brought his fist down violently on the table. "I
will never send it back! Never! You are insane!
Why, it would be acknowledging—"

"It would be confession," she agreed.

"Well! that would be ruin."

"Ruin?"

"Why, if people knew—" he began.

"It is ruin, anyhow," she said, dully. "Don't you
see? The only thing left is restitution."

"I can't make what you call—'restitution,' without
—ruin; absolute ruin! Do you realize what it would
mean to me, in this town, to have it known that I—
borrowed from the Trust, and—and had not yet returned it? On the stand, of course, I had to protect
myself; and that would be—against me. And it *would*
be known. Hammond would never let it be settled

privately! He couldn't prosecute me on the old charge; but I suppose he might make a claim of—of perjury. Anyhow, just the publicity would ruin me. And he would make it public. Trust Hammond! Besides, I've given it back ten times over in unpaid-for work to the Estate—" He stopped abruptly. Amy had fainted. . . .

Sunday was a long day of struggle. The immediate hour of violence was over; he was ashamed; and he loved her; and he was frightened. But he was immovable. His hardness was worse than his violence.

"I can not do it, Amy; I will not do it. The thing is done. It's over. It's settled. I'm sorry; I—regret it; nobody regrets it as much as I do. But I will not destroy myself, and destroy you—you, too!—by returning it." Then, sullenly, "Anyway, I don't owe it, morally. I've more than made it up to them."

Monday, the holiday (and holidays had always been such joy to them; a whole day at home together!)— Monday, they struggled to the death.

It was in the afternoon that she suddenly flagged. She had been kneeling beside him, entreating him; and he had been hard and violent and childish by turns; but he would not. And toward dusk there came a dreadful pause. Partly, no doubt, it was because she was exhausted; but it was more than that. It was a sudden blasting consciousness that the man must save or lose his own soul. If she forced him to make restitution, the restitution would not be his, but hers. If she pushed him into honesty, he would still be dishonest. If he preferred the mire, he would be filthy

if plucked out against his will and set on clean ground.
A prisoner in heaven is in hell! No, he must save
himself. She could not save him.

She drew away and looked at him; then she covered
her face with her hands. "I am done," she said,
faintly.

The suddenness of her capitulation left him open-
mouthed. But before he could speak she went away
and left him. He heard her slip the bolt of their bedroom door; and then he heard her step overhead.
After that all was still.

The afternoon was very long; once he went and
walked drearily about the snowy lanes, avoiding
passersby as well as he could. But for the most part
he sat in the library and tried to read or smoke; but he
forgot to turn over the pages, and he had to keep
reaching for a match to relight his cigar. He said to
himself that his life was over. Amy would leave him,
of course; she had said as much. Well, he couldn't
help it. Better the misery of a broken home than
public shame, and disgrace, and ruin. And he had
made restitution (as she called it); he had made it
many times over!

It was late at night, as he was saying something like
this to himself for the hundredth time, that his wife
came back into the room. She stood up in the old
place, on the hearthrug. Very gently she told him
what she had to say. She did not look at him; her
eyes were fixed on the Japanese crystal resting in its
jade bowl on the mantelpiece; once she took it up, and
turned it over and over in the palm of her hand, look-

ing at it intently as she spoke. But probably she did not even see it.

"I have thought it all out," she began in a low voice; "and I see I was wrong—" He started. "I was wrong. You must save your own soul. I can't do it for you. Oh, I would! but I can't. I shall not ever again insist. Yes, the Kingdom of God must be within you. I never understood that before."

"Amy," he began, but she checked him.

"Please!—I am not through yet. I shall pay the money back, somehow, sometime. (Oh, wait—wait; *don't* interrupt me!) Of course, I shall not betray you. My paying it shall not tell the truth, because, unless the truth is from you, it can not help you. It must be your truth, not mine. But I shall save, and save, and save, and pay it back—to clear my own soul. For I—I have lived on that three thousand dollars too," she said with a sick look. She put the crystal back into its bowl. "It will take—a long time," she said, faintly.

She stopped, trembling from the effort of so many calm words. Thomas Fleming, looking doggedly at the floor, said: "I suppose you'll get a separation?"

"Get a separation?" she glanced at him for an instant. "Why, we are separated," she said. "We can't be any more separated than we are. I suppose we have never been together. But I won't leave you, if that is what you mean."

"You'll stay with me?" he burst out; "I thought you despised me!"

"Why, no," she said, slowly; "I don't think I despise you. I don't think I do. But of course—" She looked away, helplessly. "Of course, I have no respect for you."

"Well," he said, "I'm sorry. But there's nothing I can do about it."

Amy turned, listlessly, as if to go upstairs again; but he caught her dress.

"You really mean you won't—leave me?"

"No, I won't leave you."

"Of course," he said, roughly, "you don't love me; but—" His voice faltered into a sort of question.

She turned sharply from him, hiding her face in her arm, moving blindly, with one hand stretched out to feel her way, toward the door. "Oh," she said; "oh—I'm afraid—I—"

And at that he broke. . . . Poor, weak Love, poor Love that would have denied itself for very shame; Love brought him to his knees; his arms around her waist, his head against her breast, his tears on her hand.

"Amy! *I will do it. I will give it back.* Oh, Amy, Amy—"

# GENERAL INDEXES

INDEX BY TITLES

INDEX BY AUTHORS

# INDEX BY TITLES

# INDEX BY AUTHORS